# A WONDERFUL KIND OF LOVE

---

## KRISTA LAKES

ZIRCONIA PUBLISHING, INC.

*"Are you thinking what I'm thinking?" she whispered, pushing her hips against his. The way his pupils dilated nearly did her in.*

### Ethan

There are only two things that make billionaire Ethan White's heart race: fast cars and Laura Corbett. Unfortunately, Laura wants nothing to do with his playboy ways. Ethan thinks that everyone has the wrong idea about him, including his stalker, and he's determined to prove them all wrong. When Ethan's business partner wants to open a new car R&D facility in Colorado, he jumps at the opportunity to be closer to his two passions.

### Laura

Thrust into the new responsibility of raising her siblings by the death of her parents, Laura Corbett doesn't have time for awkward hookups, let alone a relationship. So when the billionaire she had a one night stand with shows up in town, she pretends he doesn't exist. She can't let anything come between her and her family.

But nothing can prepare her for the way that Ethan connects with her brother and sister. And she can't deny the fact that jumping in his bed makes her come alive. Everything seems like it'll be normal again, maybe even better than normal.

But Ethan's stalker disagrees...

Laura couldn't get enough of him. Now that the ice had been broken, she wanted to dive in head first. Whatever had made them want each other a year and a half before was there again, and back in full.

She kept her lips against his and wrapped an arm around his shoulders. Then she slowly pulled herself on top of him so that she straddled over his lap. Ethan let out a sexual growl but didn't break the kiss. She could feel the vibration of the noise as it made its way from his throat, all the way to her lips.

Their kissing quickly became more aggressive as they lowered their walls and allowed themselves to express how badly they wanted each other. Laura felt one of Ethan's hands slide up her back, all the way to her neck. He slipped his fingers into her hair and gently squeezed his hand into a fist. The movement pulled her hair, just enough to create some tension against her scalp, but not enough to actually hurt.

With one hand in her hair, Ethan brought his other one

to her lower back. His fingers found the place between the bottom of her shirt and the top of her jeans. He touched her bare skin, and it caused her to moan softly. She wanted his touch, not just there, but everywhere.

Ethan slowly pulled his face away. He was still gripping her hair as he gazed into her eyes. His pupils dilated, growing big in the pale green. He was breathing a bit harder, too, making it clear that he wanted this just as badly as she did.

"My God, you're gorgeous," he said, his eyes moving slowly up and down Laura's front. "Something about you. I don't know exactly what it is, but this is how I remember feeling when I first saw you at that party all those months ago. You just do it for me. Why did we wait this long?"

Laura shrugged. "Let's not worry about any of that. The past is the past. We're here now, though. Why don't we savor this moment before it slips away?"

Ethan nodded. "You're right. You're absolutely right..."

*For Rong*

# A WONDERFUL KIND
# OF LOVE

# Chapter 1

$\mathcal{L}$aura

HIS HAND WENT to the back of her neck again, pulling her into him. She gasped as his hand tangled in her hair and he tugged gently as he kissed her. She felt the pull from her scalp to between her thighs, and she whimpered.

"That's a dangerous sound," he whispered, his voice dark and full of desire. He turned her to him, so her back pressed up against the glass of the Rocks, Gems, and Minerals display. She thought it had gold or something inside of it, but she really wasn't paying attention to the science exhibit once his hips pressed against her. She could feel his desire press up against her, and she moaned again.

Sweet, hot, and her tongue tangled with his as he kissed her again, stealing her moans. He gripped her hair harder, wanting still more and she arched her hips into his. All she had on under the dress was a very tiny thong. It wouldn't be hard to slip it to the side. If he undid his fly, he'd slide right in. The idea made her shiver with desire.

"Are you thinking what I'm thinking?" she whispered, pushing her hips against his. The way his pupils dilated nearly did her in.

He nodded, reaching for the hem of her skirt. His hand was hot against her thigh as he felt her skin. He took his time, tracing his palm along the hem of her dress. The waiting made her want it all the more. Slowly, so slowly it made her writhe, he slid his hand up her skirt. She held her breath as she waited for him to reach the top of her thigh.

She shifted her weight to give him better access, but he wasn't touching her anymore. She opened her eyes to find him glaring at her. He took a step back and grimaced.

"What's wrong?" she asked, confused. The heat inside her was quickly dissipating. This wasn't how it was supposed to go. This wasn't how it happened.

"I don't want this," he said, shaking his head. He took another step back, fading into the darkness. She couldn't see him anymore.

"Ethan?" she called out. Suddenly, a woman appeared. She had never seen this woman before, but she knew that it was Ethan's secretary.

"He said he doesn't want this. He doesn't want you. He does this to all the girls. You're not special."

She didn't believe a word of it, but every time she tried to get around the secretary, she blocked Laura's way.

The secretary kept talking. "Just forget about him."

Ethan was about to step through a door. "Ethan!" She reached out to him, but he was already gone, and she was alone in the dark of her bedroom.

"Laura? Are you awake?" a small voice asked, hand on her shoulder.

The dream vanished, leaving her dizzy and confused. She turned to see two green eyes inches from her own, and she yelped.

The small owner of the eyes screamed which was followed by a third smaller scream. Laura's heart pounded in her chest like an over-sized drum as she sat up and turned on the light on her nightstand. Her brain struggled to make sense of what was going on as she woke from her dream.

"Ivy, you scared the crap out of me," Laura gasped as soon as the light was on and she could see who was standing in front of her.

"I'm sorry, Laura," Ivy whispered, her lower lip trembling. Laura's younger sister clutched her small security blanket to her chest a little tighter. Behind Ivy, their little brother Dallas sniffled and looked just as miserable.

Guilt hit Laura square in the chest. Ivy was only seven years old and Dallas only five. She remembered crawling into her parents' bed with nightmares when she was that age too. She didn't want them to think she was angry with them.

"It's okay. You just startled me," Laura said, doing her best to smile at her siblings. "Did you guys have another nightmare?"

Ivy and Dallas both nodded, their eyes still full of fear. "Yeah," whispered Ivy.

"Mom and Dad again?" Laura asked, already knowing the answer.

"The usual one," Ivy replied, looking at the floor like having nightmares about their dead parents was something she should be ashamed of. They both looked so small and vulnerable in the yellow lamplight that Laura's heart squeezed in her chest, and she wished for the millionth time that she had a better way to take away the pain.

"You too, Dallas?" Laura asked her brother.

The little boy held his chin up. "I wasn't scared, but Finn was." He held up his stuffed dog for Laura to see how scared it was.

"You guys want to come sleep with me until morning?" Laura asked, patting the bed beside her. Both kids grinned and jumped into the queen-sized bed, snuggling up on either side of their older sister. One sibling under each arm, they both sighed with contentment as Laura turned off the light. The nightmares never followed them into Laura's bed, and if they did, Laura was there to keep them safe. That was Laura's job.

Laura had no doubt that they had nightmares. She had them almost every night herself. If she had someone bigger and stronger to snuggle up with after waking up, she would have gone running just like they did. To be honest, she rather liked having them with her. They kept *her* safe from the nightmares.

Dallas was back asleep almost as soon as his head hit the pillow and the light was off. He had his butt pressed into Laura's hip and his arms wrapped around Finn, the stuffed dog. Ivy usually took a little bit longer to go back to sleep.

Laura shook her head as she found a comfortable position. They should just start all going to bed with her in the first place. They kids ended up here every night anyway. It would probably give them all better sleep that way.

"Laura, were you dreaming?" Ivy whispered in the dark.

"Yeah, I was," Laura answered. "Why?"

"You were mumbling and smiling. Were you dreaming

of Ethan from Mia's fundraiser last month?" Ivy asked. "You said his name. What were you dreaming about?"

Laura felt her cheeks heat and was glad it was too dark for her sister to see. There was no way she was going to tell her innocent little sister that she had been dreaming about the one-night-stand she'd had with the guy a year and a half ago. Nope.

"I don't really remember the dream," Laura lied, shifting her weight slightly. She remembered the dream vividly. She remembered him from that night perfectly. She also remembered how he had his secretary tell her he never wanted to see her again. "And I wasn't dreaming about Ethan. You probably heard wrong."

"If you say so," Ivy said with a shrug. She yawned. "I liked Ethan. He was nice."

Laura nearly sat up. "When did you meet Ethan?"

"At Mia's fundraiser," Ivy replied like it was the most obvious thing in the world. "He helped you look for Dallas when he got lost. Remember?"

Laura needed more sleep. "You're right. I forgot that you met him during that."

Laura relaxed. Ivy didn't know Ethan from her one-night-stand. She knew him because her little brother Dallas got lost with another little boy at a fundraiser for the ranch Laura worked at a little over a month ago. The two boys had followed a dog out into a snowstorm. The entire ranch shut down to find him.

Ethan had helped her look for her brother. She was surprised he'd done it, given that he supposedly hated her. He was with her when they got the news the boys had been found, safe and sound.

She purposefully pushed the rest of the memory away. Especially the part where she'd kissed him at hearing the news. It was a stupid thing to do. She still couldn't believe she'd done it. She told herself it was all just the emotion of the moment. Hopefully, he did too.

Ivy sat straight up, bumping Laura's shoulder in the process and keeping them both from sleep. Ivy looked around, panic filling her small frame.

"Where is it?" she whispered, pulling at the sheets. Her breath came in tiny gasps.

"Where is what, Ivy?" Laura asked, sitting up. "Don't wake up Dallas."

"Dad's shirt!" Ivy wailed, pulling at the comforter. "I can't find it!"

"You had it two seconds ago," Laura replied. She felt around on the bed and quickly discovered the t-shirt Ivy now used as a security blanket. "You were laying on it."

"Oh." Ivy scooped it from Laura's hands and held it up to her face, breathing in the scent of it. It was just an old t-shirt their dad used to wear. There was nothing special about it, other than the fact that it had belonged to him. Ivy had found it in the laundry after he died and started using it as a security blanket. She couldn't sleep without it now.

"Does it still smell like him?" Laura asked. Her throat tightened with the question. It had only been about ten months since the plane accident that killed their parents. Just thinking about them still hurt. She wondered if it would ever stop hurting.

"A little," Ivy replied. "It's starting to go away, though."

Laura's heart broke a little. She sounded so sad and resigned. *A seven-year-old shouldn't have to know this kind of pain,* Laura thought. *To be honest, a twenty-five-year-old shouldn't have to know this sort of pain.*

"I know where his cologne is," Laura said after a

moment. "We can spray some on it tomorrow. That way it will still smell like him."

"I'd like that," Ivy murmured, sleep finally pulling at her. "I don't want to forget them."

"We won't ever forget them," Laura promised, smoothing the girl's hair as Ivy snuggled closer into her. "Never ever."

"Good," Ivy whispered, her voice trailing off as she found sleep again.

But now, Laura was awake. She couldn't help but think of her parents. As soon as she closed her eyes, she saw the pictures of the wreckage from her parents' flight. It was just a small private plane, but the crash had killed the two of them and the pilot instantly in the mountains.

Laura took a deep breath and tried to steady herself. She didn't want to hear the drone of an airplane engine in her dreams. She didn't want to remember having to tell Ivy and Dallas that she was going to have to take care of them now. That it was just the three of them.

It sucked, and she hated it.

Dallas mumbled and reached for her in his sleep. He rolled over, his hand finding her stomach. As soon as he found her, he quieted and went back to peaceful dreams.

She hoped she was enough for them. That was she was doing was enough. It didn't feel that way. She wasn't ready to be a parent, but here she was anyway.

Her phone vibrated on the nightstand. Rather than being annoyed at the message at such a late hour, she was grateful for the distraction. Being careful of her sleeping siblings, she reached for it and read the text.

*Going to the hospital! It's time!*

Laura smiled. Mia was not only Laura's good friend, but she was also the wife of Laura's boss. The two of them were so excited for this baby that it was all they had talked about for the past few months. She couldn't be happier for them as she sent a text back.

*Good luck. May 15$^{th}$ is a great birthday!*

Laura smiled as she turned off her phone and put it back on her nightstand. A new life in the world was always something to be glad of. She closed her eyes and tried to find sleep, this time thinking of how cute the baby was going to be and whether it would look more like Mia or more like Carter.

She wrapped her arms around both her siblings, pulling them to her as they used her shoulders for pillows. With them both safe in her arms, sleep came quickly.

# Chapter 2

than

"Becky, where's my phone charger? The one with the little climber guy etched on it?"

Ethan opened the drawer to his desk just to check that he hadn't overlooked it the first time. He liked this particular charger because it was customized. He could have sworn he had put it in his top desk drawer like always, but it wasn't there no matter how many times he opened and closed the drawer.

"I thought you kept it in your desk?" Becky replied, poking her head in through the open door to his office. She frowned. "Is it not there?"

"No," he replied, shutting the drawer a little more forcefully than necessary. He sighed. "Will you find me a different one for my trip? My flight's in an hour."

"Of course, sir," Becky replied with a cheerful smile.

He mentally wrote off the charger and continued packing his computer bag for his trip. Except, nothing seemed to be where he put it last.

"Becky? Have you seen my pens?" he called out when he discovered his stash of pens was missing as well. "Did you clean my desk?"

Becky came back to the office door. She shook her head, making her short blonde hair fall in her eyes.

"No, sir. You told me not to mess with your desk without permission when you hired me." She thought for a moment. "Maybe it was the cleaning crew? We did just hire some new staff."

"Well, all my pens are gone," he explained, pointing to the empty spot in his drawer. "I was looking for the one the President gave me."

"The silver one with the gold top?" Becky came over and handed him a backup charger.

"That's the one," he replied. He looked around his desk, and Becky started checking the rest of the office. He sighed as he closed another drawer on his desk. He wasn't just missing things. His entire desk was out of order. "Becky, will you please make a note to speak to the cleaning crew? I don't want my desk touched."

"Of course, sir." She walked around to the far side of the large office and bent over near the bathroom door. "Found it." She held up the silver pen triumphantly.

"Thank you, Becky." He couldn't figure out how his pen got on the floor. He kept all his pens in the drawer specifically so they wouldn't get lost. It was strange. He took the pen and placed it in his travel bag before glancing around the office to make sure he had everything he needed to get work done for the next few weeks.

"I've emailed you next week's schedule," Becky told him.

"And I wanted to remind you again that I'm taking off early tomorrow for my anniversary. It shouldn't cause any problems since you'll be out of town anyway, but I wanted to remind you."

"That's right. You said Mr. Jones' secretary would be covering for you. I remember." He smiled at her. She was an excellent secretary. She was calm and collected, and most importantly not interested in him in the slightest.

After the issues with Janie, his last secretary, he wasn't taking any chances on having another clingy, romance-wanting secretary who scheduled his life. Becky was happily married and, as an aside, not interested in men at all. That meant that combined with her amazing organization skills and multitasking ability, she was the best secretary in the world.

"How many years is it this year?" he asked.

Becky blushed like a schoolgirl. "It'll be seven years with Katie."

"Congratulations," he replied. She grinned like it was her very first anniversary and Ethan couldn't help but be happy for her. Love like that was meant to be celebrated.

"Thank you. Do you need anything else for your trip?" she asked.

Ethan glanced around the room. He still didn't know where the rest of his pens were, but he could manage without those. He looked back over at Becky.

"No, I think I'll be able to survive the flight," he replied with a smile. "And if I can't go the whole flight without ordering another phone charger, I'll just bill Carter for it."

Becky chuckled as she headed back to her desk. He closed his bag and followed behind her, shutting the door to his corner office as he went.

"And Becky, have a wonderful anniversary," he said as

she sat at her desk. "Dinner's on me. Use the company card and go someplace really nice."

"Thank you, Ethan." Becky grinned. "I appreciate it."

He shrugged. "Make sure you drop my name, so you get the best table," he advised. "And seriously, go all out. Seven's a lucky year."

"Thank you, sir. Katie will be so surprised," Becky replied, the smile growing on her face. "Have a good flight. And tell Mr. Williamson congratulations on the new baby for me."

"I will. Thank you again, Becky." Ethan raised his hand and headed off toward the big elevators leading down to the main floor. He stopped halfway there and turned around. "Oh, who is security for me this trip since Bruce is out for his shoulder?"

Becky looked up from the desk. "Craig. Craig Daily," she replied. "He volunteered for the trip."

"He's the one from New York, right?" Ethan asked, trying to pull up an image of the guard.

"That's David," Becky corrected him. "Craig is from San Francisco."

Ethan thought for a moment. "Tall, dark hair, very quiet?"

"That's every security guard Bruce hires," Becky replied with a chuckle.

"Good point," Ethan agreed. They all seemed to fit the tall, dark, and brooding stereotype. "He's the one who helped with the Janie situation last year, right?"

Becky nodded. "That's him. He's been very loyal. One of Bruce's best."

"Alright," Ethan said with a nod. He could place Craig in his mind now. "I like him. It'll be a good trip.

"You'd better hurry," Becky advised, tapping her watch. "You don't want to miss your fight."

He thanked her and hurried off to the elevators. It was time to head to Colorado.

## Chapter 3

$\mathcal{E}$*than*

ETHAN WAS BREATHING HARD at the top of the stairs to the maternity floor. He was in good shape, but the Colorado altitude was a deal breaker. He almost regretted not taking the elevator, but he didn't feel too badly since Craig was just as out of breath behind him and probably in better shape. His security couldn't have been more than twenty-five with short cropped dark hair and serious brown eyes.

Craig was certainly taking his job as bodyguard seriously. The man barely let him out of his sight for more than a moment. Ethan didn't mind though. Good protection was important for a billionaire. Ethan hurried up the last two steps and opened the heavy door to the second floor.

The hospital was probably the smallest one Ethan had ever seen. He was fairly sure that Mia might be the only patient in the entire building, other than the person they saw walking into the ER for stitches.

It was a short walk from the stairs to the main desk of the maternity ward. A nurse sat there like a guard, making sure that no one got past her. She looked up as she heard the two men coming and smiled.

"You must be Mr. White and company," she said as they came closer. Ethan reached for a pen to sign in, but she waved him off. "You were already logged in by the security team downstairs."

Ethan nodded. Carter Williamson, the father of the baby they were here to see as well as the co-owner to W Motors, was taking no chances. The head of Carter's security, Brian Cards, had even checked the gift bag Ethan carried the moment they stepped on hospital grounds.

"Wait here," Ethan said to Craig. "I'll be just inside."

"No leaving without me," Craig reminded him, taking a seat near the nurse's station.

"Of course not," Ethan assured him. He walked over to the only open door and peeked inside.

Carter was sitting near the window with a little bundle of pink blankets in his lap making goo-goo eyes and big smiles at the baby inside them.

"How's my wittle girly-wirly?" Carter asked his daughter in a sing-song voice that sounded strange coming from the usually stern man. Ethan couldn't have imagined something like this.

"How's the wittle daddy-waddy?" Ethan asked in a similar silly voice, pushing open the door and stepping inside.

"Don't you worry, my little baby girl. I can still beat his ass and fire him," Carter told her in the same soft baby-talk voice. He looked up from his daughter and grinned at Ethan. "Good to see you, Ethan."

"Should you be swearing in front of your kid like that?"

Ethan asked, setting his gift on the counter and coming over to see the baby. Carter held her up like she was the most precious, beautiful thing in the world. "Congratulations. She's beautiful," Ethan told the proud father.

"You want to hold her?" Carter asked, offering her out to him like it was some sort of honor.

"Um, sure." Ethan held out his arms uncertainly. He didn't want to say no to his best friend.

"Do you know how to hold a baby?" Carter asked before handing over the bundle of blankets. He looked at Ethan's open arms uncertainly.

"Of course I do," Ethan scoffed, reaching for the baby. "You just don't drop them."

Carter shook his head. "Here, put your arms here and support her head," he coached, carefully putting the baby in Ethan's hands.

Ethan felt the weight of the child pass to him, and her head suddenly rolled to the side. "Shit!"

"She's fine," Carter said in a calm voice. "Just hold her head."

"What's wrong with her neck?" Ethan asked, carefully supporting her so she wouldn't go lopsided on him again.

"Nothing," Carter told him. "That's just how newborns work."

Ethan held her like she was a ticking bomb. If her neck couldn't support her head, he was afraid that just moving her wrong would make her stop breathing or something. For the life of him, he could not figure out how humans survived as a species.

"Aww, you're a natural," Mia said, coming out of the bathroom. She wore a clean nightgown, and her brunette hair was wet from the shower. She came over and gave Ethan a side hug as she checked on her daughter.

"Hi, Mia," Ethan greeted her. "How are you?"

"Not pregnant," Mia replied with a laugh. "Which is amazing. How are you?"

"Also not pregnant." He grinned at her, and she laughed again.

"I'm so glad, Ethan," Carter said. "We were a little worried there for awhile."

Ethan rolled his eyes at his business partner.

"So, Mia," Ethan pointedly asked, turning to the nicer person in the relationship. "What did you two end up naming her? I know you weren't sure the last time I saw you."

Mia and Carter looked at one another, sharing a secret smile that only lovers have.

"Mireille Joy," Mia announced proudly. She pronounced it as "Meer-ay."

"Mireille?" he repeated. The name flowed off his tongue like music. It wasn't a name he'd heard before.

"It's French, Mia explained. "It means 'miracle,' which is appropriate. I never thought I'd have a baby. We're going to call her Miri for short."

"Well, hello little Miri," Ethan cooed to the baby. Little Miri just blinked once and went right to sleep. She was actually kind of cute, in a squishy way. "You two make good babies."

"Thanks," Carter replied. "My part was really hard."

Mia raised her eyebrows at him from across the room. Her arms crossed and she blinked slowly as she waited for him to say more.

"And I'm going to go make a phone call before my wife murders me," Carter announced, holding up his phone and quickly ducking out of the room.

"Do you want her back?" Ethan asked, holding out the

baby to Mia. As much as he was afraid she was going to stop breathing at any moment, holding her was really quite peaceful. Plus, she was asleep, and he didn't want to accidentally wake her.

"You keep her. You look very cute with her," Mia told him. She picked up a hairbrush and started working on her wet hair. "How long are you in town for Ethan?"

"As long as Carter needs me while we get things set up for the new research and development office in Denver," Ethan replied. "It'll be at least a couple of weeks. Maybe more."

Mia nodded. "It will be nice to have you here," she said, finishing up with her brush. She set it down and looked at him. "Does Laura know you're coming?"

He swallowed hard. "Laura? Why would Laura care I was in town?"

Mia just lifted a single eyebrow and waited for him to try and deny it again. Given the look he was getting, he suspected she knew the history between Laura and him. They'd had an amazing one-night-stand at the W Motors Christmas party a year and a half ago. He had called a couple times, and then after about a week, she had finally picked up. Only it wasn't her, it was a guy. Apparently Laura's boyfriend. The guy told Ethan to never call her again.

He had honored that request. He had no intention of being a home-wrecker or trying to pursue a cheater. It wasn't his fault they were both at Mia's fundraiser last month. He was fairly sure she hated his guts right up to the moment where she kissed him. Granted, she was under a lot of emotional stress at the time, but the fact remained that she'd kissed him. He wasn't quite sure what to think about her.

He sighed. "No. She doesn't know."

"Why not?" Mia asked. "I thought you two had a moment at the fundraiser."

"We had a what?" Ethan looked at her in surprise. "Did Laura tell you that?"

"She told me that you kissed when she heard her brother had been found," Mia replied.

Ethan sighed. "She was just relieved her brother was okay," Ethan explained with a shrug.

Mia snorted. "Yeah. Because I just kiss people any time I get good news. That must be it." Ethan ignored the eye roll. "She likes you."

"Then why did she tell me not to call her? Why did she tell her boyfriend to tell me off?" he asked her, trying to keep the hostility out of his voice. The baby wiggled in his arms, and he didn't want to wake her.

"Her boyfriend?" Mia asked. "Laura doesn't have a-"

She never finished her sentence because the door opened right then. In walked Laura with a big bouquet of yellow and white daisies.

She was beautiful. Her dark red hair was down around her shoulders, and her green eyes sparkled as she walked into the room with a huge smile on her face. The smile faded as soon as she saw Ethan, but her cheeks went pink.

Ethan was glad he was holding the baby, or he might have tried to kiss her right there on the spot. He had thought she was breathtaking that first night at the Christmas party. He had thought she was gorgeous a month ago at the fundraiser. He didn't know how she did it, but she had gotten even prettier. Now, standing in the hospital room, she was absolutely stunning. She became more beautiful every time he saw her.

She swallowed hard. "I didn't know you were going to be

here," Laura murmured, setting her bouquet of daisies down next to his gift bag.

"Hi Laura," Mia greeted her enthusiastically, crossing the room and giving her a big hug. "I'm so glad you came."

Ethan did not appreciate the look that was on Mia's face as she looked back and forth between the two of them. She was plotting something, and he wasn't sure what it was. Whatever she was planning, it was setting of every one of his internal "run now" alarms.

"So, actually Laura, Ethan was just about to go get me some of these cheese curds from this restaurant nearby," Mia announced.

"I was?" Ethan replied. He didn't remember agreeing to this.

"Yes, you were," Mia said pointedly. "It's weird. Even though I'm not pregnant anymore, I still have a craving for these cheese curds. Apparently, they're from Wisconsin, and I just can't get enough of them."

"Okay," Ethan shrugged, not really following what was going on. Laura looked as confused as he felt.

"Would you go with him? That way I can feed the baby and rest for a little bit." Mia smiled and fluttered her eyelashes at Laura.

"Well, I... uh..." Laura looked at her like she was crazy.

"Please, Laura?" Mia's smile grew wider, and her eyes took on a sad puppy-dog look.

"I, uh..." Laura sputtered, not knowing how to turn her down.

"Oh, thank you so much!" Mia grinned and bounced around the room as if Laura had given a resounding yes. Mia marched over to Ethan and took the baby right from him. "Just go to Sandy's off of Main Street."

Ethan stood there in shock as Mia walked off with her

baby. His arms were still cradled, but the baby was long gone.

"Cheese curds, Ethan," she reminded him with a nudge of her hip. "Go."

"Uh, right." He cleared his throat and went to the door where he held it open for a baffled Laura. Mia just smiled at the two of them.

"Oh, and you two take your time," Mia informed them, following them to the doorway. "Feeding her takes like, three hours. Yeah. So get drinks. And you can bring me the food whenever you have time. Okay. Bye!"

And with that, she shut the door firmly behind them.

Ethan stood in the hallway next to Laura unsure of exactly what to do next. He could smell her shampoo. It was soft and floral and making it hard to think. All his brain wants to think about is the kiss they shared.

He made up his mind. This was his second chance. Mia was giving him a gift right now for him to have another opportunity with Laura. He wouldn't get one like this again. It was time to put on the charm and win her over.

He smiled at her.

"So, your car or mine?" he asked.

## Chapter 4

*Sixteen months ago...*

BEST CHRISTMAS PARTY EVER, Ethan thought to himself as he stood up to look for his pants. He couldn't help but smile as he glanced back at the couch to see the most beautiful woman at the party watching him. He liked the way her eyes felt on his bare skin.

*Yup, definitely the best party ever,* Ethan thought with a smile.

He nearly didn't come to this year's event. There was so much work to be done, and the legal battle over a faulty airbag was just ramping up. His attention was on his business, but Carter told him to go. Or rather, Carter blackmailed him into it. Now that he was here, he couldn't be more grateful.

He had dutifully trod down to the California Science Museum to put in an appearance. At the start of the evening, he had fully planned on making enough of an appearance to appease Carter and make his employees feel appreciated and then going straight home to go over the lawsuit again.

Instead, she'd shown up.

So, instead of spending a night at home with his computer and a glass of wine, he'd spent it in the "Rocks, Gems, and Crystals" exhibit with his hand up the skirt of the sexiest woman he could have imagined. It would have gone further if a security guard hadn't interrupted.

That would have been the end of the night for most people, but Laura wasn't most people. She'd pulled him upstairs to the "mother's room" where they'd just had the most incredible sex of his life. Ethan wasn't ashamed to admit he'd had a few one-night-stands in his life, but this one blew them all out of the water.

And now, he was hoping it wasn't going to be just a one-night-stand.

"So, can I see you again?" he asked. He hadn't found his pants yet, but he wasn't really looking very hard either. She was stretched out on the small couch, and he was much more focused on how to never get her to wear clothes again.

"I'd like that," she replied. She gave her beautiful smooth shoulder a playful shrug. "Maybe we can go to an art museum or something."

He chuckled. Not only was she sexy, but she was also funny too. He leaned over and kissed her. How in the world had he found someone smart, funny, and this damn beautiful at a company party?

"What's your number?" she asked, reaching to find her phone on the floor. Her purse was next to her dress, which was next to her panties. He didn't help her find it because he wanted to keep her naked like this for as long as possible.

"555-1978," he told her once she'd found her phone. She carefully put the numbers in. It was his personal line- the one he almost never gave out. This line was reserved for friends and family only.

Within a couple of seconds, the phone chirped from his pant pocket. It certainly made finding his pants easier. They were tossed over by the changing station. He smiled as he read the message she'd sent him.

"Sexy Party Girl?" he asked while hitting the save new contact button. "That's what you want your contact name to be?"

"What? Are you really going to remember my real name?" she asked with a pragmatic shrug.

"It's Laura," he said. As if he could forget. He could already sense that she was everything he'd ever wanted in a woman. Even after that amazing round of sex, he was still interested in her. He wanted to take her home and learn everything about her. And, of course, have more sex.

He had never believed in love at first sight until tonight. One night with her, and he could already feel it in his bones that this was a forever kind of thing. This was a wonderful kind of love. He knew it.

"Okay, Ethan," she replied. Her voice was soft and sweet. He liked the way she said his name. He liked hearing her say it that way almost as much as he liked hearing her call it out as she trembled and came beneath him.

"I'm still saving you as Sexy Party Girl, though," he teased, keying in the name to his contacts list. He hit save with a flourish. "It'll make me smile every time I see it."

She grinned, making his heart speed up again with just her smile. "I'm okay with that," she replied, typing something into her phone.

"What are you saving me as?" he asked, watching her for a moment. His pants were now in his hands, so he didn't have a good reason not to put them on.

"Sexy Party Boy," she replied with a naughty grin. "I don't want us to get confused."

He laughed, feeling happy and light. He hadn't felt this good in months. They had a connection, and it was more than just physical. She made him laugh, and he wanted to take her places that would make her smile like she was now.

"I am so buying you another drink," he told her. He wasn't about to let her disappear off into the night like Cinderella. He was going to make sure she kept both her shoes and came home with him.

She grinned up at him, her smile matching the way he felt. "After this," she said, sitting up and motioning to the mess of clothing around them. "I'd hope so."

Ethan chuckled. They had made a mess. But, he was hoping to have a repeat of this mess in his bedroom at home in a few hours. She said she was going to be in California for another two days, and he was already mentally clearing his schedule to spend as much time with her as possible. If things worked out like he was hoping, maybe she'd even stay for longer.

After all, what could possibly go wrong between now and then?

# Chapter 5

aura

Present Day

LAURA PULLED into the parking lot of Sandy's Bar and Grill and parked the car. She was fairly sure that his security guard was right behind them, but she was doing her best to ignore everything about him. The awkward silence between them was deafening, and she could hardly wait to get out. Ethan, on the other hand, seemed perfectly comfortable with all of it. She hated him for it.

"So, this is the infamous Sandy's?" he asked when the car came to a stop. He tipped his head and peered at it through the window of her car. He didn't sound impressed.

"It doesn't look like much, but it really does have the

best food in town," she told him. She wasn't sure why she was defending the restaurant to him. It wasn't her request that had them here. She still couldn't believe Mia had duped her into this.

"Let's go on in," he said, putting on a charming smile before opening his door and getting out. Laura wondered just how many women had fallen for that smile. She knew she was certainly one of them.

Laura took a deep breath in to steady herself. She considered just putting the car in reverse and driving off without him. It would feel so good to just put him in her rearview mirror once and for all.

Except Mia would kill her. So, instead, she sighed and got out of the car.

Sandy's was built in a rustic style with a large wooden porch that wrapped around to the back. Inside, there was a big bar with TV screens positioned strategically around it. Wooden tables and chairs, all with rustic charm, decorated the rest of the space.

Ethan held the door open for her as if he were a gentleman. She tried not to laugh at the irony of that.

"Have a seat anywhere, Laura," the bartender called from behind the bar. Elena was working today. They'd known each other since high school. Laura was going to have to answer questions about her date later. "I'll be right with you."

"We're just here to get Mia her cheese," Laura announced, heading up to the bar. However, Elena was gone, and Ethan was already settling into a booth. He smiled and motioned her over.

"Okay. I guess this is what we're doing," she said under her breath as she walked toward him. "Because this won't be awkward *at all*."

Laura took the seat across from him and crossed her arms.

"What can I get you two?" Elena asked, popping up next to the table. She smiled wide like it wasn't her fault no one was manning the bar and Laura was now stuck at this stupid booth.

"I'll have a jack and coke," Ethan replied. They both turned and smiled at Laura, waiting for her drink order.

"Um, I guess I'll have the same," she said with a shrug. She didn't want drinks. She wanted to get Mia's stupid cheese and get out of here. The last thing in the entire world that she wanted was to have a conversation with Ethan. He hated her guts and didn't want anything to do with her. She still remembered the conversation that she had with his secretary, and the mean things that the secretary had relayed to her. Why he wanted anything different now was a total mystery to her, one that she didn't really want to find the answers to.

Elena waited for a second to see if they wanted anything else before thanking them and heading off to the bar. Mia crossed her arms and waited for her drink.

Ethan cleared his throat, breaking the silence between them. "I figure I'll just get this out of the way now," he told her. "I'm going to be in town for a few weeks while Carter is busy with the baby. I'm setting up the R&D department in Denver, so I'll be here for awhile."

"Okay," she said with a shrug. "Why does that matter to me?"

His pale green eyes met hers, and she felt their electric pull in. She wanted to resist, but to resist him was to resist the tide or the need to breathe.

"I want to see you."

She blinked twice. "What?"

"I'd like to see you," he repeated. "I know you said that you weren't interested after the party, but given what happened at the fundraiser..."

"Wait, what? What do you mean I said I wasn't interested?" she asked, suddenly confused for more reasons than one. She had certainly never said that after the party. "You were the one who told your secretary to let me down easy."

He frowned and shook his head. "No. You had your boyfriend tell me off when I called you."

"Uh, no." She shook her head hard enough that hair went across her face. "You never even called me. You never talked to me after the party. I didn't have a boyfriend, and you never called."

"Here's your drinks," Elena said setting the drinks down on the table. She pulled out her pad to take their order, but as she looked at the two of them staring across the table like two cats in a territory fight, she quickly pocketed it and went back to the bar.

"What do you think happened after the party?" Ethan asked once Elena was gone. His voice was calm, but there was a small tick at the base of his jaw that drew Laura's attention.

She reached for her drink and swirled the thin red straw through the dark liquid without drinking it. Slowly, she raised her eyes back to his. There was a hurt there that she hadn't seen before, or at least she had recognized.

"I gave you my phone number, and we left the mother's room," she replied. "Your secretary found you, and you had to go off to some important business thing."

"That part matches my memory," he replied. "What happened next?"

She took a sip of her drink and remembered.

# Chapter 6

 aura

*Sixteen months ago...*

HE DIDN'T CALL the next day after the party.

Laura was disappointed, but as she was nursing a small hangover combined with jet-lag for most of her Sunday morning, she wasn't too devastated. She figured he was probably in the same boat. She kept her phone on her for the whole day as she explored the area near her hotel once she felt up to walking.

It was only one day and a hungover day at that. Plus, maybe his business still needed his help. She wasn't sure what he did for W Motors, but he seemed important.

She woke up early Monday morning, eager to enjoy her

last day in California. Today they were supposed to go rock climbing, and she hoped to have another fantastic time together. Her flight home was at noon on Tuesday, so today was really her only day. She checked her messages and voicemail twice before nine am, but there was, of course, nothing.

She sat down on the foot of her bed, staring at the phone. He said he'd call, but she was getting nervous he wouldn't.

"But," she rationalized out loud, "he doesn't know that I'm leaving tomorrow. He might be following the appropriate 'wait three days' rule. I should just call him."

The thought of hearing his voice sent shivers of desire up her spine. She closed her eyes and let herself remember the feel of his touch. She was going to be remembering just how good he felt for months, she could already tell. Hopefully, though, she would have some new touches to add to her memory banks.

She opened her eyes, took a deep breath, and dialed his number.

It rang twice.

"Hello?" A female voice answered.

Laura wasn't quite ready for that, so she ended up stuttering a little.

"Um, hi. Is Ethan there?" Laura felt like she was back in elementary school trying to call the boy she liked for the homework assignment and talking to his mother instead.

"No. May I ask who is calling?" the voice replied.

"This is Laura. We met at the Christmas party." Laura smiled so her voice would sound friendly.

"He's very busy right now," the voice informed her.

"Oh, okay," Laura said, sagging a little. "Is there a time I could call back? Who am I speaking with, by the way?"

"This is his secretary," the voice replied. "And there isn't a good time until the end of this month."

"Oh." Laura bit her lip. Whatever emergency had kept him from calling must have been worse than she thought. "Could you tell him I called? And, if he gets time, to call me?"

"This is Laura from the party at the museum, right?" the secretary asked.

"Yes, it is."

The woman on the other end sighed like she was about to do something she really didn't want to do.

"I'm really sorry, sweetheart, but he's just not interested. He doesn't want to see you again. He said he'd call because it's the polite thing to do, but..." The secretary paused. "But, he told me to tell you if you called that he doesn't want you to call him ever again."

The words hit Laura like a slap in the face. "What? That doesn't make any sense..."

"Sweetheart, I'm trying to spare you the details of what he told me. The things he said about you were not kind. I'm letting you down gently. Ethan doesn't want to see you again." The secretary's voice was calm and overly sweet. It made Laura want to throw up.

"But, but..."

"I'm to tell you that if you call this number again, he will sue you for harassment," the secretary continued. "I'm really sorry, sweetie. He does this all the time to girls. Just forget you ever met him and move on."

"I don't understand..." In her mind, she could see his easy smile, the light in his eyes. He'd been so warm and wonderful. Hurt blossomed in her chest. She'd been tricked.

The secretary sighed again. "He called you a fat bimbo

in a skanky dress," she announced. "He called you an easy lay that he'd regret tomorrow."

"He did?" Laura couldn't imagine those words coming out of his mouth.

"He did. I hate telling girls the things he says about them because they are never nice. There was more, but I think you get the picture."

"Oh." Laura didn't know what to say.

"I'm really sorry, sweetie. I am," the secretary replied. "But for your own good, don't call back, okay? Just pretend you lost his number and forget it ever happened. That's my advice."

"But-"

"Did he promise to take you someplace? Buy you something?" the secretary asked. "He does that to everyone. You aren't special."

Laura felt like Mike Tyson had just punched her in the gut.

"Don't call back, okay? I'm really sorry. Goodbye."

The line clicked off.

Laura stared open mouthed at the phone in her hand. She almost wanted to call back and make sure she had the right Ethan. She thought they had fun. She went through her memories and found them to be a little hazy due to the alcohol, but there wasn't anything that had foreshadowed the conversation she'd just had. Could she have imagined things so badly?

Her hand fell, sinking onto the bed as big tears welled up in her eyes. She felt dumb. Used. The more she thought about it, the more stupid she felt. She had thrown herself at this guy. She thought there was a connection, but she never really made sure. He had used her. She'd just been an easy one-night-stand.

She went to delete his number. If that's how he felt, then there was no reason to keep it, but her finger hovered over the delete button without moving.

She sighed and just put it back in her pocket without deleting it. She felt like a total idiot, but she wanted to hear the rejection from Ethan, not his secretary. She couldn't believe that he'd actually said those things about her, or at least, she really, really didn't want to.

Laura chewed on her lip for a moment. She really considered pulling her phone back out and sending him a text message that said, "Call me if you change your mind."

But she didn't. She didn't want to be desperate. She wanted the magic she'd experienced the night before. The party had been effortless. This verged on crazy stalker girl. He didn't want to talk to her, and forcing the issue was not the right move.

Laura sighed and walked around her hotel room for a moment. She'd been planning on going climbing with Ethan today, but now she didn't have plans. She didn't want to just sit in her hotel room all day watching bad TV. It would only make her feel worse.

"I'll go to the beach," she said, making a decision. It was cold by California standards, but back home in Colorado, it was snowing. A day at the beach with sunshine and sea air would do her good.

She nodded to herself, quickly packed a bag, and headed out.

"Screw him," she said, closing the door behind her and heading out to catch a taxi. She even turned off her phone. She raised her chin defiantly and left, determined to have a good time. "I don't need him anyway."

# Chapter 7

*Present Day*

ETHAN STARED at her as she told him her story. He felt like his eyes were going to bug out and he was having a hard time from keeping his jaw from hitting the table.

"I tried to call you a week later, but the line was disconnected," she finished. She shrugged and took a sip of her drink. Her green eyes were fierce. No wonder she was angry with him. He was angry with her version of him.

"That's not what happened at all," he told her, trying his best to keep his voice level. Inside, he wanted to strangle someone.

She raised her eyebrows and took a sip from her straw. "It's not?" She didn't sound convinced.

"Not even close," he replied. He raised his hand and signaled to the bartender for another round. He was going to need a lot more alcohol.

"So what do you think happened?" she asked, setting her drink down and crossing her arms.

"I was tied up with business all that Sunday," he explained. "But I wanted to see you. I couldn't stop talking about you to my secretary. You met her at the party."

"Your secretary? You mean the lady in the red dress who wanted you under the mistletoe?" Laura asked. She pursed her lips and let out a breath. "I bet she just *looooved* that."

He had to agree with her. In hindsight, it was coming together now. The whole issue between them was all due to a jealous secretary.

"I had an interview Monday morning, so I left my phone with Janie," he explained. "I was going to call you as soon as the interview was done to go rock climbing. I was looking forward to it."

"Uh-huh," she replied, taking a small sip of her drink. She still had most of her drink left, and she certainly didn't look convinced at his story.

"You must have called while I was giving the interview," he told her. "I swear to you, I didn't tell her to say any of those things, and I never said any of what she claimed."

"Why'd she say it then?"

Ethan sighed and took a sip of his drink. "She thought we were dating. She was sure that I was falling madly in love with her and was going to sweep her off her feet Prince Charming style at any time."

"She thought you were a cliché romance novel hero?" Laura asked.

"I had to fire her because she wouldn't take no for an answer. We had to call security to forcibly remove her from the building, and my lawyers had to set up a restraining order," he replied. "It was a complete and total mess."

She played with her drink straw, mulling over his words. When she looked back up, he could see she was starting to believe him.

"Thinking about it, I can actually see her doing that," she said after a moment. "She seemed pretty possessive of you at the party. I mean, I met her for all of five minutes, but..."

She shrugged and took another sip of her drink. She wasn't even half done with it when the bartender arrived with their second round. This time, she just dropped them off at the table and bolted rather than waiting to see if they had an order.

"I called you. Or rather, I called the number on my phone for you," he amended, picking up his new drink. "It went straight to voicemail, and I couldn't leave a message due to it being full."

She frowned. "My voicemail had plenty of storage. I don't keep any messages."

"I'm guessing that Janie changed the number," he explained.

Laura's eyes widened as she figured out what had happened. He continued.

"I tried again later that day. That's when I started getting these text messages that said, *'Don't call me again'* and *'back off creep.'*"

Laura winced.

"I tried one more time that evening, and a guy answered." Ethan took a sip of his drink. The bartender was skilled. These were perfectly balanced. "He read me a riot act and told me not to call his girlfriend anymore. He said the two of you were back together and you weren't interested in seeing me ever again." He shrugged. "I stopped trying after that."

Now it was her turn to stare at him. Her eyes were wide, and her mouth hung open at what he had just told her.

"I didn't do any of that," she told him. "I wasn't even seeing anyone. I was alone in my hotel room. I didn't have anyone to make that call."

"I'm guessing it was Janie," he replied. "Or rather, a friend of Janie's."

She took a sip of her drink, nearly finishing it off. It was a big sip. "What about when I called you? When it said the line was disconnected?"

"The next day, Janie 'accidentally' dropped a lamp on my phone. The screen was completely destroyed," he said. "Being my secretary, I asked her to take care of it. She got me a new phone and a new number. I didn't think anything of it at the time."

"She didn't want me calling you and exposing what she did," Laura said, shaking her head slowly. She flopped back in her seat and took a moment to marvel at the evil genius that was Janie.

"She certainly thought of everything," he agreed. He was going to need another drink at the rate he was going. She on the other hand, had barely touched hers.

"So, you're telling me that all of the anger between us was just a big misunderstanding?" she asked, incredulous. "That I thought you were the biggest douche in the history of douches for no reason?"

"Hey, I thought you were a horrible cheater, so I guess we're even," he replied. He raised his glass for a toast. "To not being a douche. Or a cheater."

She chuckled and clinked her glass against his before taking a sip.

"Is it bad that I want to murder your secretary right now?" she asked, evaluating it in her hand as a murder weapon.

"You and me both," he agreed. He raised his glass again, tipping it toward her. "To murder."

She clinked their glasses with a chuckle, and they both sipped. The animosity between them was completely gone. The natural connection he'd experienced with her that first night was back, and it felt amazing. He had been right to think that they had chemistry. When she didn't think he hated her guts, they were a match made in heaven.

"I think I can handle you being around for a couple of weeks," she said, smiling over her glass at him. "Suddenly, it doesn't seem so terrible."

He smiled. This day was now going so much better. "Do you know any good places to go climbing around here?" he asked, lowering his voice and making it very clear he had more planned than just climbing over rocks. "I need a guide."

Her smile faltered, the light fading from her face. She set the rest of her drink down without finishing it.

"I can't," she replied. She opened her mouth to say more, but her phone started to go off. She pulled it from her pocket and silenced it. "I actually need to go. That was my alarm to go pick up my brother and sister. School ends in ten minutes."

He wasn't going to give up that easily. Not after all this.

"Dinner, then." It wasn't a question. It was a statement.

She stood up and put her phone in her pocket. "What?"

"Dinner," he repeated. "I want to buy you dinner."

"I can't." She smiled politely, but it didn't touch her eyes. "I have obligations now. You've met them, and you know that they depend on me now. As much as I would like to, I can't."

"You can't get a babysitter for one night?" Ethan asked.

"We've had a rough time. They need me," she explained, picking up her purse. "What if something happens to them? I need to be there for them. I have to say no. But, thank you."

He stood from the table and went to her side. He loved that her breath caught as he came close and took her hand. She didn't pull away. If anything she leaned in closer.

"Come to dinner with me," he repeated. Her hand was so smooth in his. "We'll celebrate Mia and Carter's baby."

"The kids..." she started to say.

"I will hire an entire security team and the best nannies this side of the Mississippi to watch your brother and sister for the few hours that we are eating," he promised, still holding her hand. "They can't be your excuse."

She pursed her lips as she thought. He could see the internal struggle. She had thought he hated her for the past year and a half. Despite the fact that he didn't deserve it, she was having a hard time trusting him. He couldn't blame her. He wouldn't trust him yet either. He needed to give her more.

So he kissed her.

It was just a simple kiss. He pulled her hand toward him and tipped his head to catch her lips. He meant to make it short and sweet, but she tasted so damn good it was hard to stop at "short." It didn't help that she moaned and pressed into him.

He was the one to step back from the kiss. Her eyelashes fluttered as she recovered from the kiss. "Um, okay..." she whispered, a smile slowly filling her face.

"Good. Tomorrow night. Five o'clock," he informed her. "I'll pick you up."

"Tomorrow? Ethan, I can't-"

"And here's my number," he said, cutting off her argument. He reached for a pen and quickly added ten more digits to the back of the card. "Now you have my work number, my cell, and my secretary's number."

He handed her the card. She carefully took it between two fingers, looking it over before meeting his gaze.

"You sure you want to give me your secretary's number?" she asked.

"This time, she's not interested in me. She really will make sure I get your calls," he replied. He wanted to kiss her again. He wanted to do their entire first night together again. "But, call the private number first anyway."

She hid her smile as she looked over the card one more time. She carefully tucked it into her purse.

"You really aren't going to take no for an answer, are you?" she asked.

He shook his head. "Not again. Never again."

Her smile twitched upward before she hid it again with a sigh. "Okay. My number is 555-1978. You might want to memorize it this time. Text me, and I'll give you my address."

He grinned, whipping out his phone and putting in the numbers so quickly he was sure his fingers blurred. His chest had this amazing feeling like he might burst with happiness that he hadn't felt in almost a year and a half.

She slung her purse over her shoulder. "And don't forget about the nannies," she told him, taking a step toward the exit. "I'm going to expect Mary Freaking Poppins."

"I'll get you two Mary Freaking Poppinses," he promised. He quickly hit send on a short message.

*Dinner at 5. Don't forget.*

HE WATCHED as she walked to the door of the restaurant, shaking her head, but smiling, as she went. She looked back in time to see him watching her, and she couldn't help but grin even wider at him.

"Remember to get Mia her cheese," she called out.

"Of course," he promised. "I like being on her good side."

She chuckled and headed out the door into the spring afternoon. He watched for a moment as she went to her old beat-up truck and started the engine. He could see her smiling as she drove away.

He sat back down in the booth, feeling like he'd just gotten a second chance at life. It was time to win her heart like he should have done the first time.

## Chapter 8

*L aura*

"ARE you ever going to park or are you just going to drive forever?" Ivy asked, watching as Laura drove past the restaurant one more time. She was making sure that Ethan and his bodyguard were definitely gone. She did not want to run into them on accident. She wasn't sure she could handle another dose of Ethan's charm without succumbing to him entirely.

"I'm parking now," Laura replied, pulling into the restaurant parking lot. The only cars were Elena's and a couple of sedans that didn't look nice enough to be rentals. She was safe.

Laura helped Dallas out of his booster seat while Ivy ran on ahead. She could already smell the hamburgers and french fries and her mouth watered. Sandy's was a favorite dinner spot, especially when Elena was working. Laura tried not to have the kids eat out too often, but it was so much easier than trying to cook for all three of them after a busy day at work. Today, however, Laura had a different reason for wanting to eat at Sandy's.

She wanted to talk to Elena about Ethan.

Elena looked up from the bar as the two kids ran inside leaving Laura in the dust. Elena's smile widened as she saw who they were.

"How are my two favorite customers?" Elena asked the two kids, coming around the bar to greet them. Ivy gave her a big hug that Elena happily returned.

"I'm doing well. How are you, Ms. Elena?" Dallas asked, standing up straight with his hands behind his back.

"I am doing well, thank you," Elena replied. She knelt down, so she was on the same level as the small boy. "Have you been working on your manners?"

Dallas nodded. "I want pizza, please."

Elena laughed and gave him a hug. "You got it, kiddo," she promised before standing up. She motioned to the far end of the room. "Go on over to your special table, guys. I'm just getting off my shift. Can I join you?"

"Of course," Ivy shouted, half way to the table already. Dallas was hot on her heels, giggling as he ran after his older sister. Elena wasn't too far behind them with menus and crayons.

"Okay, here's your stuff," she said, giving each child a box and a paper kids' menu. "Will you draw me something while I talk to your sister?"

The two kids nodded, happily pouring the crayons on the table and starting to work on the cute little puzzles and coloring designs. Elena ruffled Dallas' hair before heading back to the front of the restaurant where Laura was.

"So, what's the story with the cute guy today?" Elena asked, giving her friend a hug. "And that kiss..."

Elena fanned herself with her hand and gave a low whistle.

"Shh," Laura admonished, glancing over at the table. They hadn't even looked up, but Laura didn't want them hearing that she was kissing people.

"So, what's the story?" Elena asked. "Come with me and put in the order."

She tipped her head to the side of the bar where a touch screen was set up to take orders. Both kids were too engrossed in the coloring even to notice they hadn't joined them yet. Elena swiped her badge and started putting in everyone's usual order.

"So, who was he?" Elena asked, her eyes on the touch screen but still wanting to know what was going on.

"Do you remember the guy from the Christmas party that I told you about?" Laura asked.

Elena paused and looked up. "You didn't go to a Christmas party this year... Oh, you mean last years' party?"

Laura nodded, and Elena's eyes went wide.

"Wait, *that's* museum sex guy? That's 'best sex of my life' guy?" Elena stopped putting in the order and put her hands on Laura's shoulders. "What was he doing here?!"

"Yes, that was him," Laura replied. She glanced over at the kids who still weren't paying any attention to anything but their crayons. "And keep it down. I don't want Ivy repeating this stuff to her grandmother."

"As I recall, museum sex guy never called you back," Elena pushed one last button on the screen and turned to face her friend. "You two didn't look like he wasn't speaking to you. Or rather, you did a fair amount of talking. And then some pretty hot not talking."

Laura blushed. "Apparently, he tried to call me after the party, but his secretary changed my number in his phone."

"Seriously? Who does that?" Elena asked.

"Someone who is crazy in love with her boss and doesn't want anyone but her to be with him," Laura replied. "She sabotaged the whole thing. She made him think I was interested."

"Seriously? Damn." Elena shook her head in disbelief for a moment, but then her eyes narrowed, focusing on Laura. "So what's going on now? You aren't exactly in a position to be doing one-night-stands."

Laura followed Elena's gaze to the kids. Dallas was asking if he could borrow Ivy's green crayon since he'd broken his. Ivy was being a good sister and sharing marvelously.

"He wants to take me out for dinner."

"Nice!" Elena said with a pleased smile. It twisted into a concerned frown. "With or without kids? I'm busy this whole week. I have double shifts so I can't watch them."

"I know you're busy," Laura said quickly. "He's getting me a babysitter."

"Double nice!" Elena nudged her shoulder and grinned. "I think he likes you."

Laura shrugged and didn't reply.

"Wait a second." Elena put her hand on Laura's shoulder and turned, so they were face to face. "You are doing it, aren't you?"

Laura sighed and pulled at her fingernail before answering. This was why she needed to talk to Elena. She needed to know if she was doing the right thing or if she should run from this guy. He'd already let her down once, even though it wasn't really his fault. She wasn't sure she was in a position where she was ready to go out to dinner with someone she was actually interested in.

"I don't know. I just..." Laura shrugged again.

"You just what?" Elena asked.

"The timing," Laura replied. "I mean, dating? Dinner? I have the kids and... what if they freak out? They need me, and I can't leave them alone. They wouldn't want me dating."

"The kids are fine, Laura," Elena assured her. "They don't need you with them three hundred percent of the time."

"I know." Laura sighed. "I just don't feel right when I'm not with them."

Elena frowned. "What do you do when they're at school? You've seemed fine without them then."

"I don't feel weird when they're at school," Laura tried to explain. "School's fine. They're safe there. Mom and Dad liked their school."

Elena watched her for a moment before nodding. "So that's what this is."

"What is?"

"This is about your parents," Elena said gently. "It's about them."

"How is this even remotely about my parents?" Laura scoffed. "My parents are dead."

"Exactly. You're fine with the kids being at school because your parents approved it," Elena explained. "You're fine with me watching them because your parents hired me to babysit. You're fine with them going to the ranch with Carter because your parents liked Carter."

"What's your point?" Laura asked. Annoyance crept into her voice without her meaning it to.

"You're parents never met this guy. You never even told

them about him," Elena told her. She looked over at the kids. "You're parents also didn't hire or approve of whoever is going to be babysitting them. You are freaking out about this because you have to approve and decide this all on your own."

"That's not true," Laura replied, taking a step back from her friend. "You're reaching, Elena. I'm freaking out because this parenting thing is hard. You don't have kids. You don't know what this is like."

Elena opened her mouth to say something and then quickly shut it. She took a deep breath and gave Laura a fake smile.

"I'm going to go sit with your brother," Elena told her. "He looks like he needs some adult supervision."

She shook her head as she walked away, heading to the table with the kids. Laura immediately regretted the harsh tone she'd used, but the point remained valid. Laura was responsible for her siblings now. She'd woken up one morning and suddenly had a five and seven-year-old to care for. She couldn't just randomly go out to dinner with some guy and leave them alone with a stranger. Her parents would hate that.

Laura took a breath to clear her head. Elena just had no idea how stressful this all was. She took another deep breath and headed to the table. The food would be here soon, and she was hungry.

Elena was taking turns with Dallas playing Tic-Tac-Toe. It looked like she was even letting Dallas win when Laura arrived. She slid into her usual spot at the table.

"So, Ivy and Dallas, would you two be okay with your sister going out on a date?" Elena asked, not looking up from the Tic-Tac-Toe board.

"Hey!" Laura tried to kick her under the table but

missed. Instead of kicking Elena, Laura slammed her toes against the hard wooden beam of the chair. It hurt more than she had expected.

Dallas looked up and thought for a second. "Sure. She needs to get laid," he said with a shrug.

Laura's eyes nearly popped out of her head. "Excuse me? What did you just say?"

Dallas glanced at the two women, suddenly nervous. "That you need to get laid. That's what they say on that TV show you watch." He frowned. "Is getting laid bad? It sounded like a good thing."

Elena looked like she was going to choke on her own laughter. Laura was just glad Elena was holding it in, or she would have had to kick her again.

"He's not wrong," Elena managed to get out.

Laura glared at her. Her toes still hurt, or she would have attempted another kick.

"No, Dallas," Laura said, still shooting daggers at Elena. "It's a grown-up thing. We shouldn't repeat that phrase, okay?"

"Okay, Laura." He shrugged and then went back to studying the board to determine the best place to put his X to beat Elena's O's.

"What about you, Ivy?" Elena asked, finally in control again.

Laura gave her a dirty look. She'd hoped that Elena had gotten distracted by Dallas and forgotten what she was asking, but that didn't happen.

"Sure," Ivy replied, looking up from her drawing. "Will you come watch us, Elena? Then we can have pizza."

"I'm busy this week," Elena told her. "It would be someone else watching you. Is that okay?"

Laura held her breath. She expected Ivy to say no. That

it had to be Elena who watched them and no one else. Then, she would be justified. The kids needed her.

Ivy thought for a long moment, then shrugged. "We'd still get pizza, right?"

"I'm so glad you love me for my pizza skills," Elena teased.

"What? I like pizza," Ivy said, completely serious.

"I know you do," Elena soothed. "But, would you be okay with someone else watching you? As long as they're nice?"

"Yeah, we'd be okay," Ivy replied. She thought for a moment then turned to Laura with a huge grin on her face. "Would I be in charge? Would Dallas have to do everything I say?"

Elena gave her a smug smile. "See?"

Laura crossed her arms and glared at Elena. That wasn't the answer she was expecting. "We're not discussing this now."

"They're fine, Laura," Elena said, pushing her luck. "Go on the date. And don't feel guilty about it, okay?"

"That was low." Laura kept her arms crossed.

"Yes, it was," Elena acknowledged. She smirked. "And I have absolutely no guilt over it either. You should go on the date."

"Who wants to take you on a date?" Ivy asked, looking up again. "And why you?"

"Hey, I am very date-able," Laura informed her. Ivy just gave her a skeptical look. "I really do have a date."

"Sure. What's his name?" Ivy looked unimpressed.

"Ethan," Laura said without thinking. She nearly covered her mouth with her hand. She did not need to give Ivy that information.

"Oh. The guy from your dream," Ivy said with a nod. "That should make you happy."

Elena grinned at this new piece of information. "Oh, so you're dreaming about him?"

"This conversation is ending now," Laura informed her. She smiled, but it was the smile an alligator gave before eating its victim.

"Wait, wait, wait... Ethan?" Elena asked. "As in works with Carter at W Motors and has a secretary Ethan?"

"Yes," Laura replied. "So?"

"As in Ethan White, co-owner of W Motors and ultra billionaire? That Ethan?" Elena looked like her eyes might pop out of her head.

"Yeah." Laura shrugged, pleased to have the upper hand in the conversation for a moment. "Did I not mention that last time?"

Elena swatted her from across the table. "No! No, you did not mention a billionaire asked you out on a date today. Or that you had a one-night-st--"

Laura coughed loudly and looked pointedly at a very interested Ivy.

"A one-night *date* at the museum with a billionaire!" Laura amended.

"To be fair, I didn't know he was a billionaire at the museum," Laura replied. "I only figured it out after I googled him when he didn't call me back."

Elena looked incredulous. "When you found out he was a billionaire, why didn't *you* call him again?" she asked. "I would have freaking drove to California and sat on his porch if I had known."

"I did try to call him back," Laura explained. "But his line didn't work. And I wasn't calling him because he was a billionaire."

"You found out the guy was a billionaire, but that wasn't why you were calling him back?" Elena asked.

"I thought that the fact he was a billionaire was a part of the reason he brushed me off," Laura explained. "I'm not exactly a Russian ballerina. I'm not exactly billionaire arm candy material."

"Don't sell yourself short like that," Elena said with a frown. "You are totally billionaire trophy wife material. You are a freaking catch, and don't you ever doubt it."

Laura felt a smile cross her face. Her friend loved her.

"Thank you," Laura said. Elena smiled at her.

"Still though, please date him," Elena said after a moment. "If you don't, I'm happy to. Does he have friends that need dates? I'm very available."

Laura laughed. "I'll make sure I ask."

Elena grinned, looking very pleased with herself. "So that means you're going on the date then. So you can ask him."

Laura sighed. She did want to go on the date, but she wasn't sure she could handle more things to complicate her life. Ethan White was a definite complication to her already complicated world.

"You are going on that date," Elena informed her. "You need it. You deserve it."

Laura looked at her and knew that if she didn't go on this date, Elena would come to her house, kidnap her, and put her in Ethan's car either way.

"Fine," she said, putting her hands up in the air. "I'll go on the date."

It was better just to make everyone happy. Besides, she could see the waiter coming with their food, and the last thing she wanted was to have the waiter overhear their conversation.

"Yay, Laura's gonna get laid!" Dallas exclaimed. He

clapped his hands and looked incredibly happy for his oldest sister.

"Dallas!" Laura's cheeks heated and she could see some of the restaurant patrons turning to look at their table. The waiter raised his eyebrows as he started setting the food down in front of them.

Elena dissolved into a fit of laughter, leaving Laura to glare at her brother.

Raising siblings was hard.

## Chapter 9

 *than*

ETHAN FELT ODDLY nervous as he prepared for his day. He'd woken up that morning in a great mood, and he knew it had to do with the fact that he was going to see Laura that evening. He checked his watch. He had two meetings before it would be time for his date, and it felt like too long and yet not enough at the same time.

He stood at the foot of his bed with his dinner suit laid out on across the comforter. He held three ties in his hand, trying to figure out which one would look the best. Usually, he left this kind of decision up to his secretary, but he was on his own today.

He held up the blue one. It looked nice, but he wasn't sure if the gold one gave a better impression. He wondered which color Laura liked better and wished he had a horse tie. She would like a horse tie.

A knock on the door to his hotel suite pulled him from

his thoughts. He set the ties down and went to open the door. Peeking through the peephole, he could see Craig waiting for him. He smiled and opened up the door.

"Good morning, Craig," Ethan greeted him.

Craig handed him a small package. "This came for you, sir," he said respectfully. He smiled as he handed the box to Ethan.

"Thank you," Ethan said, taking the box. "I'll be out in just a moment."

He went to close the door but changed his mind. He needed a second opinion on the ties. Craig wasn't his secretary, but any opinion would be better than none.

"Craig, are you any good at picking out ties?" Ethan asked.

"You mean for your date tonight?" Craig gave an unassuming shrug. "My sister says I have a great eye for color. Maybe I can help."

"I need all the help I can get," Ethan replied, pulling the door open wide and letting the security guard inside. "My suit's in the bedroom."

Ethan led Craig through the living area of the suite and to the spacious bedroom. Craig glanced about as they walked, taking in all the details of the place. Ethan thought it must be the mark of a good bodyguard.

"Here's the suit," Ethan said. "And the three ties I have to go with it. I'm leaning towards the blue, but I just can't seem to decide."

Craig chuckled. "You should actually check your package."

"What?" Ethan asked, unsure of what his package had to do with choosing a tie for dinner tonight.

"Check your package," Craig repeated. "I opened it up to

make sure it was safe. I think you'll find it helps your current situation."

Ethan frowned but pulled open the box. The tape was neatly sliced open, making the item inside very easy to find.

It was a tie. A beautiful pale green, silk tie.

"As my sister would say, it matches your eyes," Craig told him. His cheeks pinked slightly as he shrugged.

Ethan lay the tie out against the suit. The pale green complimented the dark charcoal of the suit better than anything he had picked out. It was perfect.

"I think she'll like that, sir," Craig said.

He picked the box up, eager to see who had sent it. The return address was just the tie seller's address, and there was no packing slip with information.

"Was there anything else in the box?" Ethan asked Craig, holding up the box. "I'm not sure who sent it."

Craig shrugged. "I didn't take anything out once I opened it and saw it was safe. I'm sorry, sir."

"Huh." Ethan frowned until it dawned on him. "I asked Becky to pick me out some new ties last week. This must be one of them."

"Of course, sir. That does make sense," Craig agreed. "Who else would even know to send you a tie?"

Ethan nodded. "Thank you for your help, Craig. I'm almost ready. I know it's about time to leave."

"You are most welcome, Mr. White," Craig replied. "Would you like me to pack up your suit and put it in the car? That way you won't have to worry about it. I have a spot where it won't wrinkle."

"That would be wonderful, Craig." Ethan smiled at him. "I appreciate it."

"Of course, sir." Craig smiled and then quickly looked away as he put the suit into a garment bag and carefully made sure the tie was folded correctly and stored where it wouldn't get lost.

Ethan watched him for a moment and then went to find his shoes and grab his documents for the day. He was going to have to give Craig a promotion if this level of service kept up.

## Chapter 10

$\mathcal{L}$*aura*

"IT'LL BE OKAY, Dallas. I promise," Laura told her brother as she rubbed his back. "You're doing great."

He nodded weakly and continued to vomit what little was left in his stomach into the toilet. Laura kept rubbing his back and making soft words of encouragement until the little guy curled up in a ball on the floor.

"I don't feel good, Laura," he said weakly. If that wasn't the understatement of the year, she wasn't sure what was. His little cheeks were flushed, and he looked absolutely miserable.

"I know, sweetie," she said softly, pulling him up into a hug. "Let's rinse your mouth out and then we'll go join your sister on the couch. Then we can watch a movie."

Dallas nodded weakly, letting his sister take him to the sink. "A new movie?"

"Sorry, we just have the old ones," Laura said, turning on the water.

"Okay." He didn't even try to whine about it. That's how Laura knew he was absolutely miserable. Dallas reached out and washed his hands and took a small sip of water into his mouth. When he was done, she picked him up and carried him out to the couch. She could feel his fever starting as he pressed his forehead into her neck.

Out on the couch, Ivy was wrapped up in a fluffy yellow blanket with a Halloween candy bucket perched on the cushion beside her. The orange pumpkin smiled out like nothing was wrong, but Laura knew better.

The kids had the stomach flu. She was just praying she didn't catch it, too.

Laura carefully set Dallas down next to his sister. He found a matching blue blanket to Ivy's and promptly curled up underneath it, hiding everything but his eyes.

"How are you doing, Ivy?" Laura asked her sister as she got out a second pumpkin head for her brother. They made for easy cleanup if the kids couldn't make it to the bathroom in time.

"Not so good," Ivy whispered. "My stomach still hurts."

"Do you need me to clean out your pumpkin?" Laura asked, hoping that she didn't.

"Not yet," Ivy replied. Laura sighed in relief even though she knew it wouldn't be long before she had to clean it out anyway.

"Okay. I'll get you two some ginger ale," Laura told them. "It'll help settle your stomachs."

"Make sure it's the green kind," Ivy said, then looked up. "Laura? Weren't you supposed to go on a date?"

"Yeah, but I canceled it," Laura told her. "You guys are sick. I'll go another day."

"I'm sorry, Laura." Ivy's green eyes filled with tears.

"Don't worry about it, Ivy," Laura said coming over to her. "I'll be fine. I want to make sure you guys are okay." She brushed the hair off Ivy's forehead. "Let me go get that ginger ale."

Both kids just stared at the TV as she went to the kitchen. It was just on the preview screen. Usually, they both would be clamoring for her to hurry up and press the skip button to get to the movie, but neither one of them said a word. She knew they felt awful.

Laura was halfway to the kitchen when the doorbell rang.

"If it's that damn vitamin sales guy again, I'm calling the cops," she muttered as she stalked to the door. The last person she wanted to deal with was an overzealous door to door salesman today. She threw open the front door, ready to deal out some murder.

Instead, Ethan stood on her front porch with flowers. He held out the dozen red roses like a peace offering and took a step back. She realized she must look rather ferocious and she did her best to smile.

It wasn't hard to smile at him. He looked amazing. He wore a dark charcoal suit that fitted his body with lines a sculptor would love. He had on a green tie that brought out the pale color of his eyes, making him somehow more handsome than she ever remembered him looking.

He looked ready for a fancy date.

She, on the other hand, did not. She had changed into ratty old sweatpants and a t-shirt she'd won at a riding competition five or six years ago. The words were starting to peel off, but the shirt was comfortable. Her hair was up in a messy "mom bun." She was anything but ready for a date.

"Ethan?" Her hands went to her hair, and she tried to

smooth it out a little bit. "Didn't you get my texts? I can't go on our date tonight." She thought for a moment and frowned. "Actually, I know you got the texts. You answered them. What are you doing here?"

He held out the flowers again. This time they looked more like a gift rather than a shield. She took them, breathing in the sweet rose scent. It was hard to be mad when everything smelled like roses.

"I know you can't go on the date," Ethan replied, his eyes sparkling as he watched her enjoy the flowers. "The kids are sick, and you can't go out."

She held the door open for him to come inside. He stepped in and carefully removed his dress shoes by the door. She stood there, holding the door and staring at him. He knew they weren't going on a date, but there he was taking off his shoes at her door.

"What are you doing?" she finally asked, totally confused by what was going on. There was no way she was leaving Ivy and Dallas with a stranger- not when they were sick.

"I wasn't about to let you off the hook for our date," Ethan told her, coming to his full height and smiling down at her.

She motioned to the two kids on the couch. They were looking over with a little bit of interest, but neither one of them had moved an inch.

"They really do have the stomach flu," she told him. "I have the doctor's note to prove it. Are you sure you want to be at ground zero?"

He smiled directly at her, and the full power of his attention made her stomach do funny things. Her whole body heated when he looked at her like that, and it made her want things she knew she couldn't have. Like time off from being the provider.

"Yes, I want to be here." He took a step forward, and she felt her knees go weak. He smelled amazing. Clean and masculine with something spicy that made her want to smell him all day.

He waved out the open door to someone coming up the walk. Craig carefully navigated the pathway to the front door carrying several large brown paper bags in his arms.

"Since you couldn't come out for the date..." he started, letting Craig pass through the doorway. "I brought the date to you."

Laura cocked her head to the side, trying to figure out what he meant by that. What he meant by any of this. This wasn't what usually happened when she canceled a date.

Craig set the bags down on the kitchen counter, clearing a small space for the last one. She grimaced slightly. The kitchen was a mess. She had meant to clean it earlier, but having sick kids meant that nothing had gotten done. This was definitely not the impression she wanted to make on Ethan.

"Is there anything else, sir?" Craig asked, looking at Ethan.

"That should be it, for now, Craig. Thank you," Ethan replied.

"If you think of anything else, I'll be out in the car." Craig tipped a polite nod to them both. "I hope the kids feel better soon, miss."

And with that, he left, closing the door behind him. Laura stared after him for a moment, unsure of exactly was going on. Ethan, on the other hand, walked into the kitchen and began unloading the bags.

"First, I got you all some ginger ale," Ethan explained,

pulling out a big green bottle. "I also got this re-hydration drink for kids, chicken broth, saltine crackers, and for dessert, graham crackers and bananas."

Laura shook her head as she looked at all the stomach bug friendly food he had brought over. She checked the bottle of ginger ale and was happy to see it was the right kind. There was only one brand that the kids would accept when they were sick, the one with the green label. It was what their mom used to get. She knew they wouldn't drink anything else, so it was good that Ethan got the right kind.

"For us, since we can handle solid food," he continued, going to another bag. "I got cheeseburgers since I wasn't sure what you would like. The waitress from Sandy's said this was your favorite."

Laura recognized the handwriting on the outside of the to-go box as Elena's. She was going to have to thank her friend later. It was labeled with the green-chile burger that she always ordered.

"I also picked up some movies for the kids," Carter added, reaching for yet another bag. He reached inside and pulled out three DVD cases. It sounded like there were more inside the bag as well. "I wasn't sure what movies you had, so I just grabbed everything in the 'new release' section."

Laura just stared at him for a moment. They were used to scrounging the five-dollar bin for old movies and he'd just gotten them what looked like every new children's movie for the past two years. It was an amazing gift.

"Thank you," she whispered. She realized she still had the roses in her hand and she had to shake herself. This was possibly the nicest thing anyone had ever done for her.

"You brought movies?" A small, weak voice from the

couch called out. Dallas sat up a little higher, his dark hair peeking out of the top of his blanket.

Laura smiled and turned to Ethan. "You go find out what they want to watch," she told him. "I'll take care of putting the food away."

Ethan walked to the couch with the bag of DVDs while Laura put the flowers in a vase and started pulling out bowls and utensils for their meal. Her hand moved on autopilot as she watched as he took off his fancy suit jacket and sat on the floor in front of the couch. He looked completely out of place with his dress pants, dress shirt, and tie.

The two kids sat up under their blankets and smiled at him. They still looked sick, but at least they weren't pouting about it anymore. Their eyes lit up as he started to pull movie after movie from his bag. Each new DVD was a present to them, and he'd gotten them about a dozen new films. Laura knew they would want to watch every single one of them at least five times. She was going to be watching kids' movies for months now.

He held up two DVDs, one in each hand. The two kids would point to the one they wanted. If they both picked the same one, it stayed in his hand. If they picked differently, he pulled out two new movies.

It took a few minutes for them to work through the selection process and come up with the choice of movie, but Ethan had the two of them giggling by the end of it. He would make silly faces and pretend to fall over when they chose differently. Laura couldn't help but smile as she watched the three of them.

She'd finished putting out bowls and cups when she heard shrieks of laughter from the living room. She looked up to see Ethan using his teeth and growling like a dog as he struggled with the DVD plastic wrap on the case. The two kids rolled with laughter as he attempted and failed at opening the DVD wrapping. When he handed the case to Ivy, she easily opened it, making the two children laugh even harder.

"I loosened it up for you," he said.

He jumped to his feet and put the DVD in the player, pressing start before heading back over to her in the kitchen.

"They say they would like some ginger ale," he told her. "But no soup yet."

"Okay," Laura said with a smile. She poured the fizzy drink into two fun colored cups with straws. "You're really great with them."

He chuckled. "I like kids."

"You must have nieces or nephews," she remarked, putting the lid back on the bottle. She made sure it was tight this time so the carbonation wouldn't escape.

"No, I'm an only child," he said, shaking his head. "Being goofy just comes naturally."

Laura handed him the cups of ginger ale. "Well, color me impressed."

He smiled proudly, puffing out his chest a little and it made her giggle.

"Ethan," the kids called from the couch. Ivy sat up a little bit. "The previews are done. The movie's going to start."

"I'm being summoned," Ethan told her, picking up the two cups. He walked over to the two kids, handed them the drinks, and then sat on the floor in front of them.

"Laura, will you sit with me?" Dallas asked, his eyes big and hopeful. There was no way she could say no to that face.

She scooted him over on the couch so she could sit between Ivy and Dallas.

"Will you sit up here too, Ethan?" Ivy asked. She smiled when he looked back at her.

"Of course," he told her, rising to his knees and then sitting in the only open space next to Dallas.

Ivy cuddled happily into Laura, while Dallas laid his head down on Ethan's lap. It was as if the boy had known him forever. Ethan simply smiled and rubbed the boy's back as the movie started.

"I think you've got a fan," Laura whispered, nodding to the half-asleep smiling boy between them. Ethan just smiled.

"What can I say? I'm pretty awesome," he told her, making her chuckle.

"Shh, I can't hear the movie," Dallas complained. He reached for the remote and raised the volume.

They all sat on the couch watching the movie for the rest of the evening. The kids sipped on their ginger ales and managed to keep them down, which made Laura happy. The movie was about singing pigs and piano playing gorillas, and Laura found herself enjoying it. It was a good pick.

The credits rolled after the last song and Ethan reached for the remote control.

"Okay guys, what movie next?" he asked.

But there was no answer. Both kids were fast asleep. Dallas was even snoring a little bit.

"How long have they been asleep?" Ethan asked, turning the TV off rather than putting a new video on.

"Um, I think the part where the gorilla dad escapes to see his son perform," Laura replied. "It hasn't been that long."

"How come you didn't say anything?" Ethan asked her.

"Because I wanted to see how it ended," she replied. She shrugged. "It was better than I expected."

He laughed and shook his head. "Fair enough. Are you ready for some dinner?" he asked. "We can eat while they sleep."

"Okay," she agreed. Her stomach rumbled. She was definitely hungry for that burger from Sandy's.

## Chapter 11

*aura*

BEING VERY careful not to wake the small humans, Laura slipped off the couch. She gently put Ivy's head on a pillow and tucked her in while Ethan did the same for Dallas. When they were done, they both headed into the kitchen to wash their hands. Laura had them do it twice, just to be on the safe side.

While she was microwaving their food, Ethan went to the bag of DVDs and pulled out something. She wasn't sure what it was until she turned around and found that he had a little candle on the center of the table. It flickered and cast a warm light on the small wooden table.

"You didn't have to clear the table," she said gently, bringing the food over. It was still in the paper take-out containers, but she didn't want to do dishes.

"Yeah, but where else would we eat?" he asked. She

could see he'd neatly stacked all the bills, homework, and art projects on one of the empty chairs. "Next time, I really do want to bring you someplace nice, but for now, would you join me for a candlelight dinner?"

"I would love to." She giggled, feeling warm and fuzzy. It wasn't a big gesture, but it was such a sweet one that she felt overwhelmed. He was taking care of her. It had been a long time since someone had looked after her. She'd forgotten what it felt like.

He went and pulled out her chair for her to sit. She felt like a princess, rather than a harried caretaker in sweatpants as she sat down at the table.

"This burger is fantastic," Ethan announced after taking his first bite. He sounded slightly surprised as he held up the big bun to look at it closer.

"Sandy's is the best place in Silver Springs," Laura agreed. Her green-chile burger was amazing as always. Even after two hours, it was still delicious. "I don't know how they do it, but I always get good food there."

"I just picked it because it was on the way," Ethan admitted. "Now, I'm really glad I did." He took another big mouthful of burger and sighed with contentment.

Laura wiped a drop of green-chile from her chin. "Out of curiosity, where were we going to go tonight? I mean, if the kids hadn't gotten sick."

"The science museum," he said with a shrug. He looked up and winked at her before smiling. "I had reservations for us downtown at Lance's Steakhouse."

"The football guy's restaurant?" Laura asked, impressed. "I think that might be the fanciest place in Denver."

"According to the internet, it is," Ethan replied. He held up the last bite of his burger. "But this is probably better."

Laura laughed. She'd never eaten at Lance's, but it would

be hard to make a meal better than Sandy's burgers. Even a fancy one.

"So, how's work coming along?" she asked, finishing off her own burger. She was hungrier than she thought.

He shrugged, popping a french fry into his mouth. "Carter really wants an R&D office down in Denver. It's a work in progress. There's a lot of bureaucracy and zoning issues I have to work through to put it where he wants."

"Sounds fun," Laura replied. The French fries smelled amazing. They were always crispy and salty at Sandy's.

"Oh, loads," he replied sarcastically. "It's basically like a Disneyland for lawyers." He ate another fry. "And I am not a lawyer."

She chuckled. Carter was the visionary designer of the W Motor cars. He enjoyed making them and testing them. He hated the business aspect of it, which was why he had partnered with Ethan when he wanted to start his company. Ethan was now the CEO while Carter just played with cars all day.

"What about you?" Ethan asked, his green eyes focusing on hers. "How's your work going?"

"Great actually," she replied with a smile. "Mia's foster kid charity camp is set to open in a couple of weeks, so we've just been getting everything together for that."

"How is Mia going to run the camp with a new baby?" Ethan asked. "I know mothers can do anything, but that seems like a lot of work."

"She won't run it," Laura explained. "Kenna, another social worker who worked with Mia, is in charge. Mia made sure to have everything in place so she wouldn't have to run it and take care of a newborn at the same time. Once Miri is older, she'll have a more active role, but for now, she's going to work on getting more investors and raising awareness."

"And you're running the barn, right?" Ethan asked. "You're in charge of the horses?"

"Yeah." She nodded. "Mia loved what the horses did for Lily, Alexander, and Grayson, so she really wants them to be an active part of the camp. I'm making sure that happens."

"And it's going well?" he asked. She loved that he seemed genuinely interested.

"The horses are ready. We actually just got a couple of new therapy horses that the kids are going to fall in love with. They're amazing and will really help bring kids out of their shells," she gushed. "It's actually gotten me interested in equine therapy again."

"Again?" He raised his eyebrows and his eyes focused on her.

"I didn't tell Carter, but I was applying to schools before my parents died," she explained. She looked over at the couch full of sleeping kids and shrugged. "But, it's not an option right now."

"Why not?" Ethan asked.

Laura looked back at him. "The kids. I can't leave them."

He frowned. "There's no schools in-state with the program? I thought Colorado was known for ranching and horses. I would assume an equine therapy program would be easy to find here."

"I just don't have time right now," she said. He studied her for a moment as she stared at the candle flickering between them. She hated that she felt like she wasn't doing enough. Being enough. Taking care of the kids and the barn was enough work. Her dreams could wait.

"So, now you know my secret dream," she said, breaking the silence. She smiled, trying to change the mood back. "I want to become a therapist that uses horses to treat people. What's your secret dream?"

She took a sip of her drink. She expected him to want to race cars or boats. Maybe sail around the world or climb Mount Everest.

He smiled and leaned back in his chair. "Take over the world."

She rolled her eyes. "Just like you do every night, eh Brain?"

He laughed at her cartoon reference and shrugged.

"Honestly? I love my job. It's fast, it's fun, it's incredibly profitable." He chuckled and looked at the candle as if focusing his thoughts. "I don't want to do anything else. I'm lucky that I found my dream job on my first try."

"So, you have everything?" she asked.

"Not… everything," he said slowly, his brow creased as he thought about it. "What would really make my life complete is someone to spend my time when I'm not working."

His green eyes lifted to meet hers. Her heart sped up, and her insides started doing twists. In the candlelight, she could swear that he meant he wanted to be with her.

"There you go," he said, breaking contact and shrugging. "There's my secret dream. It's family."

She quickly took another sip of her ginger ale. He didn't say that he wanted it to be her, but she found herself hoping he did. She found herself wanting to be the person he was talking about. She looked back up at him, and her body heated at his gaze.

The table suddenly seemed very small. His foot was touching hers, just barely, and all she could think of was touching the rest of him. All she'd have to do is lean over, and she could kiss him. She wanted to. She wanted to with everything in her.

"Laura?" a little voice called from the couch.

She closed her eyes and waited to see what happened next.

"Laura, I don't feel good," Dallas said. He sat up and as she turned she could see his little face pale and turn a shade of green.

*Oh no*, Laura thought.

## Chapter 12

 *aura*

LAURA SCRAMBLED out of her chair and sprinted across the room. She didn't even care that she knocked her chair over or that she was fairly sure her fork hit Ethan in the face. She had to get to Dallas in time. Time moved in slow motion as she reached for the Halloween bucket and managed to get it into Dallas' lap just in time.

She was about to sigh in relief, but Ivy started making the same gurgling noise. She turned, sure she wouldn't make it in time to find that Ethan already had the bucket under her and was holding back her long red hair.

Ethan cuddled Ivy close, unconcerned for his nice pants or shirt. His lovely green tie was thrown over his shoulder, reminding Laura of a cape. He was certainly Ivy's hero as he cuddled her close and comforted her.

It was so domestic and so laughable at the same time.

She smiled at him, even though he was too busy to see it. If he wasn't here, she wasn't sure what she would have done. If nothing else, she would have had a mess to clean up. So far she'd managed to have them not both go at the same time, but that couldn't last forever.

"All done?" he asked Ivy, his voice quiet and gentle. She nodded weakly, as he wiped her face with a napkin from the table. He was far more prepared than Laura was. Ivy rested her head on his chest, her eyelids fluttering with exhaustion.

"There you go, Dallas," Laura said gently, settling Dallas back onto the pillow. He looked pale, and his little cheeks were pink.

"She has a fever," Ethan said softly, his hand cupping Ivy's small face. "I'll have Craig bring some medicine. Do you want a doctor to come take a look at them?"

"At eight at night on a Friday?" Laura asked. "The office isn't open. We'd have to go to Urgent Care, and I don't think they need it."

"I can have someone come to your house," he told her, his hand still on Ivy's face. She smiled and leaned into his touch. "I'll pay for it."

"Thank you," Laura replied. She didn't think doctors even made house calls anymore. It was a tempting offer. While it would make her feel more at ease, it wasn't necessary. It was overkill and Laura knew it.

"It isn't a problem, Laura," Ethan said, waiting for her answer.

"They already saw the doctor, so I don't think another one will tell me anything new," Laura replied. "I took them right after I picked them up from school not feeling well. Apparently, the whole kindergarten class came down with it this week. The doctor said to keep them hydrated and that a fever was probably coming. I have the instructions in the kitchen, but this is is what the doctor expected.”

Ethan nodded. “Offer still stands if you change your mind later.”

She felt calmer just knowing she had options. “Thank you, Ethan. I really do appreciate it.”

He smiled and smoothed Ivy's hair off her face. “Do you think they'll be more comfortable in bed?” he asked, noting the awkward angle of the couch. Dallas had his feet hanging off, and his head was precariously close to the edge.

“Yeah,” Laura agreed. “They'll definitely be more comfortable in their rooms.”

“I'll get Ivy,” he said, picking up the small girl. Her arms wrapped tightly around his neck, and she mumbled something into his throat that made him smile.

“Her bedroom is on the left,” Laura told him, pointing down the small hallway. “I've got Dallas.”

She picked up her brother, wrapping his legs around her hips. He felt hot against her shoulder, but not overly so. The walk was short to his room. The house was small and cute. It was just the right size for three people, which was why Laura had moved her sister and brother in with her after their parents died.

She tucked Dallas in, making sure he had a clear path through his Legos to the bathroom. She turned on his rocket nightlight and gave him a kiss goodnight.

“I'll be right back with your bucket,” she whispered, but he was already fast asleep.

She went out to the kitchen, mentally preparing herself to clean out the buckets. It wasn't going to be a fun task, but it needed to be done.

Except, Ethan had already done it. He stood in the kitchen with his shirt sleeves rolled up, tie still tossed over his shoulder, with his hands in the sink full of soapy water. As she came close, he held up a sparkling clean pumpkin bucket.

"And here's Ivy's," he said, handing her the second. "You go give them their buckets."

"Thank you," Laura replied. She felt like kissing him. Cleaning the buckets was a task she had not been looking forward to doing.

He just smiled and nudged the buckets toward her. She smiled and quickly went to each of their rooms. Dallas was snoring as she put the bucket under his hand. She smoothed his hair and then went to check on Ivy.

She placed Ivy's bucket on her small nightstand and checked her temperature. She seemed cooler now that she was comfortable. That made Laura feel better, even though she knew she was going to check on them at least fifty more times tonight.

She gave Ivy a kiss on the forehead and made sure her path to the bathroom was clear before heading back out to the kitchen.

"Thank you," Laura said, stepping into the light of the kitchen only to stand in amazement. During the few short minutes she was gone, Ethan had cleaned up her kitchen. Granted, it was mostly just dirty dishes and random cups that needed to be stacked and put away, but he had done it without asking.

"I should let you sleep," he said, looking under the sink for dishwashing soap. He found the tabs and put one in the washer for her. "You need to stay healthy, too."

"You cleaned my kitchen," Laura stated, still in awe.

"Of course I did. It wasn't hard," Ethan said. "I don't know what setting you want your dishes run on, so you'll have to do that part."

She crossed the kitchen and hugged him. He had made her load lighter. For the first time since her parents died, she didn't feel quite so overwhelmed and alone. "Thank you."

"You are most welcome." He rubbed her back. "Now, go get some rest. I don't want you catching the bug too."

"Okay," she agreed. "The last thing I want is a stomach bug. Then who would take care of me?"

"I would," he replied. "That reminds me."

He let her go and walked over to the DVD bag, pulling out one last item. It was a giant container of hand sanitizer. He handed it to her with a smile.

"You really did think of everything, didn't you?" Laura asked in amazement.

He grinned, looking rather pleased with himself. "Thank you for the wonderful date, Laura."

She loved the way he said her name. It was feminine and beautiful when he said it. Special and unique. When he said her name, it didn't belong to anyone else in the world.

He leaned over and gave her a kiss on the cheek.

"Call me if you need anything," he said, pulling back. He went to pick up his jacket from the chair and gather his shoes.

"I will," Laura promised. She put her hand to her cheek. She wanted more than just a small chaste kiss, even if the kids were in the other room. "Ethan? What are you doing tomorrow?"

He thought for a moment. "Just some paperwork. Why?"

"Would you like to go for a ride with me?" she asked. She wasn't sure why she was nervous, but she wanted him to say yes so badly she was afraid of any other answer. "The kids have school and their grandparents are picking them up from school. I have to work, but I want you to come and do it with me. I know it's weird, but-"

"I'd love to," he said, stopping her flow of nervous chatter.

"Yeah?" She grinned as he nodded. "Awesome. Meet me at Carter's ranch at eleven."

"I can't wait," he told her, putting on his suit jacket. He frowned and then tugged his tie back over his shoulder and back into place. He gave her one last smile before opening the door and heading out into the night. "See you tomorrow, Laura."

She stared out into the darkness as he walked down the path to the waiting car with Craig. She watched as he got into the car and drove off before she finally closed the front door and sighed with happiness. It was an incredible feeling.

She chuckled as she pushed off the door and headed to bed. Despite it all, this ended up feeling like a real date.

## Chapter 13

ETHAN WALKED toward the familiar barn with both excitement and a little apprehension. He was excited because he was going to see Laura, and after last night she was the only thing he was able to think of. She had filled his dreams, and he had woken up needing a cold shower. He couldn't wait to see her.

However, horses were not his thing. He liked dogs and cats. Horses were too big and unpredictable. He had never been riding and had this terrible prediction that he was going to make a fool of himself.

He should have asked if they could go climbing. Or dancing. Or anything else besides horseback riding. He sighed and coughed as he took in a big mouthful of manure-smelling air. Laura loved horses. If he wanted to be with her, he was going to have to get comfortable around them.

She was worth it, so he stood up a little straighter and

put a smile on his face as he entered the barn.

The smells of sunlight-warmed hay and horses, with the metallic tang of metal and leather for accent, filled his nose. He sneezed but kept walking into the barn.

"Ethan?" Laura asked, coming out of one of the stalls. Her face split into a big, beautiful grin as soon as she saw him. He loved that she nearly skipped as she ran out to greet him. "You're here!"

She slowed to a stop in front of him, unsure of how she should greet him. He reached out and brought her in for a hug with a kiss on the cheek. She blushed and snuggled into him before letting go.

"I have Heartbreaker all saddled up for you," she said, bouncing with excitement. She bit her lower lip, and it took everything he had not to kiss her. That lip deserved to be kissed, not bitten. "I was half afraid you weren't going to come."

"I wouldn't back out on you," he told her. "I'm not letting you get away again."

Her smile came back full force. He couldn't get over how beautiful she was.

"I guess I'm still nervous about how we ended up last time," she admitted. She shrugged, trying to look like it didn't matter when it obviously did. He hated that he'd hurt her, even a little bit. He reached out and touched her cheek.

"There are no secretaries this time," he told her. He grinned. "Unless you have a horse named Secretary that carries you off. I can't help that one."

She laughed, filling the barn with the sound. Her laughter was musical.

"This way," she said, grabbing his hand. He liked how right it felt in his as she pulled him through the barn to one of the stalls. He followed, enjoying the fact that he could check her out as they walked. She had on a cute long sleeved t-shirt that hugged her curves while still looking practical and her hair was up in a cute ponytail that bounced as she walked.

But it wasn't her ponytail that he was really enjoying. It was the tight jeans and tall boots she had on. She had a perfect ass, and as she led him along like a pony, he was able to ogle without her noticing.

"Here's your helmet," she said, dropping his hand and handing him a hard hat. He nearly dropped it because he wasn't paying attention. His mind was still on her posterior.

"Helmet?" he asked, turning it around. It looked rather goofy and not at all like something a cowboy would wear.

"It's required on campgrounds," she told him, putting her hands on her hips and giving him a no-nonsense look. "Carter wears one."

"Yeah, well, Carter does a lot of things," he retorted, but he put it on to make her happy. She grinned at him and put hers on as well. Hers looked a lot cuter than his did.

"So, where are we going?" he asked. Now that he was dressing for the ride, he was suddenly less excited about it. Plus, it meant she would be sitting rather than walking in front of him.

"I have a plan," she replied, a wonderfully wicked gleam in her eyes. "You'll like it. Promise."

"You sure?" he asked, adjusting the helmet on his head. It wasn't the most comfortable thing he'd ever worn, but he would wear it to make her happy. Plus, he probably would fall off the horse, so wearing it wasn't the worst idea.

"I want to say thank you for last night," she answered. "You went above and beyond. I want to do the same."

He touched her shoulder before she could walk off to find more gear. "You deserved it. That and so much more."

Her smile was soft and sweet this time. He couldn't resist her any longer, so he leaned over and kissed her smiling lips. It was a little awkward with their helmets, but he made it work. Kissing her was worth the work.

She pulled back with her eyes still closed and sighed with pleasure before opening them. "Come on," she said, grabbing his hand and leading him along. "The horses are out in the arena."

"How are the kids doing this morning?" he asked as they walked through the last bit of the barn and into the big horse arena.

"It's like they were never sick," she said with a chuckle. "They both slept through the night and asked for pancakes in the morning. My friend Elena's watching them today, and she says they've kept everything down and are driving her crazy with their energy."

"I'm glad," he said. "They looked so miserable last night."

"I know," she agreed. She turned as they walked through the arena toward the two horses tied to the far railing. Soft dirt smushed under his feet and the morning sunlight filtered through the rafters. "You should come by again. They asked about you. They liked you."

The compliment made his chest swell a little. It could have been ego, but he was pleased they liked him. He liked them. "Yeah?"

"Yeah," she assured him. "They want to watch that scary-looking movie with the vampire on it, but they want you around for it. Just in case they get scared."

His chest definitely puffed out a little this time. He would keep those kids safe from any vampire movie. Even the scariest ones. Even Twilight.

"Here's your horse," she said, motioning to the darker of

the two horses. He was huge. And black. And giving Ethan a gaze that said the horse was not impressed. Ethan swallowed hard. Mia looked at him and then back to the horse. "Have you ridden before?"

"Once or twice," he replied, but his voice cracked slightly. "Or never."

She giggled and reached for his hand.

"Come say hello to him," she said, putting a sugar cube in his palm. "Heartbreaker is a big softie. He's one of the horses we put newbies on. He's big, but he's a total sweetheart."

Ethan held out his hand with the sugar cube displayed in the center. Heartbreaker's ears perked up, and he opened his mouth to reveal lots of slobbery teeth. Ethan did his best not to move as the horse used its slobbery lips to take the cube from him.

He didn't know if horses could smile, but he swore Heartbreaker was laughing at him. Ethan wiped his hands on his pants. He needed to remember to wash his hands before he ate anything. Before he did anything, really. Who knew what was in horse drool?

"You're doing great," Laura told him. "Come on over here to his left side."

Carter followed her lead, going to the horse's left. Heartbreaker watched him but didn't seem too concerned. The horse seemed happy enough just munching on his sugar.

"Now, put your foot in the stirrup here," she said, demonstrating and then moving her foot out of the way. "Then, you just lift and swing your leg up and over. Hold on to the saddle horn for balance, not the reins. I'll hold those for you."

She moved to the front of the horse and Heartbreaker rubbed his head against her. Ethan felt a little jealous of the horse, but he didn't say anything as he put his foot in the stirrup and tried to do as she instructed.

It took two attempts, and he felt utterly ridiculous both times. It wasn't the strength of it that was hard, it was getting his leg up high enough to clear the big animal's butt.

"Good," Laura praised him. "Now, the rest is easy. You just use your legs. Hug the horse with your legs, keeping your knees in."

He did as she instructed. It felt a little odd, but he definitely felt more secure than when his knees pointed out. "How to I make him move? Where's the steering wheel?"

Laura chuckled and handed him the reins. "Hold these with your left hand like you're holding an ice cream cone," she instructed. "Be gentle because it's attached to his mouth. No big rein flips like you see in the movies."

He took them in his hand, and she nodded.

"Now, to make him go forward, you just squeeze your knees. If he doesn't move, or you want to go faster, kick your heels a little," she said, stepping out of the way.

Ethan did exactly as she instructed and the horse moved forward. He nearly fell over backward. He was not expecting so much movement, but he caught himself and used his core to stabilize. The further the horse walked, the more comfortable he became with the gentle rocking motion.

"Perfect," Laura said, watching him. "Now, to turn, just pull the reins in the direction you want to go. Just remember, it's attached to his mouth, so be gentle."

Ethan pressed the reins to the right side of the horse's neck, and Heartbreaker dutifully turned. It's surprisingly easy and a little bit fun.

"This isn't nearly as hard as Carter makes it out to be," he commented, turning Heartbreaker to the other side.

She laughed and jumped up into the saddle in a smooth

motion. She grinned at him as she urged her horse to run circles around him with effortless grace. There was no way he would be able to pull off what she was doing.

"Show off," he muttered, turning his horse toward the open door. She just chuckled and fell into step beside him.

Outside, it was a perfect spring day in the Rockies. A crisp chill still filled the air, but the leaves were starting to come out on the aspen trees, and the world smelled of pine. The snow from the last time he was up here was gone, and wildflowers were replacing it. Birds sang as they passed by a big pine tree on their way.

"The weather is certainly better than last time," he tells her, earning him a smile.

She shook her head. "I'd rather not repeat that ever again," she replied. He had to agree.

Two months before, he'd come up to the ranch for a fundraiser. Mia was currently building a camp to give foster kids a chance at fun. She had some amazing plans to give them life skills and an experience they would never forget. She was determined to help kids, so he had come up to support her and to help fundraise.

He thought he would be able to avoid Laura and their awkward history, but that hadn't worked out quite the way he'd planned. When Laura's brother and another boy disappeared into a snowstorm, he had been put with her to help with the search.

The two of them had walked all over the ranch looking for Dallas. It wasn't much fun given that it was snowing and that she hated him. To say the conversation was quiet was an understatement.

Luckily, her brother and the other boy were found safe and sound. When the news had come in over their shared walkie-talkie, she had been so excited that she'd kissed him.

That kiss had thrown him for a complete loop. It was part of the reason he had even considered coming back. There was unfinished business in that kiss.

"I'm tired of the snow," Laura said, bringing him back to reality. "I'm glad it's spring."

"Me too," he agreed, shifting his weight to a more comfortable position on his horse.

"Thank you for coming with me," she said with a smile. She turned the two of them onto a path leading toward the mountains. "I need to check a couple of fence posts on our route. You're really helping me out by riding Heartbreaker. He and Sweetness needed to go out for a ride today."

"You are welcome," he replied. There was a serenity to what they were doing that surprised him. He was much less afraid of looking like an idiot now that he was out here than he had been this morning.

"This way," she instructed, taking him up a hill.

The mountains were breathtaking. He could finally understand why the song went "purple mountain majesty above the fruited plain." From up here, the mountains were dark purple against the light blue sky. Wildflowers dotted the meadows with color and life. Plus, the air smelled amazing up here. It was so clean it nearly hurt after the smog of the city.

"Hold on," she said, pulling her horse to the side to check a fence post. She made a note on her phone and went to the next one. "I just have to check these couple of posts."

"Is this what you do all day?" he asked, looking around. If this were his job, he would never want to do anything else.

"Not really," she said with a soft chuckle. She put her phone back in her pocket and looked around at the beautiful scenery. "I don't get to do this very often. I have to supervise the ranch hands, order supplies, pay bills..."

"So, paperwork?" he supplied.

She nodded. "I don't just manage the horses, I manage the ranch. Even before we had kids coming, it was a fair amount of work. Now it's more."

"Did you not want the kids to come?" he asked. "Since it's more work for you?"

"Oh, I want them!" She turned in her saddle to look at him. "They're amazing kids. We had a weekend test trip with some of the kids up from Denver a couple of weeks ago, and it was spectacular. Some of them had never seen a horse. A couple had never seen the stars from anywhere but the city."

He nodded. He couldn't remember the last time he'd seen the stars. It was too bright with city lights at his penthouse in California.

"I love having them here," she continued. "It's like getting to see everything for the first time. Plus, the smiles? The kids all loved it and were asking to come back. I'm so excited to have more kids here over the summer."

"It sounds like they'll keep you busy," he said.

She nodded. "Yeah. I'm looking forward to it." She shifted in her saddle to look at him. "How are you doing? The ride okay?"

He thought about it for a moment. This was actually a lot more fun that he'd thought it would be. He was going to smell like horse, but it was wonderful being outside in the sunshine and there was something special about being out in nature with an animal. He could get used to this.

"I'm doing great," he replied.

"Good, because we're about to do the hard part," she replied with a smile and she urged her horse to go a little faster.

# Chapter 14

LAURA LED as they took the back way home to the ranch. She couldn't stop smiling. This was going better than she'd hoped. It made her glad that she was on her horse in front of Ethan, that way he didn't have to see the goofy smirk that was plastered on her face.

"Slow down there, cowgirl," Ethan called out.

Laura glanced over her shoulder to see Ethan a little way back on the trail. His smile was just as broad as hers as he held the reins. His horse was carefully navigating the rocky path, but apparently wasn't going fast enough to keep up with her.

"Whoa," she said, pulling on her reins.

Her horse came to a stop in the middle of the trail, and they waited for Ethan to catch up.

"Come on, slowpoke," she shouted. "Don't be afraid of a few rocks."

"If the horse is afraid of them, then so am I," Ethan called back. "Besides, I'd really rather not fall off. That would be ugly. You don't want to see me cry. I'm a really ugly crier."

Laura laughed at his comment as she watched Ethan trying to keep his balance. He shifted his body side to side, trying to stay centered on the horses back as they traversed the trail. She was actually pretty impressed with how natural Ethan seemed in the saddle, especially considering that it was his first time riding.

Within just a couple of minutes, Ethan got to the bottom of the hill and rode up beside Laura.

"And here I thought this horse riding stuff was easy," he commented.

Laura glanced over, noticing that his knuckles were a bit white from holding the reins so tightly. Looking at his confident smile, she'd never have guessed.

"You did well," she said, with a warm smile. "Let's head back to the barn. Just follow me and hold on. Use your core."

She then made a clicking noise with her tongue. Immediately after, her horse began to trot down the trail. Now that they were past the technical area of the ride, Ethan was able to keep up with ease. Laura stood up in the saddle and gently tapped the horse's side with her heel. Within seconds, they sped up from a trot into a gallop.

The moments when she was riding fast enough so that all she could hear was the wind as it whipped past her ears, sending her hair outward beyond her back, those were the times that she cherished the most about riding. There was nothing like it.

However, somehow it was even better knowing that Ethan was right behind her, sharing the same experience. She loved that he was there, seeing the same beautiful trees as they passed by and breathing the same, sweet summer air that she was.

At the speed they were riding, it didn't take long for them to get back to the paddocks. Laura didn't even have to tell her horse what to do. He slowed down on his own as soon as they broke through from the trees and into the pasture where the ranch was.

"Good girl," she said, patting the back of her horse's neck. "Let's get you settled in."

Ethan rode up next to her, smiling from ear to ear. "That was incredible. Especially the last part."

"It wasn't too scary?" she asked, with a playful smirk.

"I'm man enough to admit it was a little scary at first," he said. "But after a few seconds, I got comfortable riding at that speed. Thanks again for taking me out. Seriously, I have a new appreciation for horses. Makes me wish I had given them a chance a long time ago."

"Better late than never," she replied, as she walked her horse toward the barn. "Let's get these guys back in their stalls so they can get some water and rest."

"That's a great idea," he said. "Plus, didn't you say something about a surprise?"

"I did," she said, flashing a wink. "I'll show it to you as soon as we get the horses settled in."

They rode side by side into the barn, then hopped out of the saddles. Ethan passed Laura the reins, and she walked both of the animals into their separate stalls. She made sure that they had enough water and hay, and then stepped back out. She'd asked one of the stable hands to help her brush them down when she got back so she could give Ethan his surprise.

She turned to see Ethan standing in the center of the barn, dusting the front of his jeans off with his hands.

"Come with me," she said, beckoning him with a finger. He raised his eyebrows but crossed the barn with her. She led him to a ladder leading up to the hayloft. The smell of hay was strong here.

"Where are we going?" Ethan asked, looking around the barn.

"Up," she said, pointing to the ladder. "And no staring at my butt."

"I make no promises," he replied.

She shook her head, put her foot on the first rung and started to climb. It was a quick climb up to the hayloft. Sunlight filtered through the open hayloft door on the side of the barn. The ranch was quiet. No one would bother them up here.

She stepped to the side and made room for Ethan to come up. He was definitely staring at her butt.

Hay was stacked on all three walls of the loft. They were getting a new batch in a few days, so there was more room than usual. Directly in the middle of the area was a clearing about the size of a small living room. In it, there were two bails of hay for seats, and one picnic basket, filled with a homemade lunch for them both.

"Have a seat," she said, keeping her eyes on Ethan to see his reaction. "Here's your surprise."

At first, he looked a bit confused, at least until he saw the picnic basket. Then his expression softened and his lips tipped upward into a smile.

"You did this?" he asked. "For me?"

She nodded. "Yeah. I mean, it's nothing too fancy obviously. It's just lunch."

"No, no," he said. "It's not just lunch. It's better than that. Seriously, this is really thoughtful, Laura."

Her cheeks began to tingle a bit, and she knew that she was blushing. She looked away for a moment, hoping that her face would return to a normal color before he saw.

"This is the best surprise," he said. "Thank you."

"Don't thank me before you try the food," she said, giggling. "What if you hate it?"

"I doubt that will be the case," he replied. "But if it is, we'll just go get Sandy's."

She strolled over to one of the hay bales next to the picnic basket and sat down. Ethan was still standing in the opening of the hayloft. He was backlit by the blue sky and the shining sun, and she could only see his silhouette. The contrast of color seemed to accentuate just how tall and lean he was. He really looked like a cowboy as he stood there, too. The tight jeans, the shirt, and probably the fact that he was surrounded by hay, all contributed to the look. Laura enjoyed the view for a moment and felt herself suddenly more drawn to him than ever before.

For fear of being caught blatantly staring at him, though, she finally called him over. "Come sit with me. Let's eat."

"You won't hear an argument from me," Ethan said. "I'm starving."

The floor boards creaked as he stepped toward the bail of hay that was situated directly next to hers. Laura wasn't sure how he was going to react to having a picnic in a hayloft. The guy was a billionaire, after all, and she was certain that most of his lunches were probably in fancy restaurants while wearing a suit. Still, though, he appeared genuinely happy to be there, and that excited her. It made her feel good about the effort she had put into getting this surprise together for him.

"So what's on the menu?" he asked, nodding toward the picnic basket.

"Well, let's find out, shall we?" she said, as she opened up the basket and pulled out a plastic jug. "This is my home-made lemonade. I can't promise you'll love everything else I have packed in the picnic basket, but I'd be willing to bet money that you'll go nuts over this. It's a secret lemonade recipe known only to a handful of the Corbett family."

"In that case, I consider myself lucky for being able to have a taste." As Ethan spoke, it seemed apparent to Laura that he was more interested in her than he was in the lemonade. It was like he couldn't take his eyes off of her. She loved it. It made her feel beautiful and extraordinary.

She pulled two plastic cups out of the basket and filled them both with lemonade from the jug.

"Secret recipe, huh?" he said, taking the cup from Laura's hand. "What's the secret?"

She shook her head and shrugged. "Well if I told you, it wouldn't be much of a secret, would it?"

"Touché," he said, holding the cup in the air. "Cheers."

"Cheers," Laura echoed his words and then tapped the edge of her cup to his.

Ethan took a sip of the lemonade and Laura watched as his eyes widened with delight.

"Well...?" she asked hesitantly. "What do you think?"

After another swig, he dropped the cup from his lips. "This is incredible, Laura."

"You're just saying that," she said, feeling her cheeks tingle once again.

"I'm dead serious," he said. "This is unbelievable. How did you make this?"

"I won't tell you all of the secrets," she said, with a sly smile. "But I can tell you that part of it is about using lemons straight off of the tree. Once you have lemonade with fresh lemons, you'll never be able to go back."

"You're right about that," he said, shaking his head in awe. "I think you've just ruined me. I'll never be able to drink lemonade from the store again."

Laura shrugged. "I guess you'll just have to let me make it for you from now on."

She didn't really mean to say it. It just sort of came out, without her even thinking about it. As soon as the words spill from her lips, she cringed.

*God, why did I say something so weird?* she thought. *I'm so awkward.*

To her pleasant surprise, though, Ethan seemed to resonate well with the idea.

"I'd like that," he said, his pale green eyes locking with hers. "I'd like that very much." He paused. "It snows here. Where did you get fresh lemons?"

"I have a little lemon tree in my house," she explained. "It goes outside in the summer and comes in for the winter."

"I see," he replied, taking another sip.

There were a few seconds that passed, and all that they did was stare into each other's eyes. It caused a warm tingling to stir inside of Laura. She wasn't sure if it what she was feeling was similar to what she had felt the first time they met, or if it was completely different. Maybe it was just the spark of attraction, which the two of them obviously shared with each other. Regardless, she felt something. There was sexual tension in the air, and it was so thick that it was almost palpable.

"Um, so, you said you were hungry?" Laura stumbled

over her words and nearly dropped her cup of lemonade onto the floor.

Ethan smiled warmly. "Yeah, I'm famished."

"Okay, good," she replied. "Once again, I didn't make anything too extravagant. I wasn't sure what you'd like, so I just made something simple. How does a turkey and swiss cheese sandwich on rye bread sound? It's my personal favorite."

"I love turkey and swiss!" he said. "That's my go-to sandwich for when I'm eating at home."

Laura smiled wide, relieved by his response. "Whew. That's good, because if you hated it, then you'd have to fill up on nothing but potato chips and lemonade."

She pulled the two cellophane-wrapped sandwiches out of the picnic basket and handed one of them to Ethan.

"Thank you, Laura," he said. "This is perfect. Honestly, this is one of the best days I've had in a long time. Between me surviving the trail ride and then this, a nice lunch with you out here in the country, I'd say it's just about as good as it can get."

He let out a long and relaxed sigh as he gazed out the open doors of the hayloft. It made Laura feel good that she was able to please someone who could have afforded anything he wanted. It was proof to her that there were indeed many things that money could not buy.

*The best and most precious things in the world can't be purchased,* she thought. *This moment is one of those things.*

## Chapter 15

aura

ETHAN AND LAURA unwrapped their sandwiches and ate in silence. The only background noise was the light wind as it rustled through the trees outside and the occasional squawk of a lonely raven that was flying around nearby. It couldn't have been nicer. Laura's surprise lunch had gone better than she'd expected.

Once they had finished eating, Laura quickly cleaned up and put all of the trash into the picnic basket. Ethan took his final swig of lemonade and then scooted over on the hay bale, closing the space between Laura and himself just a tiny bit.

"Hope that was enough to eat," she said, pushing the picnic basket out of the way. "You devoured that sandwich in minutes."

"I'm a fast eater," he said, laughing. "Besides, I was

hungry, and it was delicious. I'm full, though. It hit the spot just perfectly."

Now that the meal was over, Laura had nothing to distract her. She couldn't change the subject and talk about the lemonade or the sandwiches. So when the sexual tension between the two once again presented itself, she had no choice but to face it head on.

Without even thinking about what she was doing, she found herself leaning toward Ethan. There was still a bit of distance between them, but it was like her attraction to him slowly closed that gap, bringing them closer physically.

"Hey, Laura, is that the raven that's been making so much noise?" Ethan asked, pointing outward toward the top of the tree where the black raven stood proudly.

Of course, Laura could easily see the bird from her current position, but she wasn't about to admit that. The raven was the perfect excuse to slide all the way over to where Ethan was seated.

"Where?" she asked. "I can't see from here."

She then moved her butt across the hay, until her left hip collided with Ethan's.

"Right there," he said, still pointing.

They were so close now that she could feel his warm breath drift over the side of her neck as he spoke. It caused a tingling sensation to dance through her, and her eyes closed halfway to the sensation.

"Oh, yeah, that's the one we've been hearing," she said, realizing how obvious it must have been that she'd only used the bird as an excuse to sit nearer to him. She didn't really care.

The sexual tension was back and as strong as ever. It was as if they'd never had the time apart after the museum.

Laura looked away from the raven and brought her gaze

to Ethan. Their eyes locked and she immediately got lost in them. She practically melted right there on the hay bale, hypnotized by his sexual stare.

All logical thought went straight out the window. Laura could only think of one thing at that moment, and that was Ethan. With their faces so close and the attraction so powerful, she quickly submitted to her desires. All she wanted was him. For the moment, nothing else in the world mattered at all.

"Kiss me," she whispered, but her words were so quiet that hardly any noise came out at all.

It must have been loud enough for Ethan to hear because he leaned in as soon as she had finished speaking. His lips touched hers as he gently pressed toward her. A soft moan eased up and out of Laura's throat while a fire ignited inside of her.

It wasn't their first time kissing, but this was ten times better than the first. Something about it was more intense, more meaningful. There was more to it this time.

The kiss started out beautiful and slow, with Ethan teasing his lips against hers. It was a perfect and meticulous dance. Laura would pull away just a bit, causing Ethan to lean into her. Then the roles would reverse, and he'd do the same to her. Soon, their tongues were darting in and out of each other's mouths, twisting and wrestling while their hands drifted all over one another.

Laura couldn't get enough of him. Now that the ice had been broken, she wanted to dive in head first. Whatever had made them want each other a year and a half before was there again, and back in full.

She kept her lips against his and wrapped an arm around his shoulders. Then she slowly pulled herself on top of him so that she straddled over his lap. Ethan let out a sexual growl but didn't break the kiss. She could feel the vibration of the noise as it made its way from his throat, all the way to her lips.

Their kissing quickly became more aggressive as they lowered their walls and allowed themselves to express how badly they wanted each other. Laura felt one of Ethan's hands slide up her back, all the way to her neck. He slipped his fingers into her hair and gently squeezed his hand into a fist. The movement pulled her hair, just enough to create some tension against her scalp, but not enough to actually hurt.

With one hand in her hair, Ethan brought his other one to her lower back. His fingers found the place between the bottom of her shirt and the top of her jeans. He touched her bare skin, and it caused her to moan softly. She wanted his touch, not just there, but everywhere.

Ethan slowly pulled his face away. He was still gripping her hair as he gazed into her eyes. His pupils dilated, growing big in the pale green. He was breathing a bit harder, too, making it clear that he wanted this just as badly as she did.

"My God, you're gorgeous," he said, his eyes moving slowly up and down Laura's front. "Something about you. I don't know exactly what it is, but this is how I remember feeling when I first saw you at that party all those months ago. You just do it for me. Why did we wait this long?"

Laura shrugged. "Let's not worry about any of that. The past is the past. We're here now, though. Why don't we savor this moment before it slips away?"

Ethan nodded. "You're right. You're absolutely right."

Then he leaned forward again. Laura thought he was going to kiss her lips, but instead, he breezed past her face and began kissing the side of her neck. Her jaw dropped, and her lips curled into a lust-filled grin.

Ethan kissed her neck, just below her earlobe. He gently nibbled at the flesh, before inching his way down just a tiny bit at a time. He kissed and nibbled with every stop and each time another wave of anticipation filled Laura. She was boiling over now, ready to explode. She knew that she'd only be able to hold off for so long before she'd *need* to have him inside of her.

Ethan gently pulled down on Laura's hair, causing her chin to lift. It forced to her look up toward the ceiling, while he gently kissed the front of her throat.

"Yes," she whispered, on an exhale. "Oh, Ethan."

He didn't hear, or at least, she didn't think so. He was too busy nipping at her neck and quickly moving down toward her cleavage. When he got there, he released her hair and brought her gaze forward once again. The way she was situated on top of his lap, put his face at the same height as her breasts. She bit her lip and watched as he kissed his way down toward them.

Ethan quickly undid the top couple of buttons and then growled as he pressed his face into her chest once again. The upper part of Laura's shirt was now splayed open, exposing everything on her breasts that her bra wasn't covering. With her hands still resting on top of Ethan's shoulders, she pulled herself close to him, pressing her chest against his face. The stubble on his cheeks tickled her sensitive skin, but she hardly even noticed. She was already lost in oblivion, overwhelmed by pleasure and anticipation.

In the very back of her mind, there was a tiny part of her that worried this would end just like it had the last time. That they'd have sex and then never speak again. It was certainly a possibility. It had happened once, so it could easily happen again. She pushed the thought away and decided to take her own advice and just enjoy the moment.

Ethan brought his hands around and fondled her breasts, gently squeezing them over the top of her bra. Laura let out a moan and leaned her head back, as his touch sent a wave of pleasure throughout her body.

She reached her hands behind her back. After pulling her shirt up a bit, she quickly undid the back clasp that held her bra together. As soon as she did, the front of her bra fell forward and slid down, just enough to expose her nipples.

Ethan groaned, and she felt him grow beneath her, hard and warm. She wanted this. She wanted this so badly she couldn't even come up with words.

Laura shimmied her shoulders until her shirt slid off of them. It now hung loosely at her elbows. The only thing that covered her front was her bra, but even that was just barely hanging on.

*Why am I not nervous at all?* she thought. *Why does this feel so natural with Ethan? It's like we've done this a hundred times, but really, it's only been once. Is this what it's like to have a true connection with someone? Is it this easy?*

Ethan slowly moved his gaze up to her eyes and then back down toward her chest. He brought his hands up and tugged downward on her bra, causing it to slip off her her shoulders. Her breasts became completely exposed. She glanced down, noticing as her nipples grew firm in an instant from the change in temperature.

His pupils dilated further, and he let out a moan of approval while leaning his face toward her once again. He kissed the top of her breasts, then made his way down until his lips grazed her right nipple. It sent an immediate tingle of sensation into her, causing her lips to part and her eyes to roll up into her head.

Ethan wrapped his lips over the sensitive nub and began flicking his tongue against it, slowly at first, and then faster with each passing second. Her head tipped back, and she reveled in the sensation. Ethan lapped his tongue against her nipple a few more times, then slowly pulled away.

Without any hesitation, Ethan moved his face to the other side and began giving her left breast equal attention. Laura found herself slowly bucking her hips forward and back on top of his lap. She barely realized she was even doing it. The friction caused waves of bliss to radiate through her. The movement felt amazing but did nothing to satisfy the aching desire between her legs. In fact, it only made it more intense.

Ethan darted his face back and forth between her breasts, lapping and gently biting at one nipple before doing the same to the other one. Laura was panting now and the spark that had ignited when they'd kissed just a moment before had become a raging Colorado wildfire.

"Take your shirt off," she whispered.

She had meant it to be a suggestion, but the way it came out it sounded more like a demand. Ethan didn't seem to mind, though. He quickly undid the buttons on his shirt and pulled it off, tossing it carelessly to the side. It landed on top of a nearby hay bale.

Laura's eyes went wide as soon as she saw his bare torso. She remembered that he was in pretty good shape, but nothing like this. He looked like an Olympic swimmer, each muscle of his abs nicely defined beneath his powerful chest.

"You look amazing," she said, dancing her fingers down his stomach.

"Not one-tenth as amazing as you do," he said.

Before she could respond, Ethan placed his hands on the underside of her thighs. Then, in one swift movement, he stood up and carried her across the hay loft to a shady corner that was hidden by the blinding sun. She held onto his shoulders, admiring the way the muscles flexed with his movements. He was so strong, so powerful. It only made her want him that much more.

Ethan's shirt was still bunched up in a pile, and he grabbed it with one hand as he passed it by. When he got to the corner, he tossed the shirt out onto a bail of hay, using it as a blanket. Then he laid Laura down on it.

He took a step back and began unbuttoning his belt. Laura watched, letting her eyes drift downward toward the front of his jeans. The obvious bulge beneath the denim had grown significantly in size. She bit her lip when she saw it. She wanted that inside of her so badly, and it was becoming hard to stay patient.

Her eyes focused on his chest, then made their way down the muscles that covered his abdomen. She continued to drop her gaze, all the way down the lines of his hips, until they stopped at the top of his jeans.

Ethan had unclasped his belt and Laura watched intently as he pulled it off. He let it drop to the floor, and the metal belt buckle clanged against the wooden decking. Her heart started beating quickly. She could feel it pumping behind her rib cage. It was pure anticipation. She couldn't wait to see him naked again.

With the belt gone, Ethan kicked off his shoes and then pulled his jeans down to his ankles, before stepping out of them. Now, he stood in front of Laura wearing nothing more than his black boxer/briefs. The thin material hid nothing.

Laura wasn't about to let Ethan stand there nearly naked all by himself. So she quickly undid the top button of her own jeans and lifted her butt from the hay bale so that she could pull them down. She kicked them off of her feet, taking her boots with them. They fell into a pile on the floor.

"Come here," she said, motioning Ethan over with her index finger.

He crawled over her, placing his hands onto the hay just above her shoulders. Underneath him, she felt so much smaller. It was a combination of his height and his physique that made him appear huge in comparison.

"This is the best surprise lunch of all time," Ethan said.

Laura giggled and brought a hand to his cheek. His hair had become a little messed up already, but it made him look even cuter. Combined with the dimples in his cheeks and his pale green eyes and Laura was like putty in his hands. She would have done anything he'd asked and probably more.

"Now where were we?" she said, with a playful smirk.

Ethan looked up, pretending to really think about it. "I'm not entirely sure, but I think it was somewhere around here..."

He then slipped his hands up to Laura's breasts and began fondling them. While he did that, he brought his lips to hers, and the two continued their kiss. This time, though, the only thing that separated them was their underwear. Everything else was bare flesh.

Laura's hands drifted up and down Ethan's muscular back. She wrapped her legs around his waist and pulled him close, feeling his bulge press against her panties. She let out a muffled groan as the friction re-ignited the sensation inside of her. They were so close now, just two layers of cloth separated Laura from what she wanted.

After a moment, Ethan broke the kiss and gazed into her eyes briefly before moving his face down her body. He slid his lips across her skin, pausing for just a second on her breasts before continuing downward. Laura watched him as he eased his way across her stomach and past her belly button, down to her pantie line.

Ethan moved down a little further, kissing every inch of skin as he went. She relaxed into the hay and closed her eyes, as Ethan slipped her panties off. The next thing she knew, an explosion of sensation filled her as he brought his tongue to her most sensitive area and began to work his magic.

She groaned as she arched her back and brought her legs over Ethan's shoulders. She writhed on the hay bale underneath her, then dropped her hands to her sides, gripping a handful of hay in each hand. It was like heaven and waves of bliss continued to wash over her.

"Oh my God," she whispered, her eyes rolling into the back of her head.

Laura dropped one of her hands down and brought her fingers through Ethan's hair. At the same time, she bucked her hips forward. Fireworks exploded in her mind as she lost herself to pleasure. She panted with the need for more.

Ethan pulled away, for just long enough to kiss the inside of her thigh.

"I want you, Ethan," she groaned. "Take me."

He let out a low growl, sending a vibration directly into her. It created a flash of pleasure that radiated into her core and caused her to gasp. When Ethan pulled away, she found that she immediately missed his touch.

"I want you, too," he said, slowly bringing himself to a standing position on the floor in front of her.

Laura opened her eyes and finally released her grip from the hay. When she lifted her hands, she noticed that they were trembling slightly.

Ethan smiled and then slipped his thumbs into the

elastic waist strap of his underwear, slipping them down and off of his legs.

He approached the hay bale once more, then stopped himself before crawling over her.

"A condom," he said. "I should grab a condom."

He spun around and snatched his jeans. After a few seconds, he appeared in front of Laura with a condom in hand. She watched him slip it on, eager to have every inch of his length buried inside of her.

"Come here," she said, gently spreading her legs to allow him closer.

Ethan got onto the bail of hay and pressed Laura's knees toward her chest. She could feel the heat radiating off of him as he gently bucked his hips forward, causing his tip to slide inside. The moment their flesh touched, Laura drew in a breath through her teeth, creating a soft hissing noise.

He slowly pressed into her, filling her body with the kind of pleasure that made her lose the ability to form sentences. Once inside, he leaned forward and kissed her. At the same time, began moving his hips back and forth, pumping himself deep into her with each thrust.

Laura became lost in a sea of pure ecstasy. Every cell in her body exploded with sensation, as Ethan slipped in and out of her body. His movements were slow and steady at first, but it wasn't long until his cadence increased.

He looked so sexy as he made love to her. The muscles in his chest and torso flexed and relaxed with each pump of his body. His hair fell over his forehead and hung loosely across his eyes. Being surrounded by all the hay made Laura feel like Ethan was a real cowboy, and he was taking her in the barn. It was a secret fantasy she'd thought about often, but never thought it would become a reality.

Laura relaxed her head back and closed her eyes, letting

the pleasure wash over her. The two were tangled in their intimate dance. Everything felt right. Nothing could make the moment any better. It was beyond perfect.

Something about him satisfied a deep need in her. He was a balm to her soul that she didn't know she needed.

She felt Ethan's pace increase a bit. He looked her over, his green eyes full of lust and beauty. It was enough to make her feel like a goddess. A light layer of sweat had begun to coat his skin, causing it to shine and accentuate his muscles even more.

"You're gorgeous," Ethan said, his words broken up by heavy breathing. "God, you're perfect."

The way he took her on that hay bale was with an aggressive and fiery passion that not many people had. It was as though Laura was the only thing in the world he wanted and he had been waiting his entire life to have it. There was eagerness in his movements, the kind of sexual thirst that could only exist between lovers who were truly meant to be together. This wasn't one-night-stand kind of sex, that was one thing that Laura knew for certain. There was something special about this. Something different.

After a bit, Ethan slowed the pace of his movements down. He was breathing hard now, his shoulders rising and falling to each inhale.

She didn't say anything. She didn't tell him to speed up or slow down or to change a single thing. She couldn't. As the ecstasy washed over her, she couldn't even use her mind to create one word. All she could do was close her eyes and submit to the pleasure.

Ethan grunted and increased his pace a little more. Their bodies continued to collide, and each plunge sent her a little closer to orgasm. She had to remind herself to breathe. It was all she could do to hold onto the edge of the hay bale.

She drew in a quick breath and held it as Ethan sent her over the top. Her face froze in an expression of ecstasy. Her lips curled into a mindless smile, and her eyes rolled into my head once more. She submitted to the pleasure, letting it pound down on her with one final, giant tidal wave. It was beyond incredible. It lasted only a few fleeting seconds, but it didn't matter because it was perfect. When she finally regained her senses, she opened her eyes.

The outside of his lips curled into a pleasurable grimace. His cheeks turned red, and he squeezed his eyes shut. An animal-sounding grunt escaped his lips that sent primal shivers down her spine.

After a few seconds, he opened his eyes and drew in a breath. He looked dazed, but content, as he pulled out and crawled up next to her on the hay. She laid her head down on his chest, listening to his rapid heartbeat slowly drop to a normal one.

Ethan kissed the top of her head. "You are something else, you know that, Laura?"

She smiled and let out a relaxed breath. "I think you've mentioned that before, but you can remind me as often as you like. I never get tired of hearing it."

"Well, then I'll remind you every single day," he said.

Her heart lifted with the idea that he wasn't going to leave. He was here to stay.

He wrapped his arm around her and held her close. They didn't say anything for a while. They just laid there naked, enjoy each others company. It was pretty clear that neither of them had any other place they'd rather be.

# Chapter 16

"Kids, the pizza's here!" Laura called out, heading to her front door. She grabbed the money she'd left on the counter to give the pizza guy and opened the door.

Except, instead of a pizza delivery person on her front step, it was Ethan holding several boxes of pizza.

"Pizza delivery, ma'am."

"What are you doing delivering pizzas?" she asked, hand on her hip and smiling. "The car business not paying you well enough?"

He laughed. "This way I get to see the neighborhood," he teased. "I intercepted your pizza coming up."

"I see that," she said. She looked past him to see the delivery car drive off. "Did you pay him?"

"Maybe," he replied with a shrug. "Maybe I just stole them."

She smacked his shoulder and held the door open for him to come in.

"I thought you were going to be late. I didn't order you a pizza," she said. She tucked a loose strand of hair behind her ear. The kids would be so excited to have a surprise visit from Ethan, but she felt bad she didn't order enough food for him.

"I skipped out of the meeting early to come here sooner. And don't worry about the pizza, I brought my own," he replied showing her the pizzas he had. There was a third box with a different logo than the ones she'd purchased.

"You didn't have to buy your own pizza," she said, shaking her head. "I would have shared with you."

"Well, how was I to know what kind of pizza you like? What if you liked pineapple on yours? I couldn't eat that," he told her, kicking his shoes off at the door and setting the pizzas down on the table.

She grinned. "Actually, I do like pineapple on my pizza. It's what I always get."

He opened his mouth and widened his eyes in mock horror. "You monster!" he grimaced and shook his head. "I don't know if this relationship is going to work out."

"You just don't know what you're missing," she replied. "It's delicious."

He rolled his eyes. "No, sausage meat lovers pizza is delicious. No sweet stuff on pizza."

"Ethan!" Ivy shouted as she came out of her room. Dallas was hot on her heels as they both ran out to greet him.

"Ivy! Dallas!" he shouted back with equal enthusiasm. He caught Ivy first, throwing her up in the air like she was a toy doll.

"My turn!" Dallas begged, his eyes bright with excitement.

Ethan tossed Ivy up one more time, making her shriek with delight before picking up Dallas and giving him the same treatment. The kids giggled and begged for more.

Laura laughed and took the pizzas to the kitchen. She smiled as Ethan played with the kids, keeping the busy and happy while she put the pizza on plates.

"Okay," she shouted over them. "Dinner time. To the table."

Dallas pouted. He was having fun, and he wasn't ready to stop. Luckily, Ethan saw the impending meltdown and tagged his shoulder.

"First one to the table wins," Ethan whispered before running to the table.

Dallas chased after him, shouting "YOU'RE FROZEN!"

Ethan slowed down, pretending to move in slow motion. "Noooooooo. I... muuuusssstt... wiiiiiiiiiiiiiinnn..."

Dallas and Ivy laughed as they easily beat their frozen companion to the table. Laura gave him a wink and brought over the plates of pizza.

Everyone dug into the food, and the room was quiet for a moment. Laura looked over at Ethan's meat-lovers pizza and shook her head. Pineapple was way better.

"What kind of pizza is that, Ethan?" Ivy asked, pointing to his pizza.

"Meat-lovers supreme," he replied, his mouth full of cheese and pepperoni. "You want some?"

"Um, no thank you. I like just cheese," she replied politely.

"I want some," Dallas piped up. "I'll eat it."

Laura raised her eyebrows in surprise. Dallas only ever wanted cheese pizza. She'd accidentally ordered a pepperoni pizza one time, and he'd refused to eat a bite of it, even once the pepperoni was off.

"Sure," Ethan said. He went to the kitchen and brought back two slices of pizza. One for him and one for Dallas.

"Thanks," Dallas told him as he dived in and ate it. Laura stared in amazement as Dallas stuffed nearly the entire piece of pizza into his mouth.

"You doing okay?" she asked, waiting for him to complain about it.

"This is great," he said after a big swallow. "I want this kind next time. Me and Ethan can share a big pizza."

"Sounds good to me," Ethan agreed. He smiled at Laura, and she couldn't help but smile back. It felt so natural to have him there. He felt like the missing piece of their world. She felt like they were a family when he was around.

The thought of family nearly made her choke. She coughed to remove the pizza from her throat. She'd been with the guy maybe a week, and she was already ready to have him be family? She should know better than that.

"You okay?" Ethan asked, reaching over and patting her back as she coughed.

"Yeah, just the wrong pipe," she replied, reaching for a glass of water. Ethan smiled at her before turning back to Dallas to talk about their pizza some more.

Yet, the thought stuck with her. Ethan felt right in their world. She was probably just reading too much into things. She usually didn't bring her boyfriends by for her siblings to approve, or at least she didn't before their parents died. Maybe that was why it was working. They'd just never met any of her boyfriends and would have liked them all this much.

"So what movie are we watching tonight?" Ethan asked, leaning back in his chair and wiping his face with a napkin.

"The ninja one!" shouted Dallas.

"The princess one!" yelled Ivy.

Laura shook her head. This was the nightly debate. The few times they actually agreed on a movie was when they had a brand new one. They still had five or six new ones from their sick day, so there was very little chance of agreement.

Ethan got up and went over to the movie pile. He thought carefully before picking one out of the stack.

"How about this one? It's about a girl from Hawaii," he said, holding up the animated movie case.

Both kids looked skeptical.

"It has a princess, kind of," Ethan said. "And it's got this guy that can change into any animal he wants. Oh, and it has the ocean in it."

"The ocean is your selling point?" Laura asked from across the room. She shared her siblings' skepticism.

"The ocean is totally a selling point," Ethan told her. "The ocean is awesome. Haven't you ever played tag with the ocean?"

All three of them shook their heads in unison.

"We've never seen the ocean," Ivy informed him. "We were going to go to Florida next year, but..." She trailed off and shrugged.

"You two have never seen the ocean?" he asked, looking baffled.

"No," Ivy replied. "There isn't one nearby. I've seen a really big lake though. That's kind of the same thing, right?"

"No. Not even close," Ethan replied, shaking his head.

"I've seen Lake McConaughy in Nebraska," Dallas said proudly. "It had waves and stuff."

"That's not the ocean," Ethan said. "How have you not seen it? Laura, you've seen the ocean, right?

"I saw it for the first time when I went out to California for the Christmas party," she replied. "I went to the beach by the hotel."

He looked at her and shook his head. "That's a terrible ocean. That's not even the good ocean. Did you go in?"

"I went up to my knees," she replied. "Until someone came by and told me I couldn't do that there."

Ethan put his head in his hands. "How have you three never experienced the ocean? That's terrible."

"We just don't live near one," Laura told him. "You'd think we've never seen the sun the way you're acting."

Ethan just looked at her like that might be the case.

"Have you ever seen a black bear?" Laura asked, crossing her arms. Ethan shook his head.

"We saw two last fall," Dallas replied. "We saw a baby a couple of years ago."

"We saw three last year," Ivy corrected. "There was the one in the park. And we saw a moose."

"Have you ever seen a moose?" Dallas asked Ethan.

"No, but..." Ethan paused, thoughtfully. "I don't think there are any moose in Colorado."

Ivy's jaw dropped. "There are too! We saw one!"

Laura could see an argument starting. She quickly whipped out her smart phone.

"Maybe it was a big dog," Ethan said.

"It had antlers!"

"Maybe it was a big dog with antlers. Woof!"

"It wasn't! Laura!"

"Okay, listen guys," Laura said, using her mommy voice. "There weren't any moose in Colorado for decades, but they were reintroduced to the state. There are now over two thousand."

"See!" Ivy said.

"I stand corrected. Secretly, I just wanted to see a big dog with antlers," Ethan said, holding his fingers up behind his head like he had antlers. That got a laugh out of Dallas.

"Well, we might not have oceans, but we have some cool wildlife. Like elk and bears."

"And dogs with antlers!" Ethan added.

"No, I told you, it was a moose!" Ivy shrieked.

"Okay," Ethan said. He let his laughter subside, and then a slow half-smile started to form on his face. "You guys need to see the ocean, then."

"What are you planning?" Laura asked. She wasn't sure she liked the look on his face. He was plotting something.

"Me? Planning something?" he asked, opening his eyes wide like he was innocent or something.

"Yes, you," Laura replied, narrowing her eyes. "What are you coming up with?"

"Wouldn't you like to know?" He grinned at her and held up the movie again. "So, Girl-With-Ocean-Movie? Let's watch it!"

Laura shook her head as he put the DVD in the player and got the kids situated on the couch.

"This time, I get to sit next to Laura," Ethan told Dallas as he scooted him over. Laura smiled and took her spot. Dallas snuggled up to Ethan and Ivy to Laura. Ethan put his arm around Laura's shoulder, and again the feeling of family overtook her.

The movie started, and Laura was instantly transported to a world she could only imagine. The ocean came to life on the screen, and she watched, enjoying herself.

"I love that color," she whispered as the ocean took over the screen. All the shades of aquamarine and blue filled the screen as the character sailed on the water toward her goal.

"Yeah?" he asked, cuddling her in closer to him.

She nodded. "You live in California. You get to see the ocean all the time. Which is better? Ocean or mountains?"

He thought for a moment. "That's hard, but I'm going to have to go with ocean."

"Yeah?"

He nodded. "California is my home, and I miss it," he explained. "I miss the sound of the waves and all the seafood. I miss my office, to be honest. I'm having a hard time working out here without it."

"Oh." Laura was surprised at the pang of hurt in her chest. He was allowed to miss things. He was allowed to miss his office. It didn't mean he wanted to leave her behind again.

He leaned over and kissed her cheek. She smiled with surprise.

"What's that for?"

He shrugged. "I just wanted to kiss you."

"I like that," she replied, feeling warm and fuzzy. She snuggled a little bit closer to him. He was safe and warm beside her. It felt good to be like this. It was a simple, ordinary thing that couples did and she liked it. She liked that it was easy and comfortable.

They watched the whole movie while snuggling, not saying a word. As the movie ended, and Dallas yawned.

"Okay, mister," Laura told him, standing up from the couch. "Time to get ready for bed."

"Aw, do I have to?" Dallas asked and then promptly yawned again.

"Yes, go put on your pajamas," she told him. "You too, Ivy."

"But I want to say goodbye to Ethan," Ivy said with a pout.

"I'll wait until you have your pajamas on," Ethan promised. "So go change."

Ivy grinned, and she and Dallas raced off to their rooms.

"What are your plans for the weekend?" he asked, slipping on his shoes by the door.

"Um, just being with the kids," she replied. "Why?"

"I have an idea," he replied. "Don't plan anything too crazy. I want to spend some time with you."

"Okay," she promised. "Do I get a hint?"

"Nope. No hints, no clues, no nothing," he replied. "You'll just have to wait."

"You're a big tease," she whispered. "Now I'm super curious."

"Too bad for you," he replied with a shrug. "But, I will tell you it's a good thing."

"Can I bribe you for a hint?" She grinned, biting her lower lip.

"Possibly," he replied.

She stepped forward, wrapped her arm around his neck and kissed him. Just touching him sent electric thrills through her entire body that made her want to gasp and ask for more. She wanted to tease him with her tongue and taste his kiss completely, but they had an audience.

"Ew, gross," Dallas announced, crinkling up his face in disgust. Ivy wore a matching expression.

"My clue is..." He paused for dramatic effect. "That you will like it. You will love it. It's something none of you have ever seen before."

"That's my clue?" Laura asked, crossing her arms. "I thought I gave a pretty good bribe."

He laughed. "If I could give you a hint based off that kiss, you'd have a detailed outline with picture descriptions," he told her. "But, I don't want to ruin the surprise."

"Fine." She dropped her arms and smiled at him.

"Good night, kids," he said, dropping down to his knees. The two children each gave him a big hug that he happily returned.

"See you tomorrow, Ethan," Ivy told him.

"I have a date with Laura tomorrow," he told them. "I'll only see you for a minute."

Ivy pouted. "But last time you had a date with Laura, you brought soup and movies. Can we have that kind of date again?"

Ethan chuckled and shook his head. "Maybe next time. This time, I get to take your sister out for something special tomorrow."

Laura grinned. She'd nearly forgotten about their date tomorrow evening.

"And it is super important that neither one of you gets sick, okay?" he told the children. "No more stomach bugs."

"Okay, Ethan," Dallas agreed. "But we do need more movies."

Ethan laughed. "I'll see what I can do."

"Have a great night, Ethan," Laura told him. "Thank you for coming over. I know it wasn't terribly exciting, but-"

"It was perfect," he finished for her. He kissed her cheek, prompting another chorus of "ews" which made Laura laugh as he opened the door.

Craig was waiting outside for him.

"I'll see you tomorrow," Laura said, the smile already filling her face. "And you're sure you can't tell me another hint?"

"No more hints," he said, stepping outside. "Bye, Laura."

She watches as he walked down the path to the car with Craig. He looked back and waved one last time before getting inside and driving off. Laura watched him. The night didn't feel magical anymore. It felt normal. Mundane. She missed him already.

She sighed and closed the door.

"Okay, time to brush teeth," Laura informed her siblings. They sighed, but since their adult friend was gone, they didn't have a reason to delay too much.

"What do you think the surprise is?" Dallas asked Ivy as they walked toward their bedrooms.

"I don't know," Ivy replied. "But I can't wait to find out!"

# Chapter 17

 aura

LAURA STOOD in front of the bathroom mirror. She brought her hands down her sides, smoothing out the silky material of her white dress. She'd been standing there for at least ten minutes, just double checking that her hair and makeup was as flawless as possible. It was important to her that she look her absolute best. She was getting ready for a date with Ethan and had a feeling that wherever he took her, it was going to be pretty extravagant. Or at least a little more extravagant than horseback riding and lunch on hay bales.

Butterflies continued to bounce around inside her belly as she stepped out of the bathroom. There was something special about Ethan. He wasn't like regular guys she'd dated, and she knew that it had nothing to do with his money. There was just something about him that got her excited. It made her light up inside and put a spring in her step that she didn't think still existed.

After pacing the room a couple of times, she glanced down at her watch.

"Oh, God," she whispered. "I completely lost track of time. He'll be here any second."

She slipped into her white high heels and then headed out of the bedroom. Her shoes made a clicking noise with each step as she made her way the living room. Dallas, Ivy, and Elena were all seated around the table in the kitchen eating dessert.

"Now that looks tasty," Laura said. "It smells good, too. What is it?"

Ivy smiled wide, and her green eyes lit up. "Elena made us our favorite! It's ice cream with broken up Pop Tarts sprinkled on top."

"That sounds... interesting," Laura said, giggling. "Maybe I'll try some when I get back."

"You look really pretty, Laura," Dallas said.

Hearing such a sweet compliment from a five-year-old caused Laura's heart to melt in an instant.

"Aw, Dallas," she said. "That's such a nice thing to say."

"I second what he said," Elena chimed in. "You look terrific, Laura. That dress is fabulous. I can't believe I've never seen you wear it before. It fits perfectly."

Laura glanced down at her dress, admiring it for the hundredth time that evening. "Thank you. Yeah, I've had it in the back of my closet for a long time but never had a good reason to wear it."

"It looks good, but you're missing something," Ivy said, resting her chin onto her closed fists, as though deep in thought. "You need to be a princess."

"What am I missing?" Laura asked.

*I did my hair, my makeup, brushed my teeth,* she thought to herself, going over her imaginary checklist.

"I think you need a necklace," Ivy said, matter-of-factly.

One would have thought she was a professional stylist with the kind of confidence she spoke with when she made the suggestion.

"A necklace?" Laura said, bringing her hands to her bare collarbone. "I guess my neck does look kind of plain without one, huh?"

Ivy nodded in agreement. "You need something sparkly."

"I tried a couple of mine on, but nothing seemed to really go with the dress," Laura said.

Her little sister's eyes widened, and Laura knew an idea had flashed into her mind.

"Why don't you wear that blue one that Mom used to wear?" Ivy asked.

Laura's throat tightened at the mention of their mother. She swallowed back a wave of emotion and blinked away the tears that immediately shrink-wrapped her eyes. At first, she was going to tell Ivy that she didn't want to wear that pendant. However, she couldn't say 'no' to that cute smile and innocent expression. She didn't want to hurt Ivy's feelings by not wearing the necklace that she suggested.

"You know what, you're right, Ivy," Laura said. "That's a great idea. I think that necklace would look really nice with this dress. I'll go grab it. Be right back."

Laura spun around and headed back to her room. She went to the top drawer of her dresser, and her hand hovered for a moment before opening it. She pulled out her mother's favorite piece of jewelry. It was a very simple necklace, with a dainty silver chain and a pendant made of blue stone. It held countless memories for Laura. She remembered her mom wearing it on every Thanksgiving, Christmas and every other event that she dressed up for, including church every Sunday.

*Miss you, Mom,* Laura thought, as she admired the necklace in her hands for a moment. *I'll wear this for you.*

She clasped the necklace around her neck and adjusted the pendant so that it sat in the center of her chest, just above her cleavage. She looked up in the mirror and smiled.

"It's perfect," she whispered.

The color, the size and even the height that the pendant hung was exactly right. Ivy knew what she was talking about when she had recommended it.

Laura smiled and leaned in toward the mirror. She could see her mother's eyes and her father's nose in the mirror as she looked at herself.

She widened her eyes to let more light in. Her green irises seemed to ignite. They were a particular kind of green, like what she imagined the rolling hills of Ireland to look like. It was one thing that she and her mother had in common.

Her smile widened, and for a moment, she analyzed the way it looked. Both of her parents had a different smile than her. She knew that for sure.

"I guess that part is all mine," she whispered.

Laura's smile faded quickly, as the memory of her parents washed over her. Thinking about them was always so bittersweet. It hurt every time, but she knew that she had to keep the memories of them alive because it was all that she had left.

Fighting back the tears, she reached up and held her mother's pendant against her chest, squeezing it tightly. Wearing that necklace almost made her feel close to her mom again, or at least as close as she could ever be now that she was gone.

*I wonder if Mom and Dad would like Ethan,* she thought. *I'll bet they would. I can imagine Dad putting him through the ringer, asking him ten thousand questions about what he does for a living. He always loved making my boyfriends as nervous as possible. And Mom, she would have made Ethan a nice dinner and invited him over for Thanksgiving.*

"Yeah, they would have loved him," she whispered to herself. "Definitely."

## Chapter 18

aura

As soon as Laura left her bedroom, the doorbell rang.

"I got it!" Ivy and Dallas shouted in unison and then began running from the kitchen to the front door. It sounded like a herd of elephants stampeding across the floor.

Laura exhaled a quick breath and ran her hands down the sides of her dress one last time to smooth it out. The butterflies continued to fly in her belly as she followed the elephant herd to the front of the house. By the time she got there, Dallas and Ivy were already clamoring for Ethan's attention.

"Those are pretty flowers!" Ivy announced.

"Yuck, flowers?" Dallas said. "You should have brought video games! Girls love that."

"Alright, alright," Laura said, squeezing past the two kids

so that she could stand in from of Ethan. "Thanks for answering the door, kids. Now can we let Ethan inside without pestering him to death?"

Ethan smiled and handed Laura a bouquet of flowers. It was a dozen of the prettiest yellow roses she had ever seen.

"They're beautiful," she said, bringing them to her nose to smell them. "Thank you."

"Of course," he said, with a warm smile. "I'm glad you like them. You look amazing, by the way. I love that dress."

"Thank you," Laura said, blushing a little bit. "You look terrific, too."

She couldn't help but give Ethan a quick once over. He didn't just look good, though, he looked like a million bucks. His tailored gray suit and light green tie, combined with his perfectly trimmed beard stubble and nicely combed hair, made him look like a movie star about to take a walk on the red carpet.

"Are you ready to go?" he asked.

Laura glanced down at the flowers. "Come on in for a second. I'll put the flowers in water. Then we can head out."

She stepped to the side to allow Ethan through the door. As soon as he was in, the kids began asking him questions again.

"Ethan, we're going to watch the Lego movie tonight," Dallas said, as the group walked toward the kitchen. "It's so good. Do you know the 'Awesome' song?"

"No, I don't think I do," he said, smiling at the two children.

"Oh man, it goes like this," Ivy said. Then she and her brother began singing for Ethan.

"Everything is awesome! Everything is awesome!" They called out in unison.

Laura found herself smiling. Even though it was a little

obnoxious, it was also pretty cute. Ethan was laughing, too. He seemed surprised by how much energy they had.

"They're great kids," Ethan whispered in her ear, but Laura could hardly hear him over the sound of the duo singing.

"In small doses, yes," she replied, flashing a wink.

The kids finished singing, and Ethan followed Laura into the kitchen. She filled a clear vase with water and put the flowers in it.

"Those are so beautiful," Elena said, as Laura walked the vase toward the dining room table.

"Aren't they?" Laura said. She smiled and moved them around in the vase. "I've never gotten yellow roses before."

"Ethan, you should stay and watch the Lego movie with us," Dallas announced. "It's the best movie *ever*."

"Yeah, please stay," Ivy said. "You need to watch this movie so that you can sing the song with us."

Ethan squatted down so that he could look at the kids eye to eye.

"You know, there's nothing more I'd love to do than hang out and watch that with you guys," he said, his tone warm and sincere. "I have a date with your sister, though. I think she'd get kind of sad if I canceled on her. Especially since I'm already here and ready to pick her up. Plus, I can tell she has put in a lot of time to get ready. Doesn't she look amazing?"

Ivy nodded eagerly. "Yes, she looks really pretty. That's why she and Elena can go on the date instead. You can stay here and watch the movie with us."

Elena chuckled in the background.

"Sorry, guys," Laura said. "Ethan and I have had these plans for a while now."

"But, Laura, you promised that we'd get to watch the movie," Dallas said, crossing his arms.

"You're going to watch the movie, though, kiddo," Laura said, ruffling up Dallas' hair. "You just can't watch it with Ethan. He's mine tonight, okay?"

"Tell you what," Ethan said, placing one hand onto each of the kid's shoulders. "How about next time we go see a superhero movie? There's one in theaters right now, and it looks really cool. Have you guys seen it yet?."

Ivy and Dallas shook their heads.

"Oh, man, it looks so good!" Ethan's smile and the way he spoke to the kids made Laura's heart melt out of her chest. "There's a man in a cape who flies around the city and takes out bad guys. Now I can't guarantee that it will have a catchy song like the Lego movie, but I can promise you'll love it. I mean who doesn't like superhero movies?"

"That does sound cool!" Dallas said, thinking about it.

"Yeah, I guess that sounds pretty good," Ivy said with just a hint of a pout.

"Then next time, I'm taking both of you to go see it," Ethan said. "I suppose your sister shouldn't be the only one who has all the fun with me."

The kid's both turned their frowns upside down, grinning as they stepped forward to give Ethan a hug.

"You're the best," Dallas said, his arms wrapped around Ethan's neck. Laura's heart melted a little bit. She hadn't seen anyone get that reaction out of Dallas in a long time.

Ivy and Dallas then turned and scurried toward the living room where they took a seat on the couch.

"Thanks again, Elena," Laura said. "I owe you big time. I shouldn't be out too late, but as always, you're welcome to sleep on the couch. You know where the pillows and blankets are."

"Sure do," Elena said, flashing a wink. "Don't rush your evening for me, though. Take your time. You guys enjoy your night out. Besides, Laura, your couch is actually more comfy than my bed. I've slept on it many times."

Ethan stood next to Laura, with his hand pressed gently against the small of her back. "You ready, gorgeous?"

Laura nodded. "Yes, definitely. Thanks again, Elena. See you in a little while."

"You guys have fun and be safe," Elena said. "I'm going to go get the Lego movie song stuck in my head."

"I don't envy you," Laura replied, laughing.

She slipped her hand into Ethan's elbow and walked beside him to the front of the house.

"Sorry about the kids," she murmured.

Ethan looked over at her. "What's there to be sorry about? They're great."

"They just get really excited and energetic around you. They like you a lot," she said. "And that says something. They don't really bond to everybody. It's good to see that they have a connection with you. I just feel sorry that they bombard you every time they see you."

Ethan chuckled. "They're just kids. We were probably like that, too. Besides, I'd give anything to have even one tenth of their energy. I'd be unstoppable."

Laura laughed as Ethan led her outside and down the driveway. She immediately did a double take as soon as she saw the car that was parked in front of her house.

"Whoa," she said, stopping in her tracks. "Is that yours?"

Parked in front of her was a car that was likely worth almost as much as her home. It was a sleek, black Lamborghini.

"I have one, but I'm just renting this one," he explained.

"I thought you might enjoy a different kind of horsepower tonight."

Laura's expression must have shown her surprise. She'd never seen anything like it, though, except in her dad's car magazines and on the occasional TV show. "It looks like the Bat Mobile."

"It does." Ethan laughed. "I had them take out the ejection seat, so it should be safer."

She followed Ethan to the car and stepped up to the passenger door. There was no handle on the door anywhere, at least that she could see. She poked and prodded for just a second before Ethan was at her side.

"Here, let me show you," he said, sliding his hand up the side of the car and then touching a spot just to the right of where a door handle should have been.

The car made a soft beep to his touch, and then the door began to open. It didn't open like a regular car did, though. Both doors slowly lifted out and upward, like the wings of a bird.

Ethan took Laura's hand and helped her into the passenger seat. Her comment about the Batmobile seemed even more fitting now than it did before. It felt like she'd just climbed into the real thing. Part of her wondered if it would have flames that shot out of the exhaust, too.

"This thing is amazing," she whispered, as she touched the sleek dashboard, which had a giant touchscreen on it. Working for Carter, she'd seen lots of nice cars, but this one was definitely one of the nicest.

Ethan walked around the car and got into the driver's seat, closing the door behind him. He glanced over at her and smiled. He reached across the center console, took her hand and lifted it to his lips, giving her a kiss there just below her knuckles.

"I've got to be honest," he said, still holding her hand. "You look incredible tonight. Seriously, this car looks ten times better with you sitting in it."

Laura's cheeks tingled as she blushed. "I don't know about that, but thank you."

"I mean it," he said.

He released her hand and started up the engine. It roared to life, sending a vibration through Laura's seat. She watched Ethan smile with delight as he kept the car in neutral and began pumping the gas. The engine revved up, and the firing pistons became almost deafening.

"You're such a kid!" Laura said, speaking loudly over the sound of the engine.

Ethan let off the gas, and the car dropped back to an idle. He was still smiling with glee as he put the car in reverse and back out of the driveway.

"It's not a sports car if you don't rev the engine," he explained.

"Oh, is that so?" Laura asked, playfully poking him in the side.

He nodded firmly. "It is. It's a proven fact, actually."

Laura watched him push the gear shift up into first. Then he dropped the clutch and slammed on the gas. The Lamborghini peeled out on the pavement as Ethan went full throttle down the road. The sudden increase in speed caused Laura to get thrown back in her seat. She felt her body press into the leather.

"Whoa," she said, giggling. "This thing is crazy."

Ethan didn't respond. He focused on his driving. As soon as he got out of Laura's neighborhood, he pointed the car down the winding paved road and opened it up even more. They cruised along, taking the turns with the precision of a surgeon. Despite the fact that they were going over the speed limit, Laura wasn't afraid. She had full confidence in Ethan's ability to drive this machine. He did make cars for a living, after all.

They came to the end of the road, and Ethan slowed the car down to a stop. Then he immediately accelerated away from the stop sign like he was racing in the Indy 500.

Laura was giggling and laughing the whole time. She had what felt like a permanent smile on her face. She was having so much fun already, and the date was just getting started.

When Ethan finally got onto the main road, he slowed down to a more reasonable speed. "God, I love this thing. I need to convince Carter to make a version for us."

Laura's heart was still beating with the excitement of the ride. "It's pretty darn cool. You've got to let the kids ride in this sometime. It would make their day. No, scratch that, it would make their entire year."

"I'd love to do that for them," Ethan said. "I'll pretty much use any excuse possible to take out a Lamborghini. Let me know when there's a good time and I'll come pick them up."

He pointed the car South down the highway. Laura still hadn't asked anything about the date and suddenly wondered where they were headed.

"So what's the plan for tonight?" she asked.

"We're going to Sandy's," he said, with a playful smirk.

"Seriously?" Laura asked, her eyebrows rising halfway up her forehead. She had dressed a little fancy for Sandy's.

"No, I'm actually just joking. I have something better." Ethan pressed on the gas, and they sped up. He didn't say another word until they exited the highway a couple of miles down the road.

Laura cocked her head to the side, immediately

wondering if Ethan was lost. He'd just gotten off onto another winding mountain road, but this one didn't lead to anywhere except a few scattered neighborhoods.

"Didn't you say we were going to get dinner?" she asked.

"I did say that," he said casually. "That's exactly what we're doing."

"But Ethan, there aren't any restaurants up here," she said.

"Says you." He downshifted the car as they headed up the incline that zigzagged back and forth across the front of the mountain.

"Yeah, says me," Laura said. "There aren't any restaurants up this way. Trust me. I'm pretty sure that I'd know, too, since I've lived here my entire life."

Ethan had one hand on the top of the steering wheel and the other on the gear shift. He quickly glanced over, flashing a wink at Laura. "Well, then I'm surprised that you haven't heard of this place."

As soon as he finished speaking, he pressed a little harder on the gas and accelerated up the mountain. The car surged forward, increasing speed as they climbed. Laura just shrugged and smiled, allowing herself to relax on the drive. She had no clue where they were headed, and part of her still wondered if even Ethan knew. It was fine either way, though. Even if they got lost or if Ethan was confused about where this so-called restaurant was, Laura was having a good time just driving around with him.

The sun had nearly set, but there was still enough light to make out the silhouettes of the trees as they flew by. It wasn't often that she got to be in the passenger seat while being on these roads. She was usually the one driving, with Dallas and Ivy in the back. It was really nice, though, to be able to soak up the view.

*I sometimes forget how beautiful it is around here,* she thought.

The trees, the hills, the wildlife. She loved all of it.

"It sure is pretty up here," she said.

Ethan nodded. "It really is. Gorgeous. I can't imagine what it must look like in the fall when all of the leaves change color."

"Oh, you should see it," she replied. "There's nothing like it. The aspen trees turn everything to gold. It looks more like a painting than real life."

"Sounds really beautiful," he said. "I'll have to check it out when fall comes around."

They cruised along for a few more minutes in silence. Finally, they got to the top of the mountain. Ethan turned down a paved driveway. Next to the drive was a sign that read, "No Outlet."

"Ethan, I'm pretty sure this is a dead end," Laura said, with a worried tone. "There's a sign."

"Oh yeah," he said. "It's definitely a dead end."

She laughed and shook her head. "You must know something I don't. I'm extremely confused right now."

"Just be patient," he said, reaching over and placing a hand on the top of her knee. "We're almost there."

Laura kept her out the window until a small house appeared at the end of the driveway. Ethan pulled the Lamborghini up to it and parked. Silence immediately replaced the noise of the engine and all Laura could hear was the whispering trees outside as the wind blew gently through the leaves.

"And now I'm even more confused," she said. "I'm pretty sure this is a house, Ethan."

"You sure?" he asked, the side of his mouth curling into a boyish smile.

"I'm nearly positive," she replied. "At the very least, I can promise you that it's *not* a restaurant."

"Says you," Ethan said, winking at her again.

He stepped out of the car and walked around to Laura's side, opening the door for her. She took his outstretched hand, allowing him to help her out. As soon as she was standing, she glanced over to her right, toward the side of the mountain that they'd just traversed.

"Oh wow," she said. "Ethan, look at this view."

The sun was nearly down now, and the sky had turned from a bright orange into a dark purple. There was still enough light, though, to illuminate the sprawling view that laid before them. There were tree-covered mountains for as far as the eye could see. Miles and miles of land. It was so beautiful and serene.

"We're standing at one of the highest points in Silver Springs," he said. "You've never been up here?"

"I've been up to this mountain, but never here," she said, unable to pry her eyes away from the view. "I didn't think anybody had a view like this."

To Laura, it felt like she was on top of the world. It was truly breathtaking.

"There's more to see," Ethan said, holding out his elbow.

Laura slipped her hand onto his arm and followed him toward the house. She still had absolutely no idea whose home this was and how in the heck Ethan had gained permission to use it. When they approached the front porch, a security guard stepped out of the shadows.

"Good evening, sir," the man said, nodding to Ethan.

"Ah, good evening, Craig," Ethan said. "Nice to see you. Is everything set?"

"Of course," Craig replied. "Everything is just as you specified."

"Good," Ethan replied. He nodded, and Craig disappeared back into the shadows of the trees by the house. Ethan brought her closer to the door, and she couldn't wait to see what happened next.

## Chapter 19

*aura*

THE FRONT DOOR opened and an elegant man in a dark tux opened the door. Laura was sure this was what butlers must look like. "Good evening, sir. Ma'am."

He held the door open and then carefully closed it behind them before escorting them through the home. Laura glanced around, surprised by how beautiful the interior was. It was fully furnished, with beautiful and extravagant paintings covering every wall.

"Whose house is this?" she whispered to Ethan.

He just glanced over and smirked, without saying a word. She shook her head. Him and his secrets.

"Right this way, sir," The Butler said, approaching a door at the very back of the house.

Ethan and Laura walked through and onto the screened porch. There were two heat lamps, one on each side of the deck, which made the area entirely comfortable despite the fresh mountain air outside. Situated in the center, was a small white table and two chairs. There was a beautiful flower bouquet in the center, surrounded by candles, which flickered lightly in the breeze.

"Ethan," she said, shaking her head in awe. "This is beautiful. You did this for me?"

"Yeah, I mean, you surprised me with lunch, and I wanted to surprise you with dinner," he said. "You like it?"

"It's amazing," she said. "Nobody has ever done anything like this for me before. Let me get this straight, though. You got me a private restaurant? You rented a house up on the top of this mountain and turned it into a restaurant?"

Ethan smiled. "Would you prefer a public restaurant? I called around, but there was one big problem. Not a single one of them had this view. I decided I'd figure out a way to give you both dinner, and a view."

As he spoke, he motioned his hand outward beyond the railing of the deck. Laura stepped forward, letting her eyes adjust to the dim lighting outside. As soon as the view came into focus, she gasped with surprise.

"Holy cow," she whispered.

From where she stood, she could see the entire city of Denver and all of the surrounding area. The lights twinkled out on the prairie, making it seem like they were much closer to town than they actually were. In fact, they were forty miles away, but from that deck, Laura felt like she could reach out and pick up the entire city with one hand.

"I'll take it you like it." Ethan stepped up beside her and placed his hand on her lower back.

She blinked back tears of joy as she turned to face him. "I've never seen anything like it."

"It's funny, that's the exact thing I said to myself the first time that I saw you," he said.

Laura practically melted in front of him but managed to stay composed enough to keep standing. She was shocked and overwhelmed with the deepest feeling of joy imaginable. For the first time in her life, she felt like a princess.

Ethan lifted his hand and cradled Laura's chin between his thumb and forefinger. "You're just as gorgeous as the view." He then leaned in and kissed her, sending an electric wave through her body. His lips pressed against hers, the smell of his cologne, the view nearby. Everything was perfect. Everything was right.

When he pulled away, Laura's lips were tingling. It was as though they missed his touch even though it had been less than a second since he'd broken the kiss.

"Are you ready to eat?" he asked.

She nodded slowly, still trying to regain her senses from all of the surprises that Ethan had presented her that evening. "Yeah, I could eat."

"Good," he said, walking her toward the table.

He pulled out the chair for her and Laura sat down. Her entire body was tingling with excitement. It had already been the best night of her whole life, and they hadn't even eaten yet.

Ethan walked around and took a seat on the chair across from her. "I hope you like what's on the menu."

"Menu?" Laura asked. "You mean, you actually did turn this place into a restaurant?"

Ethan nodded, and at that same time, a new man wearing a black tuxedo stepped out onto the deck. He carried himself with prestige as he walked toward them and placed a menu in front of each of them.

"Good evening," he said, with a light British accent."What can I bring you to drink, Ms. Corbett?"

She tried to think of something fancy, but she was used to beer and cheap vodka. Neither one of those seemed appropriate for a fancy dinner. "Do you have Cabernet?"

"Of course," he said. "We have several kinds, but there's one, in particular, that's quite good. It's a private stock, made from a small family in Sicily."

"I'll take that one," Laura said, with a smile.

"And you sir?" The waiter turned to face Ethan.

"I'd like an Irish Whiskey, please," Ethan said.

"Very well," the waiter said. "I'll be back with your drinks and to take your order in just a moment."

He turned and then disappeared into the house.

"Ethan, this is crazy," Laura said with excitement. "This is the best surprise of all time."

"By the way, he's not just our waiter. He's also my personal chef," he said. "You may not know this about me, but I'm not the best cook in the world. If it weren't for Daryl, I'd probably starve. That guy makes me all of my meals and is by far the best cook I've ever known."

Laura glanced down at the menu. The top of the paper read, "Ethan and Laura's Second Date Menu."

"How cute is that?" she said. "I might have to keep this as a souvenir."

"By all means," Ethan said. "Any of the food sound good to you?"

She glanced down the list. There were three options laid out for each course.

*1<sup>st</sup> course*

- Ahi Tuna Tartare, Hamachi Sashimi
- Royal Ossetra Caviar
- Ahi Tuna, Maine Lobster, & Mussel "Paella" 24
  Baked Saffron Risotto, English Peas

*Main course*

- Boulder Natural Chicken "Wellington" 42
  Brioche Baked Breast, Braised Chicken &
  Mushroom Duxelle, Foie Gras Mousse,
  Sunchoke Puree, Pinot Noir Reduction
- Colorado Lamb Rack, Loin & Braised Shank 68
  White Truffle Infused Heirloom Polenta,
  Ratatouille Vegetables, Goat Cheese, Lamb Jus
- Ruby Red Trout, Diver Caught Scallops 38
  French Green Lentils, King Trumpet
  Mushrooms, Berkshire Bacon, Caper Brown
  Butter Emulsion

*Dessert*

- Sticky Toffee Pudding Bourbon Toffee Sauce,
  Vanilla Bean Ice Cream With Badia a Coltibuono,
  Vin Santo del Chianti Classico
- Triple Chocolate Terrine Flourless Dark
  Chocolate Cake, Milk Chocolate Marquise,
  White Chocolate Mousse, Raspberry Sauce

LAURA STARED at the menu for a bit, overwhelmed with how amazing everything sounded. "I'm not even sure where to start."

"Take your time," Ethan said. "Pick whatever you like. The chef is prepared to make all three options."

She looked up from the menu. "Wait, you mean I could order all three?"

Ethan shrugged. "Sure, why not?"

"In that case, I think I might want to order everything," she said, her face beaming. "Then we can try them all."

He grinned. "I like it. Let's do it."

Daryl came back out with the drinks a moment later. "Have you two decided?"

"Yes," Ethan said, as he handed the menus back to Daryl. "Bring us one of everything."

"Everything?" Daryl said, raising a single eyebrow, but otherwise showing no emotion at the request.

Ethan nodded. "Yes, please. We'll take it all." Then he glanced at her. "Are you okay with sharing? It's a lot of food."

"You mean so that the two of us can eat three meals instead of six?" she said, with a smile. "Yeah, I think I'm okay with that."

"Very well," Daryl said, with a polite nod. "You two relax and enjoy the drinks. I'll be back soon with your meal. In the meantime, don't hesitate to get me if you need anything at all. I'll be in the kitchen."

"Thank you so much," Laura said.

"You're quite welcome, dear," he said, then shuffled back into the house.

Never in her life had Laura been exposed to something so romantic. They had privacy on the porch, and it felt so cozy with the heaters. The only light that filled the area came from the candles and the moon, giving it a beautiful ambiance. As she gazed across the table, she realized that she had the best view of all time. It wasn't just the backdrop of Denver that had her memorized either. It was the handsome man in front of her, with his dark hair and sexy smile, that really had her attention.

"I really like your tie," Laura said, after a moment of gawking. "It brings out the color of your eyes."

Ethan smiled and brought a hand to his tie, smoothing it down against his chest. "Thank you. It's new. I normally wouldn't have worn a green tie, but Craig suggested that I wear it tonight. He said that green is a good color on dates with beautiful women."

Laura chuckled. "So wait, Craig is not only your security but also your personal stylist as well?"

He nodded. "Apparently so. To be fair, though, I don't know him all that well. I had to leave my personal entourage in California. I'm making do, though."

"Where is Craig anyway?" Laura asked. "I haven't seen him since we got here. Is he somewhere in the woods, fending off bad guys?"

Ethan's smiled faded. "Actually, no. He's in the trunk of the Lamborghini right now."

"Very funny," she said. His face didn't move, but he bit his lip like he was afraid of being judged. "Seriously?" she asked.

His face relaxed once again, and he started laughing.

"Almost had you," he said.

"You're right," she admitted. "I actually did almost believe you."

"No, he's not in the trunk of the car." Ethan took a quick sip of his drink, then continued. "I'm sure he's around here somewhere. He came up here earlier, before you and I got here, to make sure the place was secure. My guess is that he's just making his rounds. Pretty standard protocol."

"That makes sense," she said. She sipped at her drink and leaned forward. "I've got to ask, what is it like having someone watching over you all the time? I think it would drive me crazy. I'd feel like I didn't have any privacy whatsoever."

Ethan shrugged. "You know, it's not as bad as you'd think. These guys that work as bodyguards, they don't care what you do with your time. They're really good at just doing their jobs and staying out of your business. I've never really felt like it has invaded my privacy. To be honest, I feel like I have much more privacy because of them. They keep the public away, which is something I could never do on my own. At this point, I think I'd feel weird if I didn't have security somewhere nearby. I'd be pretty vulnerable."

Laura parted her lips to respond, but before she could utter a sound, Daryl came stepping out of the door and onto the deck. He was balancing two trays, one in each hand. As soon as he set the dishes down onto the table, the smell of the amazing food entered Laura's nostrils.

Her mouth watered as she looked at the plates. Ahi tuna, caviar, and lobster. There was a beautiful spread on the table, with just about every color of the rainbow in the form of food. And this was just the first course.

"Thank you," Ethan said. "This looks great."

"Anything else?" Daryl asked.

"I think we're okay for now," Ethan replied. "We'll let you know if we need anything."

"Very good," Daryl said, then turned to leave.

"I don't even know where to start," Laura said.

"I recommend the lobster first," Ethan said. "It's one of my favorites."

"Agreed," she said, putting some of the lobster on her plate and dribbling some butter over it.

The first bite was nearly orgasmic. It melted in her mouth, and the flavor was so fresh that it was like Daryl had taken the lobster straight out of the ocean.

"Oh my lord," Laura said, shaking her head in awe. "This is so good."

"There's nothing quite like fresh Maine Lobster," Ethan replied. "I'm glad you like it."

The two filled their plates with the first course and dove in. Every bite had Laura in further disbelief. It was the best food she had ever eaten. She decided right then and there that if she ever became a billionaire somehow, she would steal Daryl from Ethan and hire him as *her* personal chef.

*I wish that could happen,* she thought. *Because I don't know if I'll ever be able to go back to macaroni and cheese mixed with frozen peas after a meal like this.*

It didn't take long for Ethan and Laura to finish the first course. They blazed through it and set the plates to the side. Ethan took a slow sip of his whiskey and relaxed back into his chair.

"Tell me something I don't know about you, Laura," he said. "I'm sure there's a lot."

"I don't know about that," she said, smiling meekly. "I'm not that exciting."

"Somehow I doubt that." Ethan kept eye contact with her as he spoke. He seemed genuinely interested in her.

"Well, I like horses," she said. She shrugged.

"I already knew that," he replied with a smile. "I was thinking something more personal. You know, something that helps me get to know you on a deeper level. Like what was your childhood like? Any special memories?"

Laura glanced up as she thought about it for a moment.

"To be honest, my childhood was kind of a mess. I mean, my parents did the best they could, but it was hard. They both had to work two jobs just to keep food on the table. Neither of them had a college degree, so the work that they were able to find never paid very well."

"That must have been tough," Ethan said.

Laura nodded. "It was. Did you know that my mom had me when she was only eighteen? My parents weren't ready for me at all. I don't blame them either. At eighteen, they were kids themselves. They didn't know what it would take to raise a daughter. What eighteen-year-old does?"

"Not many," Ethan agreed.

"My parents did their best. I was happy, but I spent most of my childhood watching them struggle financially, barely scraping by just to make ends meet and keep a roof over our heads. When I finally turned eighteen, I made a promise to myself that I would never be a young parent. I've seen how hard it can be to go down that road."

Ethan leaned forward, bringing his elbows to the table. He listened with interest. She knew she was spilling her guts, but she wanted to share with him. She wanted him to know her. She wanted to know him.

She sighed. "But even though I swore I wouldn't be a young parent, I ended up being one anyway."

"For Dallas and Ivy?" he asked, taking a sip of his drink. "But you're older than your parents were."

"Ivy was born just a few months after I turned eighteen," she said. "Dallas was a couple years after that. I didn't have to raise them from eighteen to twenty-five, but I still have a child that was born when I was eighteen that I take care of."

"You're doing a great job," he told her. He reached out and took her hand. "They seem happy."

"Thank you," she said with a shrug. She took a sip of her wine. "You said you wanted to know something about me?"

"Everything," he replied.

She smiled and played with her wine glass. "I feel like I'm failing them," she said. "Like the universe is determined to put me in my place. I have to take the place of my parents, and I don't know what the hell I'm doing."

Ethan shook his head. "Laura, you're not failing them. I've seen the way they look up to you, and it's obvious how happy they are. You've been through things that most people on this earth will never have to go through and yet, you've managed to create a life for two kids who lost their parents. You are doing a fantastic job. Don't sell yourself short."

A tear slid down Laura's cheek, and Ethan reached forward, wiping it away with his thumb.

"You know," Ethan continued. "If anything, I think you need to learn to live your own life a little, too. You've spent so much time taking care of everybody's happiness, that I think you've forgotten about your own."

Laura's face softened, and she chuckled. "That's what Elena is always telling me, too. I'm trying, though. I just never want to take away any attention from the kids. All I care about is doing right by them because I think that's what my parents would want."

"Your parents would be proud of you," Ethan said. "Their daughter is the most courageous and strong person I've ever even heard of. I mean, jeez, I'm proud just to be sitting here with you."

"You're way too sweet," Laura said, with a sniffle.

Right then, Daryl appeared back on the deck with the main course.

"Chicken Wellington, Rack of Lamb and of course, Ruby

Red Trout," he said, as he carefully set each plate down onto the table. "Please, enjoy."

"We will," Laura said, eyes widening.

Daryl left Ethan and Laura to themselves. The main course looked even more incredible than the first and Laura could hardly wait to dig in.

"Looks good, doesn't it?" Ethan said. "I hope you enjoy it. Before we jump in, though, I want to tell you that I have a surprise for you."

"More surprises?" she said. She motioned to the view."This is already over the top. You don't need to get me anything else."

Ethan waved off the meal. "This is nothing. The surprise I have is much more exciting. I'll give it to you after we eat but before dessert. It will give us something to look forward to."

*This guy sure has a way of spoiling a girl,* Laura thought. *I could definitely get used to this.*

# Chapter 20

aura

THE MAIN COURSE turned out to be just as amazing as Laura thought it would be. She especially loved the rack of lamb and couldn't believe how tender the meat was. After they'd eaten, Daryl came out and cleared the dishes then went back inside to get dessert ready.

"I'm stuffed," Ethan said. "However, I'm going to eat dessert one way or the other. I can't resist his toffee pudding."

"I'm so full, too," Laura said. "You're right, though. Dessert is going to happen one way or the other. I have an insatiable sweet tooth."

Ethan's eyes lit up, and he reached for his pocket.

"Oh, I nearly forgot," he said. "Your surprise."

She smiled. "You really didn't have to, Ethan."

"I know I didn't have to. I wanted to." He slid the white envelope across the table.

Laura opened it up and pulled out a blank piece of thick stationery. It was folded in half, and something was inside of it.

"What is it?" she asked, carefully opening the stationery.

Two plane tickets fell out onto the table. She didn't notice anything specific about them at first glance, except for what was written underneath the line that said "Destination."

"The Caribbean?" she whispered, then immediately brought her gaze up to Ethan. "Ethan, I don't understand."

He smiled. "What's there to understand? I want to take you to the Caribbean. Everything's already paid for and arranged for us. All you need to do is pack your swimsuit."

"Oh, Ethan," Laura said, glancing back down to the tickets just to make sure she had actually read it right. "You're serious."

"Completely," he said casually.

Her initial excitement and surprise quickly faded as a realization flashed into her mind. "I want to go. Oh, God, do I want to go. This is such a nice offer, Ethan. But I don't think I can take you up on it."

She put the tickets back into the envelope and slid it toward him.

Ethan looked confused. "Why not?"

"The kids," she said, shaking her head. "There's no way I can leave them."

The expression on Ethan faced softened immediately. "That's why they're coming with us."

"Wait, what?" Laura said, raising an eyebrow.

"My plan was to have us fly out there two days before

they do," he said. "They'll be in school for those two days, and then after that, they'll fly out to meet us."

She stared at him in silence for a moment, just allowing herself to soak in what he was saying. She didn't know what to say. She'd never even dreamed this could happen.

"The kids have never seen the ocean," Ethan continued. "I'm going to change that. I want to show it to you."

She could feel her heart beating in her chest as excitement flowed through her. This wasn't a dream at all. Ethan was really there, and he was going to take her to the ocean.

"This is crazy," she said, smiling. "You're taking us all to the Caribbean?"

"I have all of the details planned out," he said, gently squeezing her hands. "There's nothing you need to worry about. I'll come and pick you up that morning. You just have to have your bags ready."

"I don't know what to say," she said. She was still trying to process the idea. It was so big a gesture she was having a hard time believing that it was real.

"Just say, 'yes.'" Ethan kept his eyes locked on hers as he spoke. He was so genuine and caring. She felt safe with him.

"Okay," she said, her smile widening. "We will go to the Caribbean with you."

"Excellent." His eyes sparkled with excitement. "This is going to be a great trip. There's so much I want to show you. I think Dallas will love snorkeling and Ivy will have so much fun feeding the fish."

Laura was officially on Cloud Nine. Surprised with both a fantastic meal and a trip to the ocean all in one night had her dazed with excitement. She felt loved and adored by Ethan, a feeling she'd never experienced. It wasn't just the beautiful things he bought for her either. It was something in the way he looked at her. It made it seem like there was nowhere else in the world he'd rather be than with her.

Daryl showed up with dessert a few minutes later. Laura and Ethan had a few spoonfuls of each dish, but it didn't take much until they were so full that they couldn't eat another bite.

"Can I take the rest home?" she asked. "Dallas and Ivy will go crazy over these desserts."

"Yeah, definitely," Ethan said. "I'll have Daryl pack it all up for you."

He turned in his chair and glanced toward the house, giving a nod. Almost immediately, some slow and soft music filled the air. It was a slow swing music song from their night at the museum.

Laura's jaw dropped. "You remembered."

"Of course I did," Ethan said. He stood up from his chair and held a hand out toward Laura. "Can I have this dance?"

"Yes," she said. "Yes, definitely."

She took his hand, and they walked to the far side of the deck. Moonlight poured in through the screens and over the two of them. It was almost like a spotlight had clicked on, putting them on center stage. It felt like that, too. For the moment, there was nothing else that mattered.

Ethan took the lead and they slow danced to the song. Laura closed her eyes and moved her body to the rhythm. She could feel the heat radiating from Ethan's chest as she leaned in. The smell of his cologne met her nostrils, too. It was intoxicating, and she found herself wanting more than just a dance. She had a feeling that she would feel like this every time they danced to this song.

The song began to slow down, and Ethan leaned in, giving her a kiss. He dipped her backward but kept his lips pressed against, all the way until the song finally ended.

Then it was quiet as he carefully lifted her back up and broke the kiss. The only sound on the deck was their breathing and a handful of noisy crickets somewhere out in the grass.

"You know we have the house to ourselves, right?" Ethan said.

She knew what he was suggesting. It was like he had read her mind, or maybe he'd read her body. Still, she didn't understand how they could possibly have the house to themselves. A few minutes before, they were most definitely not alone.

"What about Daryl?" Laura asked.

"He left as soon as I had him turn on the music," he explained.

"How do you know?"

"Because, that was the plan," he said. "I told that him once I had cued the music, he could head out for the night."

"Isn't Craig still here?" she asked.

"Don't worry, he's outside right now and will be for most of the night. He won't bother us," Ethan said, then took her hand and led her into the house.

*How could a girl say 'no' to this?* Laura thought.

# Chapter 21

aura

LAURA AND ETHAN stepped off of the porch and into the house. She squeezed his hand as they made their way down the hall and into the large living room. When they'd first come in, she hadn't even noticed the little fireplace in the corner. Now, though, there was a warm fire burning inside, and its soft glow illuminated the entire room.

"Was this on when we got here?" she asked.

Ethan shook his head. "No, I told Craig to get that started after we'd sat out on the deck for dinner."

"Well, aren't you clever?" she said with a smile.

Located directly in front of the fireplace was a sheep skin rug. They both kicked off their shoes and then walked over onto the rug. The warmth from the fire radiated outward against Laura's bare calves. It was so nice and cozy there, with her toes digging into the fur beneath her feet.

She held both of Ethan's hands as they stood there for a moment, just enjoying the fire and each other's company.

"Are you sure Craig is outside?" Laura said, glancing at the dark windows. The curtains were up to showcase the view.

"I'm positive," Ethan said. "Although, he might be looking in through one of those windows."

"Ethan! Stop that," Laura said, playfully pushing against his chest. "That would be so creepy."

"Yeah, it would," he said, laughing. "I guess if he's looking at us, then we might as well give him a show."

"Very funny," she replied. "I'm going to go ahead and pretend you never even mentioned that possibility."

"I'm positive he's in his car sleeping, actually," Ethan said. "Either way, though, he's not coming in, and he's not watching from the window. I promise."

He tucked a stray strand of hair behind her ear and caressed her face in the process. The feel of his skin on hers ignited coals deep in the pit of her stomach. He leaned in and pressed his lips against hers. Their tongues darted quickly in and out of each other's mouths, in a delicate but aggressive dance.

Laura's hands had a mind of their own. They drifted up and down Ethan's muscular back, as though just touching him wasn't enough. She wanted to feel him, taste him and to absorb every aspect of him in one swoop.

Her body burned with desire. The entire evening had been foreplay in a way. From the time he picked her up at home, throughout the drive and dinner, and of course the dancing, they'd been making love in a sense. It was all part of it. Laura was no dummy, and she knew that real sex, the good kind, was a lot more complicated than just their physical bodies connecting.

Ethan broke the kiss, just long enough for Laura to noticed that his pupils had blown. It was a look she'd seen before, and she knew what it meant. He was going to take her right there in the living room. Needless to say, she wasn't about to argue.

Without even two seconds going by, he kissed her again. With his body against hers, he took a step forward, pressing her back against the wall near the fireplace. Ethan took her hands and lifted them above her head, gently pinning her wrists against the wall.

He brought his lips to her neck and began to nibble his way downward. A pleasurable chill filled Laura and goose bumps popped up over her skin. She loved the way he kissed her. It didn't matter where it was on her body either. The sensation of his lips against her flesh was enough to send her to the moon with pleasure.

Ethan still had her pinned to the wall, as he eased his face down toward her cleavage. He kissed the top of her breasts, and she felt her nipples grow hard in anticipation. It was like every part of her body was reaching out to him, fighting for the attention.

Finally, he released her wrists. He brought his hands down her sides, then slid the soft satin up her legs, pulling it upward toward her waist to reveal the upper part of her thighs.

She moaned as his hand caressed the sensitive skin just below her hip. He kept working the dress up until it was bundled around her belly button. Her little white panties were now fully exposed. His hands were everywhere, and his kisses grew more insistent.

She felt so needed at that moment. Ethan couldn't get enough of her. Both of his hands and his mouth were on her body, and the rest of him was pressed against her. She loved how it felt. It was safe and sexual, all at the same time.

After a moment, Ethan pulled away from her chest. He clenched his jaw and glanced down her body. "My God, you're hot."

Laura blushed and giggled. The way he said it was with pure sincerity and she wasn't quite used to those type of comments.

"You are, too," she said, cocking her head. "Now take off that suit of yours."

"Oh, I like when you're bossy," he said, with a smirk.

He removed his suit coat and set it on a wooden bench nearby. Then he undid his tie and began getting to work on the dress shirt. One button at a time, starting at the top, he unclasped the buttons to reveal his chest. Laura watched intently, unable to take her eyes off of him, even for a second. It was like watching a male model taking his clothes off. He took his time, making her wait.

She let her dress fall back down over her body as she chewed on her lip, watching him. She licked her lips as he undid the last button. He reached up and pulled the under-shirt off in one smooth sexy motion that made Laura whimper with desire.

Laura watched as he let it slide carelessly off of his shoulders and onto the ground behind him. Her eyes made their way down his front and just like the first time. She was shocked by the kind of shape he was in.

He reached for his belt, but she stepped forward and stopped him.

"Let me take that off for you," she said with a smirk, her hand on his belt buckle.

He grinned and lifted his hands, giving her free access.

Slowly, with her eyes trained on his face to watch his

expression, she dropped to her knees in front of him. His eyes dilated, and he swallowed hard, knowing what was coming next. She loved that she could have that kind of effect on him.

Laura pulled the belt off, then went to work on the button and zipper for his slacks. Ethan stood in front of her, watching her intently. She looked up at him, noticing the way his abs and chest tightened with every move she made. He was holding himself back from taking her right there.

Laura reached up and slipped her fingers into the waist of his slacks. She pulled downward, allowing them to fall into a heap around his ankles. Now the only thing left between her and what she wanted was his briefs.

She slid her hands up the length of his thighs, all the way until her fingers landed on the elastic waistband of his underwear. As soon as she had a grip on it, she pulled them down to his knees. She looked up as she took him in her hand and began to stroke.

Ethan's head fell back, and he groaned. The muscles along his stomach tightened. His breathing was shallow as he held still for her. She grinned and brought her mouth to him, excited to see his reaction.

He let out a low moan as his sensitive tip slid across her tongue. She allowed him in just a little and then pulled away. Ethan glanced down immediately.

"Don't stop," he begged.

She dipped her head again, this time taking him just a little bit further inside. He breathed hard, tangling his fingers in her hair to help guide her as she worked her mouth.

Each movement caused Ethan to groan in pleasure. It was like she was conducting an orchestra. She had complete control of everything. The pressure of her tongue, the pace of her movements were hers to use as she wished. And she was able to tell how he liked it based purely on the guttural sounds he made.

He was panting when she pulled back. She smiled up at him as he opened his eyes and shook his head in disbelief. "How did I get so lucky?"

Laura bit her lip flirtatiously as Ethan helped her to her feet. He pulled her close and when he did, her belly collided with his erection. It was as hard as could be and it made her smile to think that she was able to turn him on that much.

He kissed hers, soft and slow, his fingers still in her hair. Then Ethan crawled onto the rug, positioning himself so that his back was to the flames.

"Come lay with me," he said, patting the floor beside him.

"Now who's the bossy one?" Laura asked, with a flirtatious smile.

Ethan chuckled. "I'm sorry. Will you do me the honor of laying next to me, madam?"

"That's better," she said, flashing a wink.

The warmth from the fire felt wonderful, as Laura crawled up next to Ethan on the rug. The wood crackled as it burned, but the room was silent other than that. As Laura turned toward him, some of her hair fell into her face. He gently tucked the runaway strands of hair behind her ear and looked into her eyes.

"Thanks for a great night," Ethan said. "There's nobody else I would rather be with right now."

"I should be thanking you," she said. "The fact that you'd set all of this up for me just blows my mind. The dinner, the private chef, the plane tickets, this gorgeous cabin with the incredible view of Denver. It's like a dream."

"It's all just stuff, really," he said with a shrug. The firelight danced across his skin, and all she wanted to do was touch it. "The stuff didn't make it great. What actually made it great is the fact that you were there to enjoy it with me. That's the only thing that really matters."

Her heart pitter-pattered behind her rib cage. Those eyes, those beautiful eyes. They were just so hypnotic. And that smile and the way he spoke to her with such sweetness. She was pretty damn sure that if she wasn't careful, she would fall head over heels for this guy. It might have already been too late. No one had ever treated her this well. Nobody had ever seemed to care as much.

"Kiss me again," she whispered.

Ethan did as she asked. He leaned in and pressed his lips to hers, drinking her in. It was so romantic in front of the fireplace, too. To Laura, it felt like something out of a movie or a dream. Still, though, the powerful need to make love to him egged her on. Kissing wasn't enough. She needed to feel him deeply.

Laura broke the kiss and slowly got to her knees. She glanced up and down Ethan's body. He was completely naked, and his skin glowed orange from the nearby flames. She wanted to kiss every inch of him all over again.

"You should take off that dress," he said, with eagerness in his eyes.

She nodded in agreement, then stood to her feet. With one quick movement, she grabbed the bottom of her dress and pulled it over her head.

"God, yes," Ethan gasped, his jaw dropping.

She bit her bottom lip and reached behind her, unclasping her bra and letting it slide forward off of her shoulders. His eyes were fixated on her, and she loved it. It made her feel like the sexiest person to ever walk the Earth.

She slipped down her white lace underwear, all the way

to her ankles. Then she picked it up and playfully tossed them toward Ethan. He snatched them out of the air immediately and kept them in his grip.

"Now come back over here," he said, beckoning her with a finger. She grinned.

Laura dropped to her hands and knees and began to crawl toward him. She went slowly, savoring the moment. Even though there was nothing more in the world she wanted to do than jump straight onto his lap, it was still fun to hold off for as long as she could handle.

"Don't tease me," Ethan begged. "You're killing me right now. Come here."

"Or what?" she asked, stopping in her tracks and grinning at him as she stayed just out of reach.

"I'll just have to come get you," he said, slowly sitting up.

She shrugged. "Maybe that's what you should do then."

Ethan crawled to his knees and then lunged at her, wrapping her up with his powerful arms. She squealed and giggled, while he spun her around and laid her on the rug. He made sure his hand hit the floor before she did.

"I like when you do that," she said, gently touching his lower lip with her index finger.

He held himself over her, using his body weight to press her into the soft fur that surrounded her. He brought his face forward and kissed her. It felt as amazing as the first. In fact, each one was getting better.

"Condom?" he asked.

She sighed. "We probably should."

He nodded in agreement. "Yeah. I guess you're right."

Luckily, he had one in the pocket of his slacks.

*I guess I wasn't the only one hoping for things to turn X-rated tonight,* she thought, with a smirk.

Ethan slipped on the condom and then resumed his position over the top of her.

"Yes..." she groaned, dropping her hands to her side and gripping the carpet.

He pressed into her all the way. Her jaw dropped slightly, and she let out a gasp as a wave of pleasure washed over her. She brought her hands to his forearms, holding on as he began making love to her.

Ethan held himself over her with his hands just above her shoulders. He dropped his head a bit and kissed the outside of her neck. The movements of his hips were slow at first but quickly sped up.

Laura wrapped her legs around his waist and began pulling him deeper into her with each thrust. The two were entwined in an intimate dance, while that romantic fire crackled nearby.

Laura let out a moan of pleasure while she dug her fingernails into his back. He let out an animal-sounding growl that heated her to the core. She was the source of his lust, and she knew it.

Because of the heat of the fire and the heat of the moment, it wasn't long before both of them were coated with a light layer of sweat. It made their skin slick. Laura's hands continued to find their way around Ethan's back, occasionally dropping down his arms so that she could admire the way his muscles flexed as he held himself over her.

Ethan lifted his eyes to meet hers. She lost herself to the pale green of his soul and forgot to breathe. He slowed his pace down, all the way to a stop. Then, in one movement, he brought his hands to her hips and rolled over onto his back, making it so that Laura was now on top of him.

She straddled his lap and brought her hands to his

chest, using it to hold herself up. Then she began to ride him. The look on Ethan's face was priceless as she took his complete length. He just kept moving his eyes up and down her body, and it was clear that he was shocked by her beauty.

Ethan's hand went to the top of her thighs, then drifted up past her belly button, finally landing on her breasts. He fondled them, letting her nipples slide between his fingertips. He stayed there for just a moment, then continued the journey upward until his hands were on top of her shoulders. With that, he pulled her down toward him and began kissing her.

The two moaned out, their lips and tongues intertwined, while Laura continued to drop her weight over his lap. It wasn't long before she felt herself rise to a climax. She rode the waves of ecstasy all the way to the top. It was the sound of him that did her in. It was his gasp and primal groan as he lost himself to her that tipped her over the edge. Her entire world dissolved into nothing but bliss. When it was over, she opened her eyes and took a shaky breath.

"How do you do that to me?" she whispered, still in a daze.

"You do the same to me," he said.

The two cuddled up next to the fire. Ethan put his arm around Laura while they both lay on the rug and watched the flames flick up against the brick chimney. It was so peaceful and serene, just laying there with him. Everything was perfect. The aching desire between her thighs had turned into a tingling contentedness.

She smiled as she squirmed against him, cuddling as close as possible. "I can honestly say, this was the best evening I've ever had. Every part of it. You seriously made my night. I don't know if I've ever been this happy."

Ethan kissed the top of her shoulder. "Me either, Laura. This is just so perfect."

Between the warmth of the fire and the feeling of safety with Ethan's arms around her, Laura faded off into a deep and peaceful sleep.

# Chapter 22

$\mathcal{L}$*aura*

Laura woke up to the morning sun shining in through the window of the cabin. She slowly opened her eyes and glanced around the room. It was the first time seeing it in the daylight. The fire had gone out, but it was still smoldering and putting out enough warmth to take the chill out of the air.

*Well, I'm awake and last night was most definitely not just a dream,* she thought. *That makes me happier than I've been in a long time.*

Ethan's arm was wrapped around her. She felt as he pulled her close him so that her back pressed against his chest. Then he kissed the top of her shoulder, sending a tingle through her.

"You awake?" he whispered.

Laura nodded. "Yeah, just woke up actually."

"What time is it?" he asked.

"No clue," she said. "I guess around eight."

"We should just lay here all day," he said, chuckling.

"God, I wish that I could." Laura sighed and pressed her back against him, snuggling as close as possible. "I've got to get back to the kids, though. I told Elena that I wouldn't be out late, and here it is, already the next day."

Ethan lifted his head up a bit. He brought his hand to her shoulder and began tracing patterns with his fingertips. His touch felt nice, and Laura closed her eyes for a moment, just trying to enjoy it.

"I had such a great time with you last night," Ethan said. "Best date of my life."

"Mine too," she said, gazing toward the window on the opposite side of the room from them. "You surprised me with so many good things."

It was right then that Laura remembered the trip to the Caribbean that he had surprised her with. At first, she'd been excited about it. She'd agreed to go, and everything about it sounded spectacular. Now, though, something in her gut made the idea of getting on a plane and heading thousands of miles away from home made her more anxious than anything else.

"Ethan," she said, after a few moments of silence.

"Hmm?" he grunted, still drawing imaginary circles on her shoulders.

He was obviously as happy as could be, but she needed to be completely honest with him.

"I don't think I can go to the Caribbean with you," she said, as she rolled over so that she could face him.

His relaxed smile turned into a frown immediately upon hearing the news. "How come? I thought you were so excited about taking the kids out to see the ocean."

"I was excited," she said, tears welling in her eyes. "But I can't get on that airplane. The thought of boarding that thing and sitting in those seats, the same kind of seats that my parents were in during their crash... It terrifies me. I can't even think about it. I'm sorry. I just..."

Ethan slipped his arms around her and held her tightly against his chest. "Shhh, shhh. I get it, Laura. I completely understand. If you don't feel comfortable going, I won't make you. I'd never force you to do something that you didn't want to."

He held her there for a moment, and Laura closed her eyes, pressing her cheek against his bare chest. Having Ethan with her helped to ease the anxiety in her heart. It was tough because there was nothing more in the world that she wanted to do than to go to the beach with him and the kids. But memories of her parent's death haunted her, and even the remote possibility of having Dallas and Ivy's lives end in a similar way was enough to send her into a panic attack.

"Are you okay?" Ethan asked as he began to rub her back gently.

She nodded. "Yeah, I'm fine. I wish I could get over this fear, but it's just so hard. I've thought about that accident so much that it was almost like I was on that plane myself. That's the only thing that makes me not want to take the trip with you, though, I promise. If it weren't for that, I'd go with you no matter what."

"For what it's worth, Laura, the tickets are for a private jet," he said. "It wouldn't even feel like a plane. It's a completely different experience."

"What do you mean?" she asked.

"You're not strapped down to your seat for half the flight," he said. "You can get up and walk around as much as you want. We'll have the plane to ourselves, too. You don't have to worry about anyone. And unlimited drinks."

He flashed a wink, and for the first time since they were talking about airplanes, Laura smiled. "Unlimited drinks, huh?"

"And it's all the good stuff," he said. He brushed a hair from her cheek, his eyes soft as he touched her. "It'll be you, Craig and me. But Craig will probably spend most of the time up in the cockpit, hanging out with the pilot."

She was silent for a bit, her mind whirling with possibilities and worse case scenarios. Suddenly, the sound of an airplane engine filled her ears. It came out of nowhere, like a flashback in a scary movie. The deafening roar surrounded her. Ethan was still talking, but she could only see his lips moving. She couldn't hear a word he was saying over the sound of the airplane motor.

All at once, images of her parents laying in the flames of a plane wreck entered her mind. She saw her mother there, wearing what used to be a beautiful white dress, but was now just a charred piece of cloth that hung desperately to her body. Her father was nearby, surrounded by flames that were too high for her to reach him. It was her worst nightmare. She was there but could do nothing to help. She was forced just to stand there and face the reality that they were gone and were never coming back.

A tear fell down her cheek, and Ethan reached forward, wiping it away with his thumb. "Hey, you alright?"

The engine sounded faded away, and Laura snapped back to reality. She looked around in a daze until she finally regained her senses.

"Yeah," she said, sniffling. "Sorry, I was just thinking about planes. It's never a fun thing for me to think about."

Ethan stroked her cheek with the back of his hand. He

gazed into her eyes. *If I ever feel safe again, I know that it will be with him,* she thought. Still, though, everything inside of her screamed at her to never get on an airplane again. It was, of course, just fear that filled her mind with these ideas. Regardless, fear was one powerful influence, and it had a grip on her that was so fierce it was impossible to ignore.

"I'd be with you the entire time," Ethan said. "If you got scared, I'd be right there. Anything that would make you feel more comfortable on the flight, I can make happen. I don't care what it is. Movies, games, drinks, food, a mariachi band. I'll figure out a way to make it happen, and it will get done. I promise you that."

Laura wanted to say 'yes' again so badly. She really did. She wanted to pretend that everything would be okay, but in all reality, she had no clue how she might react the moment she stepped foot on that airplane. Having a full blown panic attack in front of Ethan wasn't exactly the kind of impression she wanted to make on him.

"I don't know, Ethan," she said, shaking her head. "I just don't know."

"Look, Laura, if it's that difficult for you, then we don't have to go," he said. "As I said, I don't want you to do something you're not comfortable with. But if there's even a tiny part of you that feels like you can do it, please consider it. I promise it will be safe and also that it will be worth it. The ocean can heal you. It heals me, anyway. Every time I go there, I leave feeling so much better about life. It puts things in perspective. I'd love nothing more than to show it to you."

"You know, I've technically seen the ocean before," Laura said. "I don't remember it making me feel that way, though."

"That's because you saw the industrial city ocean," he said. "That's not where I'm taking you, though. This is completely different. Where we're going in the Caribbean is unlike any other ocean in the world. The house is built over the water. We can snorkel with dolphins that live in the area."

"Dolphins?" she asked, perking up. "Really?"

"Yes, really." Ethan's eyes lit up as he spoke. "The coral reefs there are gorgeous, too. I've never seen so much ocean life in one spot. It's like taking a swim in an issue of National Geographic Magazine, only a million times better because you're actually there to experience it."

"It sounds lovely," she said, with a sigh.

"The water there is so clear, Laura," he said. "When you swim out beyond the reefs, you can see all the way to the bottom. It's not uncommon to look down and see whales swimming underneath you. It's happened to me before. Twice, actually. It's not like California ocean either. It's not cold at all. Picture crystal clear water the temperature of a nice bath."

"I've got to be honest, you're making this place sound like a paradise," she said.

He smiled and nodded. "That word wouldn't even do justice to what this little piece of the Caribbean is like."

Laura rolled over onto her back and stared up and the ceiling. Doubt still loomed in her mind, but somewhere, in the depths of her heart, something more powerful illuminated. It was dim at first but slowly got brighter. Something inside of her began to make her feel like maybe it was time to face her fears and start to live out her future instead of her past.

"So if I were to agree to go, all I'd have to do is get onto the plane?" she asked softly.

Ethan nodded. "That's it. Nothing else. Will you try? If you get there and change your mind, that's okay, too. We can turn around, and I'll take you back home without question."

Laura looked over at him. She gazed into those beautiful green eyes of his and sensed his sincerity. If she was going ever to have a chance of facing this fear, this was going to be it. She felt safer with Ethan than anybody else and with his reassurance, she realized she might just have a chance at getting through this.

"I'll try," she finally said. "If you're with me."

He slowly smiled. "Always."

"Thank you, Ethan," she said, feeling the tension in her shoulders relax.

"You are most welcome," he said.

Then he leaned in and kissed her. It was a profound and meaningful kiss, and to Laura, it reassured her that his words were true. That he was with her always and that he would keep her safe.

When the kiss was over, Laura snuggled into him, with her face against his chest. She listened to his heartbeat and his breathing. She realized right then, as Ethan held her against his body that she wasn't scared. He had made her feel so secure about everything. For the moment at least, the anxiety that had filled her with the idea of flying on a plane seemed to disappear.

*I can face this fear,* she thought. *With Ethan, I feel like I can face anything.*

## Chapter 23

"Sir? Do you need anything?" Craig asked, walking into the space Ethan was currently using as an office.

He'd rented out an office space in a building next door to his hotel, but it didn't feel like an office. It had a desk and chairs, but no people. It was just Craig and Ethan. He got more done here than in his hotel room, but not by much.

Ethan missed the hum of his old office. He missed having coffee with people and not having to drive all over town to attend meetings. Plus, he missed his desk at home. He missed his nice pens and the way he had everything set up. He couldn't find anything in his current space.

He couldn't wait for the R&D office to finally be set up. He was enjoying his trip to Colorado, especially the parts with Laura, but he missed his workspace. He wished there was a way he could have both, but for now, he was going to enjoy his time with Laura.

"Can I ask your advice?" Ethan spun in his chair to face the other man. This chair turned more than his office chair at home and had a tendency to tip over if he leaned in it.

"Anytime." Craig smiled and leaned against the door frame. "I can't guarantee it will be any good, but I'm happy to give it."

"What do you think about Laura?" Ethan knew it was a loaded question, but he wanted to hear an outsider's opinion.

"Laura?" Craig repeated as if that wasn't the question he was expecting. He shrugged after thinking for a moment. "She seems nice. A little high maintenance, but nice."

"What do you mean, 'high maintenance?'"

"The kids," Craig explained. He pushed himself off the door frame and sauntered across the office to sit in one of the chairs. "The kids limit what she can do."

"So that makes her high maintenance?" Ethan asked. "I thought high maintenance girls liked expensive things and lots of money."

Craig laughed. "I'm sure most of them do. She's a different kind of maintenance," he explained. "You can't jet off on a surprise trip to Vegas because someone has to watch her kids. Your romantic evenings have to be scheduled. She can't go to things because she's got other people she has to work around. Dating a single mom is harder than dating a regular girl."

"You sound like you've done it before," Ethan observed.

Craig shrugged. "I dated this girl who had a four-year-old daughter. The kid was great, the girl was great, but I was always second. The kid came first for everything. It didn't work out for other reasons, but kids definitely complicate things. You aren't committing to just her. You're committing to her and her kids."

Ethan nodded. He had to agree with that. Dating with kids around was not what he was expecting. Just watching the movie at her house was different. If he were with a childless girl, he would have made out with her by scene two and had their clothes off by scene four. He'd watched the whole movie with barely a kiss.

He liked Dallas and Ivy a lot, but they did make things more complicated. In any other relationship, he would have jetted off to Fiji by now for several overnight trips, but they hadn't had a single one.

Yet, he loved getting to be domestic. He couldn't remember the last time he'd actually had pizza and a movie, and he'd thoroughly enjoyed the experience. It felt more like a family, which was what he secretly craved. It was different than he was used to. Harder, but it seemed like it might be better.

"But other than the kid thing?" Ethan asked, returning to Craig.

"Other than her having a ton of responsibility that comes before you?" Craig asked. Something about the way he said it ruffled Ethan's feathers. He didn't like the tone.

"Yeah. Other than that," Ethan said, crossing his arms.

"She makes you happy. If someone makes you happy, you don't let go of that." Craig put his hands on either side of the chair and looked directly at his employer. "You keep them close to you. You fight for them. Even if it is harder. Even if it doesn't completely make sense."

Ethan's irritation faded, and he sat back in his chair. It was harder, but Laura was worth it. He knew that.

"Why do you want to know what I think?" Craig asked. "I'm just your security."

"You're more than just security," Ethan said. The man was with him constantly and probably knew more of

Ethan's secrets than Ethan did. He saw a hint of a smile cross Craig's face that disappeared in just a moment.

Ethan sighed. "She's only seen the ocean once. And it was at a crappy city hotel. I want to make her happy."

"Happy is good," Craig agreed. "You sound like you're having trouble with a decision."

"I got us tickets to the Caribbean. To give her the best experience of the ocean possible," Ethan told him. He sighed again. "I"m just thinking it might be too fast."

Craig thought about it for a moment, then shook his head. "No. It's not too fast. You two have history, right?"

Ethan nodded. "Yes."

"And you know her through Carter, so you at least know she's not psycho or just after your money," Craig continued. "I think you're good. It's definitely faster than most couples, but then you aren't most people. Neither of you are."

"Thank you, Craig," Ethan said.

"What about the kids?" Craig asked. "She won't want to leave without them."

"They're coming out two days after us," Ethan replied. "I got them a special kid-friendly flight plan. I have a professional princess and football player that will entertain them onboard. Plus, all the kid-friendly food and drinks I could find."

Craig whistled. "Damn. I want to go on that flight. I'll date you for that kind of treatment."

Ethan laughed. "I want them to have a good time."

"I like it," Craig told him with a nod. "You'll get your time with Laura, and you'll make her and the kids happy. If the kids are happy, she's happy."

"That's the truth," Ethan agreed. "She never stops thinking about them."

"I think you have a recipe for success. So what is making

you rethink this?" Craig asked. "I mean, I'll be there, so you've got the best security possible. What's the problem?"

Ethan chuckled. He sighed before answering. "She seems excited about it, but a little apprehensive too. Her parents died in a plane accident last year. She's still struggling with it. She's unsure of getting on a plane. If she's not sure, I don't know how the kids will handle the flight."

Craig considered Ethan's words. "I am not a psychologist. I don't even play one on TV," he told Ethan, getting another small chuckle. "She may balk. The kids may refuse, and she won't go without them. Planes are probably still the scariest thing in the world to her right now. Don't get your hopes up too high."

"So what do I do?" Ethan asked. "Not fly? I'm not driving."

"Come up with a backup plan," Craig advised. "One that doesn't involve flying. Be creative. Chicks love creativity."

"Creative, huh?" Ethan thought for a moment and then smiled as an idea came to him. It was crazy, but he had a feeling he could pull it off if Laura couldn't get on a plane. "Craig, you are a smart man."

"I'm working for you, aren't' I?" Craig replied.

"What would I do without you?" Ethan asked, getting up from his desk. Now, Craig couldn't hide his smile. He beamed at Ethan from the chair. He rose as well once Ethan was standing.

"Can I help with anything else, sir?" Craig asked.

"Not right now, thank you," Ethan replied, walking around his desk and toward his jacket where he had his phone. "I need to make some phone calls."

"Of course, sir," Craig replied. He paused at the door. "I'm glad I could help, Ethan."

Ethan looked up from his jacket and smiled with a nod.

Craig carefully closed the door behind him, and Ethan began his phone calls with a smile on his face.

## Chapter 24

*L*aura

LAURA LOOKED down at the two faces of her younger siblings and felt her heart break. They were staring back up at her with tears streaming down their little cheeks. Their eyes were puffy from crying. Each of their sobs caused Laura's heart to break a little more.

Dallas was sitting on the ground, with his arms wrapped around her left leg. He was squeezing her so tightly that she was pretty sure her foot would go numb soon. Ivy was doing the same thing but on the right. She couldn't move. It was like both of her feet had been cemented into the floor.

"Guys, please," Laura pleaded with them. "Just hear Ethan out. He's trying to give us a gift."

Laura and Ethan had gotten back to the house a few minutes before. The kids had been so excited to see them initially. They were prancing and dancing around the house with giant smiles on both of their faces. Things changed immediately, though, as soon as Ethan presented them with their surprise trip to the Caribbean.

At first, the kids were just shocked and almost seemed excited about it. Of course, that was because they didn't know exactly where the Caribbean was. As soon as Dallas asked if it was far away, and Ethan replied with a "yes, it's far from here. We'll ride a plane there," all hell broke loose. Both Dallas and Ivy just lost it, and their smiles turned to sobs of fear in a matter of seconds.

"It's okay, you guys." Laura knelt down and wrapped her arms around her siblings, pulling them close. Their tears soaked her shoulders as soon as their little faces got close. "It's totally safe. As Ethan said, it's not a regular airplane. It's a private jet. It's different."

"It's not safe!" Ivy shouted, through a wall of tears.

"We don't want you to go," Dallas said, squeezing her even more tightly.

"You get to come too, though," Laura said. "Don't you want to see the ocean? Ethan said we can see dolphins and whales and that the water there is so warm it's like taking a bath. Doesn't that sound incredible?"

"NO!" little Dallas shouted. "Planes crash! Mommy and Daddy got on a plane and didn't come back!"

"Yeah, we're not going," Ivy shouted. "Dallas and I are staying here, and so are you! Ethan can't take you away from us."

Ethan was standing just a few feet away, watching the interaction. Laura felt horrible for him because he had been so excited to present the surprise to the kids. This wasn't the reaction he had hoped for.

"Dallas, Ivy, I'm not taking her away from you," Ethan

said, kneeling down. "I just want to give you guys a fun experience."

Neither of the kids responded to him. They just gripped Laura even more tightly than before. She couldn't be mad at them for their reaction. She'd felt pretty similar earlier that morning when she thought about boarding a plane. Her heart hurt as the kids continued to cry because she knew exactly what they were going through.

In fact, their fears were probably even more intense than her own. They were young and didn't have the capacity to think things through in the same manner as she did. They had never been on a plane before. Their only experience with the giant metal birds that fly in the sky was that they crashed.

"You can't leave us, Laura," Ivy said, hesitantly releasing her grip from around Laura's shoulders. "You can't go. What if something happens? We wouldn't have anybody."

Ivy's words seemed to strike a chord in Laura's heart. She winced. The idea of those two kids being without her, being left alone in the world, was her greatest fear. Still, though, she had to see past that. She couldn't allow them to live in a world full of fear and pain. There was more to life than that. There were so many things to see. She knew that she wouldn't be doing either of them any favors by sheltering them forever.

"Guys, what if we all went at the same time?" Laura said calmly. "That way we'd be together."

"No, no, no!" Ivy said, stomping her feet in frustration. "That's even worse! What if the plane crashes then? We'll all be dead!"

"Ivy, please," Laura said, stroking her back. "Please, just hear me out right now. Do you think I'd ever suggest anything that might hurt you or your brother? I love you guys more than anything in this entire world. There's nothing I wouldn't do to keep you safe. You've got to understand that planes aren't dangerous."

Dallas pulled away and looked at Laura like she'd lost her mind. "Then where are Mom and Dad?"

Ivy and Dallas both stared at her, waiting for an answer. Their eyes were overflowing with tears, and they looked legitimately scared. She hadn't seen this level of fear in them before, and it scared her. Their lower lips trembled, while they attempted to hold back another wave of sobs.

"Please, please don't do this, Laura," Ivy said. "We need you."

The sincerity in Ivy's voice caused the shattered pieces of her heart to turn into dust. She couldn't do it.

Right then, Ethan approached them. He knelt down and wrapped his arms around all three of them.

"It's okay, guys," he said. "No planes."

Laura lifted her gaze and looked at Ethan. Ivy did the same and wiped the tears from her cheek with the back of her hand. Dallas and Ivy were still crying and clinging onto Laura as though she was about to vanish in a puff of smoke.

"No planes?" Ivy said, sniffling.

Even Dallas released Laura a little bit and looked over at Ethan. For the first time that morning, Laura could feel a sense of relief in the two kids.

"It hurts me to see you guys like this," Ethan said. "I don't want any of you to have to do something that scares you this much."

Laura frowned. The last thing she wanted to do was to cancel the trip and let those plane tickets go to waste. She couldn't even imagine how much money it took to buy four tickets on a private jet.

"Ethan, what about the tickets?" she asked.

He shrugged. "Don't worry about the tickets. When you own a jet, they're refundable. Besides, I have a pretty good backup plan."

Laura cocked her head to the side. "You do?" She wondered what in the world someone planned instead of a trip to the Caribbean.

"It's actually pretty good," he said with a shrug. Ethan put his hand on Laura's shoulder and gave it a reassuring squeeze. "The whole point of the trip was to make you guys happy, and if it's not doing that, then I don't want to go."

"Thank you, Ethan," Laura whispered. A sense of relief washed over her. It wasn't just the kids that were anxious.

"Besides, we can always go another time," he promised. He looked down at the children still clinging to Laura. "It's pretty clear, though, that the time is not now."

She was disappointed that it wasn't going to work out. However, there was still a not-so-small part of her that felt relief because she wasn't going to have to face her fears quite yet.

"Ethan, thank you so much for understanding," she said. "You're the best."

He smiled and shrugged like it was nothing. To Laura, it was anything but. He cared. This meant almost more than him making the offer for the trip.

"I've got to make a quick call," Ethan said, as he stood up and pulled his cell phone from the front pocket of his slacks. "But I've got a question for you kids first. What do you think about heading to the movie theater in a bit and going to see that new superhero movie we were talking about?"

The kids sniffled, but slowly pulled their faces away from Laura's neck. They didn't release their kung-fu grip from her, though. They weren't quite ready for that.

"Superhero movie?" Dallas asked, in the cutest voice Laura had ever heard in her life.

"Yeah, remember the one about the guy in the cape?" Ethan asked. "I'm going to take all of us to see that tonight. Sound good?"

Dallas looked over to Ivy, and it was as though they had a quick conversation with just their eyes. Finally, they both nodded.

"Yeah, let's go see the superhero movie," Dallas said, then sniffled again.

"Alright," Ethan said. "Sounds like a deal. Oh, one more thing, I need all three of you to be ready for the beach tomorrow morning."

Laura frowned. "Ethan, we just talked about this."

"I didn't say anything about a plane, did I?" he said, with a playful grin. "All I said is be ready for the beach. I'll be here at ten in the morning to pick you three up. Have everything ready. Everyone needs swimsuits, sunscreen, and beach towels."

Laura was beyond confused and so were the kids but based on Ethan's smile. He once again had something fun planned up his sleeve. Before anybody could say a word, Ethan turned and began to walk toward the front of the house.

"I've got to make this call," he said. "I need to coordinate some things for tomorrow's plans. Go ahead and start getting ready for the movie. I'll be right back."

He left Laura and kids sitting there on the floor, all three of them with a confused expression on their faces.

"Laura, what's he talking about?" Ivy asked. "I thought nobody was going on the trip. You said we didn't have to fly on a plane."

"We don't, honey," Laura said. "Ethan has another

surprise for us and apparently, this one doesn't involve any planes at all. It sounds to me like it's going to be a lot of fun. What do you guys think?"

Dallas wore a thoughtful expression, but at least the tears were gone. Ivy wiped at her face, but her eyes were already drying.

"I guess it could be fun," Ivy said. She smiled. "As long as there are no planes, I'm good."

Dallas nodded in agreement. Despite her brave words earlier, Laura couldn't agree more.

# Chapter 25

*aura*

THE NEXT MORNING, Laura and the kids were all gathered in the kitchen. They'd already eaten their breakfast and were dressed in their swimsuits. Laura had on her favorite two-piece suit, which she'd only ever worn one other time. It was white, with giant black strips going across it. The bottom part was like a little skirt, which fell just below her butt. Over that, she had on sweatpants, because it happened to be the middle of May and still pretty cold outside in the mornings. Colorado winters never ended when they were supposed to and this year was no exception. One day it was warm and sunny, then the next day there would be a blizzard.

"Laura, is it going to be nice today?" Ivy asked. "It looks cold outside."

"Yeah, it will warm up soon," she replied. "The sun will

show up here any minute. At least that's what the weather says."

Sitting on the kitchen table nearby was Laura's giant gym bag that she'd had since high school. It was stuffed with everything she could think of that was swimming related. Since Dallas still wasn't a confident swimmer, she'd brought his inflatable arm floaties and a small paddle board.

In addition to that, she'd packed goggles for the kids, three beach towels, every bottle of soda she had in the fridge and of course, some water toys. There was a Frisbee, a football and a giant blow up beach ball.

*I hope this is everything we'll need,* she thought. *Since I don't really know exactly where we're headed, I'm not sure what else to bring.*

Despite having pressed Ethan the night before for some clues as to where he was taking them, he'd kept his lips sealed. He said it was a surprise and that she was going to have to wait. She'd racked her brain, trying to figure out where they could go that involved a real beach but didn't include a plane. They lived in the middle of Colorado, after all. So a beach without a plane wasn't exactly a possibility unless he was about to take them on a thousand mile road trip to California.

She heard a car pull up in the driveway and she glanced out of the kitchen window to see a big, black SUV with tinted windows and shiny chrome wheels.

"Hey, guys, are you ready?" Laura asked. "Looks like Ethan is here."

She gathered up a few last minute things, including her purse and cell phone. The kids stood by her side, at least until the doorbell rang. Then all hell broke loose.

"I'll get it!" Dallas shouted, then sprinted toward the door.

"No, let me!" Ivy replied, following him as though they were fighting over a million dollars.

Laura chuckled to herself and heaved the gym bag over her shoulder, then made her way toward the front. The kids pulled open the door, to reveal Ethan standing in the doorway.

She usually saw Ethan in a three thousand dollar suit, or at least an expensive pair of jeans. When she saw him standing in her doorway wearing bright red swim trunks with Hawaiian flowers on them and a white t-shirt, she nearly fell over from shock.

"Hey, hey!" Ethan said, holding out his arms as he knelt down to receive hugs from Dallas and Ivy. "You guys ready to hit the beach? Do some swimming?"

"Yeah!" They both cried out in unison.

In addition to his outrageous swim trunks, Ethan also had a giant silly beach hat on. It was made of straw and was so big that the sides flopped down a bit. To top it all off, there was an obvious smear of white sunscreen plastered over his nose.

Laura couldn't stop laughing as she walked to the front door.

"The kids say that they're ready, Laura," he said, with a broad smile. "Now the question is, are *you* ready?"

She nodded, but couldn't seem to stop chuckling. "I don't know if I'm as ready as you are. You look very prepared for this adventure."

"To be fair, I had to stop at the store and buy this outfit," he said. "I asked for something that would make me look cool at the beach, and the girl there recommended all of this."

"Was she blind?" Laura asked, with a playful smile.

Ethan cocked his head to the side. "You know what? I didn't think about that, but now I'm kind of wondering."

"Hey, Ethan," Dallas said. "You've got a little sunscreen on your nose."

Ethan pretended like he hadn't noticed, reaching his hand up to touch the blob of sunscreen. "I do? Oh jeez, how silly of me. I'm such a klutz."

All four of them started laughing. Laura locked the door, and they all headed to Ethan's car in the driveway. Craig was in the front seat of the SUV, and as soon as he saw the group, he hopped out and walked swiftly toward Laura.

"Good morning, Laura," he said. "Here, let me get that bag. It looks heavy."

"Thanks, Craig," she said, handing him the gym bag.

Craig grunted as he lifted it over his shoulder. "Jeez, what's in here? You packing bricks or something."

"I didn't know where we were going, so I packed everything I could think of," Laura said, giggling. "I might have overdone it, though."

Craig tossed the bag into the back of the SUV and then opened the rear door for them.

"Alright, I can fit adults in the back row. Car seats go in the middle row," he said. "If anybody wants to sit up front with me and listen to good music, feel free."

"Not it," Ethan said. "Craig stinks."

"Eww, not it," Dallas said. "And I ride in a booster seat. Not a car seat."

"Not it!" Ivy chimed in.

Laura laughed. "Fine, I guess I'll sit up front. We don't want stinky Craig getting lonely."

"Hey, now, just because I'm a big oaf, doesn't mean I don't have feelings," Craig said, flashing a wink. "Just joking. I actually do kind of stink."

He made his way to the driver's seat and sat down.

"Sit in the back row with me," Ethan whispered dramatically to Laura. "It's a bit of a trip, and I'll get lonely back there all by myself."

"You sure Craig will make it alone?" she asked, with a pretend concerned face.

"I think he'll live," Ethan said, flashing a wink. "Is your car unlocked? I'll grab the kid seats."

She pulled her keys out of her purse and hit the button to unlock her car. Ethan ran over and removed the car seats and balanced one on each arm as he walked back to the SUV.

"I can get those," Laura said, hurrying over to help.

"No, I got it," he said. "Take a seat in the back and relax."

She shrugged, then crawled into the car, sliding toward the back row. Meanwhile, Dallas and Ivy stood outside, watching Ethan wrestle with the car seats.

"So wait, this buckle goes where?" he asked. "No, this can't be right."

Laura sat silent for a moment, just enjoying the show. Finally, though, she realized she had better help him. Because after five minutes, he wasn't any closer to getting the seats in than when he had first started.

"You sure you don't want me to do it?" she asked. "I've done it a million times."

Ethan let out a defeated sigh, then nodded. "Yeah, you'd better. I'm getting nowhere."

"I think it's cute that you tried, though," she said, squeezing his arm as she scooted up front to install the seats.

"You'd think I'd be good at it," Ethan said, shaking his head. "Considering I run a car company and all."

"You run a car company," Laura told him, putting the last buckle in place. "Not a car seat company."

As soon as they were all secured, Dallas and Ivy hopped in and buckled themselves up. Ethan and Laura sat next to each other in the row behind the kids.

"Alright, Craig," Ethan called out. "We're ready to hit the road."

"You got it," Craig said, then pressed on the gas to begin their trip.

Laura turned to Ethan. "So you still won't tell me where we're going?"

He shook his head and wrapped his arm around her shoulder. "No way, Jose. It's a surprise."

"Well, I thought about it a lot last night, and I think it's important that I share something with you," she said.

He suddenly looked concerned. "What's that?"

"I checked and re-checked the Colorado map, and I'm about one hundred and ten percent positive that there is not a beach here. At least not one that isn't currently full of ice and absolutely freezing. I didn't want to burst your bubble, but now I think you should know."

"Very funny," he said, reaching his other hand over to tickle her right above her hips. "Believe it or not, I actually *knew* that. Now, if you could just trust me, we'll be there before you know it."

Laura leaned in and kissed his cheek. "Okay, but don't blame me if we drive for eight hours and don't see water."

Ethan chuckled and relaxed his head back into the seat, closing his eyes. "I promise I won't blame you if that happens."

They rode in silence for less than five minutes and just a few miles before Dallas spun around in his seat and gazed at Laura.

"I have to go potty," he said while crossing his legs as if to hold it in.

Her eyes widened. "Dallas, are you kidding me right now? You just went, right before we left the house."

Dallas let out an exaggerated sigh and rolled his eyes as he faced forward once again. "Fine. Never mind, I guess I can hold it."

Ethan leaned close to Laura. "Can he hold it? We can pull over somewhere. I'm sure there's a gas station or something on the way."

"No, it's alright," she said. "He'll be fine. As long as we're not in the car for too long. Speaking of which, how far away is this secret location that you're taking us?"

"It should only take us about forty-five minutes or so," he said.

"Yeah, Dallas will be fine then," she said. She shrugged innocently. "Forty-five minutes, though? Where exactly are we going?"

"Nice try," Ethan said. "But you're not going to get it out of me. Remember, it's supposed to be a surprise."

Laura wasn't one for being patient and certainly not when it came to surprises. She was the kid who, on every Christmas morning, got up long before sunrise and stared down at the Christmas tree to see if she could spot Santa. It wasn't to catch a glimpse of the old gray-bearded man either. No, she knew what he looked like. Her real reasoning was to try to find out what her gift would be before anybody else in the house was awake.

So being taken to some mystery beach had her curiosity turned up to level ten.

*Maybe he's taking us to a lake?* She thought, sitting back in her seat. There were a handful of lakes near Denver, but all of them would still be half-frozen this time of year.

While Laura was busy trying to figure out where they were going, Ethan was having fun with the kids. He was taking one of the foam, bendy noodles that Laura had brought and was poking them with it. He started off by pressing it into Ivy's side and then as soon as she spun around, he hid the noodle out of sight.

"What?" he asked, with an innocent expression.

"What was that?" Ivy asked.

"I don't know what you're talking about," he said.

She turned back around and once again, Ethan poked her with the noodle. Every time he did it, he looked like he hadn't done anything. Dallas saw him, though, and soon the little game had him laughing. As soon as Ivy realized what was going on, she started laughing too. Watching the way Ethan interacted with them made Laura smile. It also helped to pass the time and the next thing she knew, Craig was looking up in the rear view mirror to tell them that they had arrived.

"We're here," he said. "I'll drop you off in the front."

*Finally, I get to see where this so-called beach is,* she thought, gazing out the side window of the car.

Her eyes lit up as soon as she saw the sign, which loomed high above the parking lot.

"Water World," she said, then turned to face Ethan. "Oh, my God. Ethan! I love Water World! How did you know?"

He smiled with delight. "I didn't know, actually. But when I tried to find beaches in Colorado, this was about the closest I could get."

"It's perfect!" she wrapped her hands around his neck.

"Dallas, did you hear that?" Ivy said. "We're going to Water World!"

"Yes!" he squealed and kicked his feet in excitement. "This is the best day ever!"

The mood in the car was one of pure joy. Everybody had a huge smile on their face. Laura couldn't have been happier, or more surprised, by Ethan's choice. Sure, Water World didn't exactly have a traditional beach, but she didn't care about that. They had water, a wave pool, rides and everything in between. In a lot of ways, it was actually better than a plain old beach with a bunch of sand.

"I would never have guessed," she said, hopping out of the back seat. "You definitely did a good job of not giving any clues."

"I thought for sure you were going to figure it out," Ethan said. "I'm glad I was able to surprise you."

"I honestly had no idea," she said, shaking her head. "This is really great, though. Thank you, Ethan." She stood up on her tiptoes and kissed his cheek.

"Anything for you," he said, with a smile. "Now, what do you say we get in there and start doing some rides? Huh, kids?"

"Yeah!" Dallas and Ivy shouted, as the unbuckled themselves from their car seats and hopped out onto the sidewalk. "Let's do it!"

Ethan went to the back of the car and grabbed the gym bag, slinging it over his shoulder. Before he closed the door, he told Craig that he'd text him when they were ready to go.

"It'll probably be sometime this afternoon," Ethan said to him.

"No problem," Craig said. "Take your time. I'll be around. Just let me know when you're ready."

Ethan walked up to Laura and the kids, with a smile on his face as wide as she had ever seen.

"You guys ready?" he asked.

"Let's do it!" Ivy said.

Laura hadn't felt that happy in quite some time. She

realized that she didn't feel that way because she was about to go and have a relaxing time at Water World, though. She was happy because Dallas and Ivy were happy. That was enough for her.

"This is going to be so much fun," Laura said.

Then the four of them headed toward the gates, to begin a fun-filled day on the beach.

## Chapter 26

ℒ*aura*

ETHAN, Laura, Dallas, and Ivy and made their way down the sidewalk and toward the front gates of Water World. Laura remembered many happy summer days at this water park as a kid. It was a quite good backup plan to come here.

As they walked, Laura realized that something didn't feel quite right. There wasn't the sound of any kids laughing or water splashing on the other side of the fence, where the park was. In fact, it was pretty much silent except for their own feet as they scuffed across the pavement.

That was when she glanced back toward the parking lot. She saw Craig driving away in the SUV, cutting across the parking lines on his way to the exit. He was the only car in the lot, though. Not a single other one was parked.

*That's weird,* she thought. *This place is usually packed.*

She reached over and touched Ethan's arm to get his attention.

"What is it?" he asked.

"Look," she said, nodding toward the empty parking lot. "We're the only ones here. I'm pretty sure it's closed."

Ethan smiled. "Oh yeah, it's closed. It actually doesn't open up for another week."

"If it's closed, then we can't get it," she whispered. "What will we do? The kids are so excited. Maybe we can find another pool somewhere."

"It's actually a good thing that it's closed," he said.

"How so?" Laura asked, not understanding. Closed was bad.

"Because," he said, taking her hand. "If it weren't closed, then I wouldn't be able to do *this*. Come with me."

Ethan took Laura in his right hand and Dallas in his left. Ivy held onto Laura as they approached the gate. As soon as they got close to the main entrance, a young man in khakis and a blue polo shirt stepped out to greet them.

"Good morning, Mr. White," the man said with a friendly smile.

"Good morning," Ethan replied. "Is everything ready?"

Laura's jaw hit the sidewalk.

*No way,* she thought. *Did he do what I think he did? Did he rent out Water World for us, before anybody else could get in?*

She glanced past the employee, noticing that none of the rides were moving. There wasn't anybody else there at all.

"We have everything set up for you as requested," the man said. "I'll go ahead and notify everyone that you're here. We aren't fully staffed today, as you can imagine, but please let me know whenever there's a ride you'd like to try, and I'll make sure that someone is there to start it. We do have lifeguards on duty. The park is all yours today. Please let me know if there's anything we can do to make your stay more enjoyable."

Ethan glanced at the kids who were ready to jump up and down with excitement. "I think we're ready."

"In that case, please follow me," the man said, then turned around to lead the group through the turnstiles. He walked for a few feet and then stopped. "Oh, and Mr. White, the wave pool with the adjustments you requested is just around the corner there. Just go past the funnel cake kiosk, and it's on the right. You can't miss it. It's all ready to go, just like you requested. Hope you enjoy it."

"We most definitely will." Ethan squeezed Laura's hand.

She stood next to him with an expression of pure joy mixed with a little bit of shock. If she had learned anything about billionaires, it was that they could afford anything they wanted. This was beyond amazing. Water World was one of the most popular parks in the entire state, and he'd somehow managed to get them to open early *and* have it stocked with employees to run the rides. It must have cost him a small fortune, and he did it all for Laura and the kids. She felt all warm and fuzzy.

"So, if I heard that guy correctly, we have this entire park to ourselves," Laura said, facing Ethan. "Did I hear that right, or am I going crazy?"

"You heard it right," Ethan said. "It's all ours for today. No lines on the rides, no screaming kids, just the four of us hanging out and enjoying the sunshine."

She didn't know what to say. She was overwhelmed with happiness, and tears of joy made their way out of her eyes and down her cheeks.

"Sorry," she said, wiping the tears away. "I don't mean to cry. I just can't believe how sweet you are. You're way too good to us. You know that?"

"Not true," he said. "I can never be good enough. That's a fact."

"Laura, can we go on the water slides?" Ivy asked, her face beaming with excitement. "I want to go on the dinosaur one!"

"Of course, Ivy," Laura told her. "We can go on any ride we want. Ethan made it so that we won't have to wait in any lines. The whole park is ours for the day. Can you believe that?"

Ivy seemed confused at first, and so did Dallas. She stared at Laura and then back to Ethan.

"Wait, so we're the only ones who are allowed in here all day?" Ivy asked.

Ethan nodded. "Yeah, kiddo. It's just us. We can do whatever we want. Also, I heard through the grapevine, that in about an hour or so we'll be getting some ice cream. It could just be a rumor, but I'd like to believe it's true."

The two kids got so excited they started skipping across the sidewalk and whooping. From where Laura stood, it seemed that they were happier than they had been in almost two years.

Ethan and Laura walked hand in hand toward the funnel cake kiosk.

"This is so amazing," Laura said, looking around the park. She was so used to waiting in lines for each ride that the idea of having the place to herself felt like the most extravagant thing she could imagine. "Thank you."

"You haven't even seen the best part yet," he said. "You ready?"

"You mean renting out this whole place wasn't the best part?" she asked.

"Not even close," he said and began walking a little

faster. "Hey, kids! Hold up a second. There's something I want to show you."

The kids stopped skipping and turned around, running back up to Laura and Ethan.

"What is it?" Ivy asked. "We're ready to go swimming."

"Oh, then you're going to love this," Ethan said.

He led everyone past the kiosk and turned to the right.

Laura had been to Water World a couple of times in her life, but it had been years since she had gone. The last time she'd gone was in high school, so she expected some things to have changed. However, even though it had been so long, she knew something was different as they approached the wave pool. Where there was once just cement along the water's edge, there was now white sand.

The wave pool looked like a legitimate beach. The sand was silky smooth, and there were four outdoor lounge chairs situated in the center, complete with a giant umbrella. It looked like paradise.

"What do you think?" Ethan asked.

"This sand," she said, shaking her head. "This was never here before."

"I know," he said, walking toward it. "Feel it."

Laura followed him and kicked off her flip flops, letting her bare feet sink into the sand. It was already warm with the morning sun. It was so soft and fine compared to the sand she was used to.

"I couldn't take you to the beach," Ethan said, motioning to the white sand. "So I brought the beach to you."

"Ethan, you did this?" she asked.

"Yeah." He shrugged and managed to look a little bashful. "I mean, I promised you and the kids that you were going to see the beach and I wasn't about to break that promise."

She ran toward him and wrapped her arms around his neck. She kissed him right there, overwhelmed with happiness.

"How on Earth does someone bring in enough sand to make a real beach?" she asked, as soon as she'd broken the kiss.

Ethan shrugged. "I just made few phone calls and got in touch with some friends who owed me a couple of favors."

Laura glanced over, to see that Ivy and Dallas were already busy playing in the sand. They'd found some plastic toy shovels and were clearly in the process of making a sandcastle.

"I can't believe this is real," Laura said, reaching down to touch the sand. "It's magic. Thank you. For everything."

"You are very welcome," he said. "Just wait, though. Any second now, the waves should start."

Just like that, the wave pool whirred to life. Laura turned to face the water, watching as it lapped against the sandy shore. If she didn't know that she was standing in a water park, she would have believed that she was on a real beach.

"How is it not cold?" Laura asked. It was still only mid-May. It wasn't unheard of to get snow this time of year, yet she was perfectly comfortable in her swimsuit. Warm even.

"Infra-red heaters," Ethan replied, motioning to tall iron palm trees. "They put out heat."

Laura stared open mouthed at him. He had thought of everything.

"Laura, look what Dallas and I are building," Ivy called to her. She had to shake herself to walk over. She strolled along the sand, feeling it squish between her toes to see their sandcastle. They already had a pretty decent start.

"This place is so cool," Dallas said. "When you were a kid, was this your favorite place to go?"

Laura chuckled and took a seat next to him in the sand. "No, I only got to go a couple of times, and it was never like this. There wasn't sand here at all, and there were always huge lines of people. This is a lot different than when I went."

"I want to live here," Ivy said, with a huge smile. "Can we just move here? We can play on the beach all day every day."

"I wish," Laura said. "That would be fun."

Ethan walked up and took a seat next to Laura. He wrapped an arm around her shoulder and pulled her close. The two of them stared at the water, admiring the waves. Laura relaxed into him and let out a nice, long sigh. For the first time in a while, she felt completely at ease. Her worries were gone, and the only thing that mattered to her was that present moment.

"It's peaceful, isn't it?" Ethan said.

"It really is," she agreed. "You want to go swimming?"

"Do I?" he said, quickly standing up and taking her hand. "Do you even have to ask?"

Laura stood up, and as soon as she was on her feet, Ethan grabbed her by the waist and lifted her from the ground. She squealed and giggled as he carried her toward the water.

"It's going to be freezing!" she said. "Don't throw me in!"

Ethan laughed and increased his pace. He was taking giant steps through the sand, with Laura draped over his shoulder.

"Dallas! Ivy! Save me!" Laura called out, laughing the whole time.

The kids looked up from their sandcastles but didn't run to help. They just giggled as they watched Ethan playfully throw Laura into the water. To her surprise, it wasn't cold at all and in fact, was quite warm. When she stood up, her hair had fallen into her face. She pushed it to the side to see Ethan standing there with a playful smirk. He was still completely dry, except for his feet.

"I'm going to get you," Laura said, running toward him.

Ethan took a step back, but Laura was too fast. She tackled him in the waves, and they began to wrestle in the water playfully. The kids finally came in with them, and all four started splashing each other. Within seconds, they were all soaked.

"I love the beach," Dallas said randomly.

Laura laughed as she lifted him into the air. "I love it, too, buddy. Now, what do you say we go finish that sand castle you guys started?"

"That's a great idea," Ethan said. "I'll race you guys. Last one to the sand castle is a rotten egg."

Laura set Dallas back down, and all for of them sprinted out of the shallow water and back to the warm sand. Ethan let everybody else get there before him and pretended to be panting with exhausted as he approached the castle.

"You guys beat me," he said.

"You're a rotten egg," Dallas said, giggling.

"I know," Ethan replied, laying on the sand. "That's a bummer, huh?"

They spent the next hour or so building the sandcastle, and by the time they were done, it looked like the Taj Mahal. It was at least as big as a dog house, with two stories and intricate windows engraved in the walls by Ethan.

"I need a picture of this," Laura said, pulling out her phone.

"Wait, hold on," Ethan said, hopping up from the sand. "I'll take the picture with you and the kids next to the castle. It'll be a family picture for you."

"We want you in the picture, too, Ethan," Ivy said.

Laura shrugged. "You want to be in it?"

"Sure, yeah," Ethan said, smiling. "Let me just grab an employee."

He jogged off and a moment later came back with a young lifeguard. Laura handed him the phone and then all four of them situated themselves around the castle.

"Okay, say cheese," the kid said, holding out Laura's phone.

"Cheese!!" the group shouted.

The employee took a few pictures. "There you guys go. Such a good looking family."

Laura smiled. "Thanks for taking those."

"Not a problem," he said.

Ethan walked up to him a moment later. "Hey, do you think we can get some ice cream?"

"Of course," the lifeguard replied. "I'll be back in a few minutes. I'll just bring all of the flavors, and you guys can choose."

"Perfect," Ethan said.

The rest of the day was spent eating ice cream, going down water slides and playing in the waves. At one point, the kids even decided to dig a giant hole in the sand. They somehow convinced Ethan to get into the hole feet first and then they buried him up to his neck. After that, Laura and the kids turned Ethan into a giant beach mermaid, by creating a fish-like outline in the sand below his protruding head. He was a good sport about it, though, and even smiled for the dozens of pictures that Laura took with her phone.

For lunch, they ate pizza and funnel cakes. The kids smiled the entire day and Laura did, too. So much so that by the time the afternoon came around, her cheeks were sore from it.

Ethan had gone out of his way to make the best day for

her and her siblings. He had spoiled her non-stop for the past twenty-four hours and made her feel like she was a princess. For once, her heart didn't hurt, and she wasn't sad. Everything finally just felt right. Needless to say, she had a whole lot to smile about. It was, in every sense of the word, a perfect day.

# Chapter 27

 aura



EVERYONE WAS quiet for the ride back home from Water World. Laura and Ethan relaxed in the third-row seats, while Dallas and Ivy slept soundly in the middle row. Laura hadn't seen the kids this tired in years. A day of fun in the sun, going on rides and building sandcastles had taken it out of them. They weren't the only ones who were feeling it, though.

Laura was beat. She could feel a sunburn on her nose and couldn't seem to stop yawning. She was just glad it wasn't her that was driving because she wasn't sure she was going to make it home awake. It was the good kind of tired, though. The kind of tired that meant you'd spent the day the right way and squeezed every drop of life out of it that you possibly could.

"Pass the bucket…" Dallas mumbled in his sleep. "I need to make the castle bigger."

Ethan nudged Laura and pointed toward Dallas. They both listened in, watching as he stirred.

"It's my turn to go on the water slide," he whispered, then smiled right before falling back asleep.

"That's the cutest thing I've ever seen," Ethan whispered.

"You really made them happy today," Laura said, turning to face him. "I know for sure that they're going to remember this 'beach' day for the rest of their lives. I will, too. It was so much fun, Ethan."

She leaned her head against his shoulder and let out a relaxed breath. This was what love felt like. He tipped his head and kissed the top of her hair. The gentle gesture made her smile.

"It means the world to me that you spent the time, effort and money to make this happen," she said, softly so she wouldn't wake the kids. "I want you to know that, Ethan. I can't even begin…" She stopped short of finishing her sentence as a wave of emotion filled her. She couldn't remember ever feeling this loved. "Just, thank you a million times over."

Ethan stroked her cheek and gazed into her eyes. "For you. Always for you."

Her heart melted at the sound of his words. She realized right then, that for the very first time since her parents' deaths, that she was deeply happy. Her mind, body, and soul felt like they were in perfect harmony and her heart was at ease. It was like nothing in the world could harm her or her siblings as long as she was with Ethan.

More than that, though, for the first time she wasn't worried about what her parents thought. She wasn't thinking that they were looking down on her from above and seeing that she was failing Dallas and Ivy.

*This is what they would want,* she thought. *They would be so happy to see Dallas and Ivy having such a good time with Ethan and me.*

Laura closed her eyes and nestled her head into Ethan's shoulder. She thought about her parents. She imagined her mother's warm embrace and the way she used to laugh at all of her own jokes. She remembered her father's face, and the way the corners of his eyes wrinkled when he smiled. Every Christmas morning she had ever spent with them flashed through her mind.

For once, Laura didn't think about the plane crash as she remembered her parents. It was like her mind had healed, and the only images that flashed in her mind were good ones. There was no fire, or death, or carnage. There was only love and peace, hugs and kisses, smiles and 'I love yous.'

She hadn't realized that part of her mind still existed until that very moment. For the past few months, she was confident that the warm fuzzy feeling she used to get from being excited about life was gone. But it wasn't gone. It had just taken a little break and thanks to Ethan, it was back.

"Oh boy," he said, causing Laura to open her eyes. He was holding up his phone to what looked like a news story.

"What is it?" she asked sleepily.

He chuckled. "Look at the latest news article."

Laura took the phone from his hand to see a picture of the four of them at the 'beach' at Water World. It wasn't the photo that the spiky-haired kid had taken for them, though. This one seemed to have been shot from a distance. It had Ethan with his arms wrapped around Laura. She was looking up at him with stars in her eyes. In the background, Ivy and Dallas were splashing each other with water.

"Who took this?" she asked,

"Who knows?" Ethan said. "It looks like a telephoto lens."

Her eyes moved down to where the title of the article was. In big, bold letters it read, "Billionaire creates beach escape in Denver, Colorado."

*If you're made of money, you don't ask how to get to the beach. You ask how to bring the beach to you. That's what Ethan White said today when he decided to have truckloads of white sand delivered to Water World, all in an attempt to create paradise in the desert. It's hard to say why he did it, but many are thinking it has something to do with the beautiful woman who's with him. Who is this lucky lady? We don't know. What we do know, is that they look like the perfect, happy family. The two were seen kissing and holding hands throughout the day. Sorry ladies, but bachelor Ethan White is no longer on the market.*

*Sources confirm that this was not a publicity stunt brought on by Ethan White, and also not an attempt at a photo shoot. But could you ask for a better picture? Clearly, this is one happy couple and why wouldn't they be? I think all of us would be pretty happy if we could have a private beach created for us whenever we wanted.*

THE ARTICLE WENT on a little further, but Laura stopped reading. She handed the phone back to Ethan and sighed.

"Wow," she said. "Well, since the entire world knows now, I suppose that we should probably tell Carter about you and me. I expect you'll have to have a serious talk about what your intentions toward me are."

"My intentions are quite impure," Ethan assured her with a naughty wink. "Though, I'll have to wait until tomorrow to ravage. I'm a little tired."

She gave him a gentle push. "Shh, no talking about ravaging me in front of the kids. Even if they're sleeping."

He chuckled and wrapped his arm around her. He smelled like sunscreen, but she found it a nice reminder of the day.

"Are you okay?" Ethan asked, stroking her hair.

"Yeah, I'm fine," she said. It was strange to know she was in a news article for everyone to read. "Just weird that there was someone there with a camera that we didn't even know about."

"That's just one of the many perks of dating me," he said. "You get to have your picture taken when you least want it. I've actually gotten kind of used to it. Eventually, you just let it slide off of your back. They aren't hurting anybody. They just want a silly picture so that they can have content for their websites and newspapers. They're just doing a job."

Laura shrugged. "Yeah, that makes sense. At least they decided to pick a flattering picture of me. I think we look pretty cute there. Imagine if they'd posted one of you carrying me over your shoulder, right before you threw me into the water."

Ethan laughed and pulled her close. "God, I can only imagine what that headline would have read. *'Ethan White throws petrified girlfriend into icy water in an attempt to calm her down. Abuse? Probably."'*

"Oh, stop." Laura poked him in the side. "They can't just make stuff up like that, can they?"

"They can, and they do," he said. "All the time, actually. Even though they aren't supposed to."

"Well, whatever then," Laura said. "I guess since it's all made up anyway, I'm not going to worry about what they say."

Ethan leaned over and kissed her cheek. "It's a little tough getting used to, but I'm glad you're okay with it."

Laura shrugged. "There's not a whole lot I can do about it, is there? Unless I hire my own version of Craig to follow me around and make sure that nobody within ten miles has a camera." She put her head back on Ethan's shoulder. "Don't worry, though, Ethan. This day was way too perfect to have some silly news article ruin it for me. I'm still as happy as can be."

Ethan squeezed her into him and stroked her back. "Then I'm happy, too, Laura. I'm happy, too."

# Chapter 28

aura

"Are you sure you have to go?" Laura asked. She sat on the edge of the hotel bed watching as Ethan packed up his things. He was meticulous in where he put everything, and she could see why he wouldn't want anyone else to do it. The man was a little bit of a control freak about his things.

"Yes," he said, looking up. "It'll only be for a couple of days. You'll barely even notice I'm gone."

Laura made a visible show of pouting. "I just like having you here."

He chuckled and stopped packing to lean over and kiss her.

"I like being here," he told her. "However, W Motors is still based out of California. I have things I have to do there."

"And you're sure you can't do those things here?" she

asked, still pushing out her lower lip. "I mean, telecommuting is a real thing."

"Believe it or not, I have done it," he replied, going back to his suitcase. "I have to do this in person. Not everything can be done through a computer screen."

Laura crossed her arms and pouted, doing her best impersonation of a three-year-old. It made Ethan laugh.

"I'll be back before you know it," he said, closing the lid to his suitcase and zipping it up.

"Promise?" she asked, still keeping her pout going.

He smiled. "Promise."

He came around and kissed her again, wiping the pout from her lips. It wasn't possible to pout and kiss him at the same time. It wasn't possible to be anything but happy when he kissed her.

"Now I really do have to leave, or I'll be late for my flight," he said, giving her a stern look.

"I thought it was a private jet? Don't you get to pick when you take off?" she asked. She fluttered her eyelashes at him. "Maybe in, I don't know, thirty minutes?"

"You temptress woman," he told her shaking his head. "I have meetings. And a flight plan. And we already went once today."

"So?" She grinned, and he chuckled.

"So... you are a bad influence," he told her. He paused, obviously considering his options. He checked his watch. "You have ten minutes."

Laura grinned. It took seconds for her to have her shirt and bra off. As she bent over a bit to unbutton her pants, she could see Ethan lick his lips, then begin to unbutton his own shirt. He was being far too slow, and as soon as Laura had her pants down, she stepped toward him, grabbing onto the bottom of his shirt and beginning to undo the buttons.

"Come on, come on! Ten minutes isn't a lot of time to work with!"

Ethan grabbed her hands and stopped her. She looked up at him to see him smiling. "I appreciate your enthusiasm," he said. "Like you said, though, I get to pick when I take off."

Laura smiled back at him. "Do you get to pick when you get off also?"

"Of course I do, it's just whenever the plane la-" He stopped, then laughed. "Oh, you weren't talking about the plane, were you?"

Laura bit her lip and shook her with a naughty smirk. "Nope."

"Well, in that case, I do get to pick when I get off."

"Oh, is that right?" Laura asked, with a bit of a mocking tone.

"Yep. There are some perks to being a billionaire."

"Well then, *sir*. Do you want to get off now?"

He shrugged. "I guess that depends on you. Am I cleared for take off?"

Laura went back to undoing his buttons. "I *was* trying to take off your clothes, but you stopped me!"

Ethan laughed. As Laura kept messing with his shirt, she leaned up and kissed him. He reached around her, running his hands up and down her bare back. She loved the feel of his fingers against her skin. It almost tickled, but it felt so good she shivered. Finally, when she got the last button undone, she pulled the shirt over his broad shoulders and down his arms, nearly tangling him up in the process.

He flicked his arms free and resumed touching her skin. His hands went down to her butt, feeling her silk panties for a moment before going to his own pants. She heard the soft sound of the metal buckle slide across leather and before she knew it his pants were down around his ankles.

Laura pushed him back, insistent with her kisses. She had ten minutes, and she wasn't about to waste them. He fell back onto the bed, her body on top of his. She wanted him all to herself, and she wasn't about to stop.

"Wait, Laura. Wait!" he insisted, chuckling as he held her back.

"What?"

"Let me at least get my pants and shoes all the way off," he said with a laugh.

She waited impatiently, checking him out as he bent over to remove the last of his clothes. She loved the way his lithe muscles flexed and moved with even the most simple of tasks. If she were an artist, she would have insisted on painting him every second of the day. He was her own personal David.

She realized as he finished removing his shoes that she should have used this time to take off her own panties, but she had been too busy looking at his body. She shrugged. They still had at least eight minutes left.

She was back in his lap, her legs straddling his perfect naked body beneath her. Her hand touched his smooth skin, trying to feel every part of him she could reach. He was sprawled out beneath her and hers for the taking. She wanted to touch and kiss every inch of his skin. There were, of course, some impressive inches that she wanted to touch more than others.

Ethan's hands were back on her ass. His fingers grabbed at her through the silky fabric in the back and his manhood pressed against the fabric of the front. Heat rolled up her spine and straight into her brain. All she could think about was getting him inside of her.

"Condom?" Laura asked, sitting up and looking around for his pants.

He held up the small square between his two fingers. "Grabbed it while I was taking off my pants," he told her, ripping it open. He quickly sheathed himself.

She was panting with need now. She only had five minutes to make him hers forever. She had five minutes before he was gone. She was determined to make the most of them.

Laura leaned down to put her lips next to his ear. "There. Now, you're clear for take-off."

He chuckled and thrust deep. Laura's world condensed into one purely of pleasure. She gasped and writhed as he plunged within her. How did every time he filled her it felt better than the last? He groaned and bucked his hips to meet her, heat rising in them both.

There wasn't much time left.

"You feel so good," he said, his voice deep and husky with desire. "I could stay here all day."

"No, sir! The clock on the wall says you only have..." She pretended to strain to see the clock, but she had lost track of time anyway. "Three minutes to get off."

He laughed, then hugged her tight. He thrust his hip up, flipping them both over so that she was on her back and he was on top. He placed his arms on either side of her head, giving her the perfect view of his muscled arms. He was in complete control, and she liked it.

She felt safe and wanted like this. He leaned forward and kissed her before starting the motion with his hips that left her gasping. Their bodies moved in tandem, each seeking the edges of rapture. Skin to skin, his lips fused to hers as they crescendoed to their fabulous ending. Her body was ready to be his completely.

He felt so good it was unbelievable.

Together, her legs wrapped around his waist and his arms straining to keep him up, they came apart at the seams and joined. Heaven wrapped itself around the two of them and held them tight for a moment of bliss.

She hated that it was over, but happy it had happened. She wished she didn't have to wait for the next time she had him like this, but he had a plane to catch. Their ten minutes in heaven were up.

"Time to get going," she whispered, but she didn't move to help him up. She liked the feeling of his weight like a blanket on top of her.

"Just five more minutes," he muttered into her ear.

"Don't make me use my mom voice," she warned. He opened one eye and looked at her. She raised her chin up so she could look down her nose at him. "Ethan White, you get up and get on your plane right this instant."

He laughed and said, "Yes, ma'am." In a moment, he had pulled out of her, then staggered to the bathroom.

Laura saw his tie on the ground. She couldn't help herself. She reached down and grabbed it, quickly slipping the loop over her head and tightening it back up so that she was wearing the tie, and only the tie.

Ethan came back and began pulling on his clothes. Laura sat on the bed, just waiting for him to notice, but he really was in a hurry now. When he had his button-up shirt back on but still open, he began lifting up pillows and searching under his pants. "Laura, have you seen my tie?"

"Yes, I have," she said.

"Where is it?"

"Right here," she said, thrusting her chest forward a little bit. It rested on top of her breasts, and when he finally looked, she saw his eyes dilate again.

He leaned forward and grabbed it. At first, Laura thought he would just lift it up over her head. Instead, he grabbed hold of it, pulling her in for a kiss. The kiss was long, passionate, and for a moment Laura wanted to go again.

*Billionaires don't have a refractory period, do they?* She thought to herself. *What was another ten minutes anyway?*

# Chapter 29

aura

SHE PUT her clothes back on and watched as Ethan did the same. It was a wonderful and sad thing to watch. Wonderful, because he was such a sexy man that seeing him naked was a treat, and sad because he was putting clothes on rather than taking them off.

"Okay, this time I really do have to go," he said, buttoning the last button on his shirt.

"Can't blame a girl for trying," she replied, and he chuckled.

"You can only use that tactic for so long," he said. He grew quiet as he looked at her. "I'm going to miss you."

Her chest tightened a little. "It'll only be for a couple of days. You'll barely even notice I'm gone," she said, repeating back his own words to him.

He kissed her cheek. "Would you like to come to the airport with me? The kids won't be home from school for a while yet."

Laura hated the airport. Especially this one. It was the last place she knew her parents were alive. They'd taken off in their small little twin engine plane from that airport and never come back.

She almost said no. She almost shook her head and ran from the memory, but she knew that it wouldn't change anything. She needed to get over her fear of that place.

"I'll just ride with you," she said. "I don't really want to go inside."

He nodded and offered her his hand. She took it and together they left the hotel room.

Downstairs, Craig was waiting with the car and driver. He didn't look surprised to see them running late. He sat in the passenger seat while Laura and Ethan climbed into the back. Laura put her head on Ethan's shoulder as the car pulled away from the hotel and headed toward the airport.

They didn't say much on the ride. They didn't need to. Laura's mind was going a million miles per hour, and she wasn't sure she could have carried a conversation anyway. With every mile closer to the airport, the more her chest tightened. The anxiety and fear were living things inside of her.

She took a deep breath and did her best to clear the memories of driving her parents to this same airport. The way they smiled and laughed as they boarded the plane with their friend. The roar of the engine as they took off. The way they had never come home.

"You okay?" Ethan asked.

She shook herself to find she was staring out the window and her hands were clammy.

"I'm fine," she said, more to prove to herself than Ethan.

"Okay," Ethan slowly. "We're here."

"We are?" She looked out the window to see they were in front of the airport and the car engine was off. Craig wasn't even in the car anymore. "How long have we been here?"

"Just a couple of minutes," Ethan replied. "Are you sure you're okay? I'll have the driver take you straight home."

Laura forced a smile. "I'm fine, really. Just thinking. I'm sorry."

"Thank you for coming with me," Ethan said, kissing her temple. "I'll call you as soon as I land."

"That would be great," she said. She let out a nervous chuckle. "I would really appreciate it."

An airplane flew overhead, and Laura winced. Coming to the airport was a bad idea. She wasn't ready for this. She knew she shouldn't have come, but it was too late now.

"Can I see your plane?" she asked. Maybe if she saw it wasn't the same as her parents her anxiety over him flying would go down. It was at least worth a shot.

"Sure," he opened the car door and then helped her out. "It's right over here."

Together they walked to a chain link fence with a gate. Craig was on the other side waiting for Ethan. Behind him was a beautiful, sleek jet that didn't look anything like the tiny plane her parents had left on. This one looked more like a miniature jet. It didn't really help as much as she'd hoped.

"Please call me as soon as you land," she whispered, wrapping her arms around him. He seemed surprised but hugged her back.

"Of course," he promised, kissing her temple. "I really do have to go."

She nodded but didn't release him. She took in a deep

breath, memorizing everything about him. The way he smelled, the way he felt, the heat of his skin, the way he made her feel. She didn't want to forget a thing.

Using every ounce of self-will in her body, she pulled away from him. "Go. Have a safe trip."

He kissed her cheek one last time before quickly hurrying through the gate and walking up to the jet's stairs. She watched as he climbed the stairs with Craig right behind him. He turned at the top and waved before disappearing into the airplane.

A tear trickled down her cheek. What if it happened again?

She couldn't stand there and watch it take off. She hated that she had even come here. This was a horrible idea, and she should have just said goodbye in the hotel. The memories of her parents assaulted her from every side.

The parking lot where she parked to drop them off. The way they waved and laughed as they carried their bags to the small plane. The smell of asphalt and fuel. The hum and throb of airplane engines as they took off and landed.

It was too much.

Laura ran past the car and into the airport. She knew there was a restaurant with a bar right off to the left of the entrance. She needed a drink, or she was going to have a meltdown. She didn't feel like she could keep it together without something to dull the pain of her memories.

"I need a shot," she told the bartender. "I don't care what. Anything. I just need something."

The bartender raised his eyebrows, but pulled out a glass and pulled a bottle from the shelf. He poured a nice splash of liquid into it. She didn't even wait for him to completely pull the bottle away before reaching for it and chugging it down.

Whiskey. It burned as it went down but she didn't care.

"Again." She put the glass down, holding it in place while the bartender poured her another.

Behind her, she could hear the whine of a bigger plane's engines start. She assumed it was Ethan's jet, but she didn't want to look. She didn't want to look and see his plane take off. The last plane she'd watched take off had crashed and ruined her life.

She didn't want to do it again.

She chugged the second shot. It still burned like the first. "Again."

"You okay, miss?" the bartender asked, pouring her a third.

"I have a problem with flying," she replied. "My boyfriend is on a plane, and I'm freaking out a little."

"We get that a fair amount around here," he said. He put the bottle away. "Hopefully he doesn't have to fly much."

Laura's heart sank.

Her boyfriend was a businessman in California. He was going to be flying all the freaking time. He couldn't just come and stay in Colorado. Even if he did relocate to the new R&D department, he would still have to fly back and forth until it was ready. There was no way flying wasn't a part of his life for the near future.

She downed the third shot. She felt sick to her stomach, and it wasn't because of the alcohol. She was going to have to do this again. And again. And again.

"You should have something to eat," the bartender recommended, pushing a menu and some bar nuts towards her.

"I'm just going to go home," she told him. She pulled out some bills and threw them on the bar. It was more than her bill would be, but she didn't want to wait around for the change. She just wanted to curl up under her blanket and forget the day.

## Chapter 30

"LAURA? ARE YOU HOME?"

Laura cracked open an eye and pulled the pillow off her face. It smelled like whiskey. She groaned as she sat up. She'd fallen asleep and now felt terrible. Drunk sleep was the worst.

"I'm here, Dallas," she said, moving slowly as she swung her feet to the floor. She glanced at the clock to see it was almost five. They'd gone over to a friend's house after school, but now it was almost dinner time.

Dallas' small face peeked around Laura's bedroom door as he looked for her.

"How was school?" Laura asked. She was just glad she wasn't hung over. Just exhausted, both physically and emotionally.

"It was movie day," he replied, standing in her doorway. He frowned as he watched her. "Are you okay?"

"Yeah." She ran a hand through her hair to find it super tangled. "Why?"

"You look sick."

Laura looked over at the mirror hanging on the wall and had to agree with his assessment. She looked awful. Her hair was a mess, and her mascara was all over her cheeks.

"I'm okay," she told her brother. "I just fell asleep."

"In a tornado?" he asked. "'Cause that's what it looks like."

She threw her pillow at him. He ducked, and it bounced harmlessly off the door.

"Where's your sister?" she asked. She wanted to go back to bed, but she had to get up and be the parent. At least she didn't feel too hung over. She stood up and stretched.

"Getting a snack," Dallas answered. He picked up the pillow and chucked it back at her.

"A snack?" Laura caught the pillow and put it on the bed. "No. It's almost dinner."

Laura hurried past Dallas to the kitchen where Ivy had a bowl and cereal out. She was just pulling the milk from the fridge when Laura caught her.

"Ivy, what are you doing?" Laura asked, putting the milk back in the fridge.

"Getting a snack. I'm hungry," she explained, looking annoyed.

"It's basically dinnertime," Laura informed her. "Can you wait twenty minutes while I make dinner?"

Ivy sighed dramatically and rolled her eyes. "I guess."

Laura looked at the bowl and raised her eyebrows. Ivy sighed again but put the bowl and cereal away like it was the hardest thing she'd had to do all day. Laura shook her head.

She was not looking forward to the teenage years with these two.

"You two can watch a movie," she offered. "Dinner will be ready in just a little bit."

Ivy fell onto the couch, but Dallas happily went over to their selection of DVDs and picked one out. Laura stopped paying attention to them and pulled out her phone expecting to see a message from Ethan. But there wasn't one.

She rechecked the time, trying to ignore the way her stomach tightened. He probably just forgot or got busy. She did make him late, and he did have meetings. Still, she was nervous.

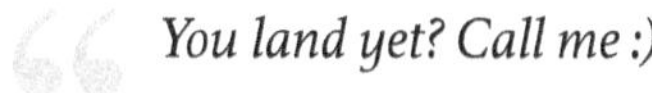

*You land yet? Call me :)*

SHE HOPED the smiley face at the end made the text message sound less needy. She'd already texted him twice since he took off. She knew it was overkill, but she couldn't stop the feeling that something bad had happened to him. She needed to know he was okay.

She pulled out some chicken breasts and started some Rice-a-Roni in a pot. She had some broccoli in the freezer that she would add to the simple dinner. She tried to focus on cooking rather than the fact that he hadn't called her yet.

*What if the plane went down? What if there was bad weather? What if there was an earthquake when he landed and it swallowed up the plane?*

She rolled her eyes at the last thought. Even that was a bit much. She laughed to herself as she cut into the chicken.

*What if he never comes back? What if he leaves just like they did?*

She froze knife in midair and raw chicken all over her hands. Icy fear ran down her spine, and the hairs on the back of her neck stood upright. She was used to him in her life. She wanted him in her life. She wanted him in her siblings' lives. The idea of him not coming back was terrifying.

She remembered coming home from work and having to tell her sister and brother that their parents were never coming home. She wasn't sure she could do that again if anything happened to Ethan. She wasn't strong enough to do it again. It would destroy her, and she knew it.

She thought she could handle him flying, but this was more than that. If anything happened to him, on an airplane or a car or even just walking down the street, she wouldn't survive it. She'd lost too much. She couldn't lose him too.

Panic rippled up and down her skin like she was covered in ants. She threw the knife in the sink and washed her hands, trying to take deep breaths. She was too close to him, and she just realized the danger now.

He could hurt her without meaning to. He would hurt her without meaning to.

Her text message alert went off, and Laura let out a sigh of relief. She dried her hands and reached for the phone, relieved that he had finally messaged her.

Except it wasn't a message from him. It was a picture of baby Miri in the outfit Laura had bought her. She looked absolutely adorable, but it wasn't what Laura was looking for. She texted Mia a thank you and then pulled up Ethan's number.

HER STOMACH WAS in knots as she set the phone on the counter. She closed her eyes and searched for strength inside of herself.

"It's just a plane ride," she whispered to herself. "It's just a plane ride. He's fine. Millions of people fly every single day and are absolutely fine. It's safer than driving."

She still felt the ball of ice in her stomach grow. Who cared about millions of people? She cared about one. Anything could have happened to him.

She jumped as her phone began to ring and vibrate. Her hands shook as she picked it up and saw Ethan's number on the screen. Her relief was palpable as she sighed and nearly collapsed into the kitchen counter.

"Ethan?" she answered before the second ring even went off.

"You messaged me?" He sounded annoyed. She could hear voices in the background.

"Are you okay?" she asked, her hand on her stomach and her knees weak with relief.

"Of course I'm okay," he replied. "Why wouldn't I be?"

A tear trickled down her cheek, and she wiped it away with the back of her hand. "I didn't get a message, and I kept thinking the worst had happened."

"I'm fine, Laura. I don't know why you didn't get my text, but I did send one as soon as I landed," he told her. "I must have been in a dead zone and it just never sent."

"I was just worried." She tried to keep her voice level and happy, but it betrayed her and quivered.

"Laura, you realize I will be traveling a lot, right?" he asked.

"I know," she said quickly. She felt a little silly now for all the text messages, but she had been worried. "I thought I could handle it. I just got worried when I didn't get a message."

"I did send you a message," he replied. "Look, I'm in the middle of a meeting. I can't be on my phone right now. I'll call you back."

Laura stared at the screen as the line disconnected. She was glad he was okay, but not so impressed by the call itself. She had been legitimately worried about him, and he'd just blown her off. That wasn't how the phone call was supposed to go.

Her chest squeezed hard against her heart, and she wiped another tear from her cheek. She really cared about him, but did he care about her? He had to know how worried she would get with him flying, yet he just brushed her off. Maybe he didn't care as much as she thought he did. Did she make a mistake?

Laura took a shaky breath and checked her messages to see if she just missed his message, but there wasn't one.

Did he really send one?

She hated that she even had to wonder. Of course, he sent one. It would probably just come through in an hour, and she'd chuckle and laugh at how late it was. It happened all the time, especially up in the mountains where she didn't get good reception.

Still, the niggle of doubt remained. Anger bubbled up, and even though she knew it was irrational, it didn't stop her from feeling it. She knew she was overreacting about him not messaging her, but she wasn't most people. Most people didn't have a history of losing loved ones to airplanes. She had a valid reason to be worried when people she cared about got on a plane.

Laura hated this. She hated feeling like this. She slammed the phone down on the counter and went back to her chicken. The butter in the pan was burning, and she needed to get dinner going, not worry about a stupid message. She tipped the chicken into the pan, covered it and washed her hands before going to the couch.

She hugged Ivy and Dallas to her as she sat on the couch between them and let dinner cook. They both leaned into her, smelling of sunscreen and grass. They were safe. They would never do this to her. They were the only thing in her world that was constant.

She needed to focus on them. She needed to focus on people that wouldn't leave her.

## Chapter 31

IT FELT good to be back in his office. Things were where he expected, and his life made sense here. He knew where his pens were. He knew where the coffee was. He didn't have to hunt and search for everything. Plus, the hustle and bustle of the office were the soundtracks to his life.

It felt like home.

Ethan leaned back in his chair, and it didn't tip over. His chair spun exactly the amount a chair should. He smiled, closed his eyes, and let himself relax for a moment. There were still meetings to go to, and he'd only come into his office to grab a file, but it he was enjoying his moment of calm.

"Ethan?" Becky opened his door and put her head in. "You've got five minutes before your meeting."

"Thank you, Becky," he replied, not opening his eyes. He could reach out and find exactly what he wanted in his desk from this spot. He didn't even have to think about it. He hadn't realized how much he'd missed his organization here.

"I wanted to thank you for my anniversary dinner," Becky said, leaning against the door. She smiled at him. "Katie loved eating at Le Chat. I don't think she stopped smiling the entire time."

"Le Chat? That's a nice place. Good pick. I'm so glad you had a good time," he said, opening his eyes and smiling at her. "That reminds me, thank you for my tie. It was perfect."

Becky frowned. "What tie?"

"The tie. The green one you sent to my hotel," he explained. "It was perfect."

Becky shook her head slowly from side to side. "I didn't send you a tie. I know you said you needed some, but the ones I ordered haven't shipped yet. I didn't think you needed them until you were back in the office."

He sat up straight in the chair. "You didn't send the tie?"

She shook her head and shrugged. "You must have a secret admirer."

"I guess so," he replied. He thought for a moment, but it didn't really bother him too much. "I'll figure it out eventually. It was probably Carter. Or Mia."

"I'm sure you will. Four minutes, now," Becky warned, heading out of the office. Ethan chuckled. He'd missed having her around. He leaned back in his chair again, enjoying the moment of quiet before he had to head back out and work again.

The door opened again, but instead of his secretary, it was his head of security in his office. Bruce Flagg was a big man, and he'd run Ethan's security for as long as Ethan could remember. He had a bald head and his arm still wrapped in a sling from his injury.

"Hello Mr. White," Bruce greeted him. "How did Colorado treat you?"

"It was great," Ethan replied, standing up to greet him. He shook the man's non-sling hand. "I've missed this place though."

Bruce chuckled. "This place is a good one," he agreed. "How did Craig do for you?"

"He did fantastic," Ethan answered honestly. "He was a model employee. Why? Is there something wrong?"

Bruce shook his head. "No, nothing wrong. He's just got a lot of overtime hours already this month. It's going to kill my budget. I wanted to check with you before I cut back on his hours."

Ethan frowned. "You're in charge of scheduling. I don't want you going over budget. You know you have complete control."

Bruce frowned slightly. "Craig said that you'd be upset. That you'd requested him."

Ethan raised his eyebrows. He couldn't remember ever actually saying that, but it was certainly possible. The two of them had spent a lot of time together. "Well, Craig is great, but I can take someone else with me on the next trip if it keeps the budget. It's not a big deal."

"You sure?" Bruce's face lightened. "It would help out my scheduling mess until my arm's better."

Ethan waved his hand through the air. "Of course. It's not a problem."

Bruce smiled. "Well, that was easier than I thought," he said wiping his brow with his good arm. "I'm glad it's going well in Colorado. I'll let Craig know you'll be taking someone else back."

"Make sure to tell him he did a great job," Ethan replied.

"Will do," Bruce assured him. He looked out the door

and chuckled. "Becky's pointing at her watch. Have a great meeting."

"Thanks, Bruce," Ethan said, standing up from his desk as Bruce headed out of the office.

Ethan picked up a pen and the file he needed, loving that he knew exactly where both were and he didn't have to search for them. It was so nice to be back on his home turf. He smiled and went to pick up his personal phone.

He sighed and went to check the messages and was glad to find there weren't any new ones. He still couldn't believe Laura had messaged him six times for a one and a half hour flight. He understood that she had some fears about flying given her parents' history, but this felt extreme.

He shook his head and put the phone in his pocket. He was going to have to have a talk with her about it. When he was here, he had to work. She couldn't be messaging him and expecting phone calls while he was working.

But that was a talk for later. He was late for his meeting. He'd been in meetings non-stop since landing and had barely even had time to go to the bathroom. Everyone was trying to get caught up while he was in the office. He was planning on calling her later tonight once the meetings were wrapped up.

But, all in all, things were going well now that the was back in California. He glanced around his office and smiled. It was good to be home.

## Chapter 32

ETHAN WALKED onto the elevator to the parking garage in a daze. He couldn't remember the last meeting that had gone on that long. All he wanted to do was go home and sleep for a week. Unfortunately, he was going to get about five hours before he had to come back and go back to work.

There were going to be more meetings tomorrow that were just as important as the ones today. The new R&D department was causing issues with investors, and he had to make sure everything worked out. It was stressful, but that was his job. He was good at this. He knew he would make it work, but it would mean a lot of hours in the office for the next few days.

He was seriously just considering sleeping at his desk. He felt like he might actually get more rest. He sighed and stepped out of the elevator and into the parking garage. It would be good to go home. He could call Laura from the comfort of his car on the drive home. He was already looking forward to it.

Ethan waved to Bruce in the security office. Bruce and another security team member waved back before going back to their discussion. Ethan rolled his shoulders trying to get the kink out and headed out the heavy door separating the building from the garage. It was a quick walk from there to his personal parking space.

He checked to make sure he had his keys with him. He had left his Corvette in his work parking spot when he left for Colorado. It was a secured lot with cameras, so he knew it would be as safe here as it would be in his garage at home.

Except, when he got to the car, he found out it wasn't as safe as he thought.

Ethan let out a loud expletive that echoed through the empty parking garage.

Deep gouges ripped across the glossy blue paint like deadly wounds. All four tires were flat, and eggs decorated the windows. Ethan's mouth opened in horror as he walked around his beloved vehicle. Not only was the paint job ruined, but whoever had done this had also scratched up the windows and windshield. It wasn't just vandalized. It wasn't safe to drive.

He noticed a piece of paper taped to the driver's side door. It looked like a typical 8x10 white piece of office paper with something printed in black and white. Being careful not to touch anything he got close enough to see it was a picture of him with big X's across his eyes.

He stepped back so fast he nearly fell over. Whoever did this wanted him dead. The message was clear and easy to understand. This wasn't just someone keying a car and

slashing tires because they were mad at his business prac-
tices. Someone was mad at him.

He fumbled for his phone and quickly dialed Bruce.

"My car's been keyed," he said as soon as Bruce answered. His voice was calm despite the fact that his heart was pounding in his chest. "Can you pull up the footage?"

"What? Of course," Bruce replied. Ethan could hear keys tapping in the background and then a long pause. "You're never going to believe this."

"What?" Ethan's eyes closed. There was nothing good that was going to come out of Bruce's mouth.

"It's gone," Bruce said, sounding shocked. "The security footage is gone. It's been deleted."

Ethan pinched the bridge of his nose. This was bad.

"Bruce, I'm going to need you to call the police. There's more than just my paint job messed up," Ethan told him. "There's a threat on my life."

"Get out of the garage and get up here," Bruce ordered. His voice had gone dark and dangerous. "And don't hang up until I'm with you."

"Of course," Ethan agreed. He turned on his heel and went straight to the heavy door leading inside.

He'd barely pulled it open and taken three steps inside when Bruce met him. The man's face looked like a thunderstorm, and he had four of the biggest, meanest-looking security personnel behind him. Bruce motioned the four to keep going.

"Are you okay?" Bruce asked, his eyes going up and down Ethan, checking for any injuries.

"I'm fine." Ethan waved him off and put his phone back in his pocket. "I thought we had new cameras after what happened with Carter?"

Ethan shuddered. Two years ago, Carter's car had blown up in this very garage. A creepy picture and a keyed paint job were infinitely less scary than that.

"We did. They're all gone," Bruce replied. "Someone knew the system. It has to be an inside job or someone who knows our systems."

"What does that mean, Bruce?" Ethan asked. His stomach clenched and ice ran through his veins. He knew this wasn't just a bored teenager. This was a real threat.

"It means we have a problem," Bruce said. "You aren't safe. I'm increasing your security. You aren't going home tonight."

Ethan sighed and felt his shoulders sag. So much for a restful night. He wasn't going to get that call to Laura. He checked his watch. It was already too late anyway.

"I guess I *am* sleeping at my desk tonight," Ethan told him. He was just glad he'd put a cot in his closet. It wouldn't be nearly as comfortable as his king bed at home, but it was better than the floor by leaps and bounds.

"Hold up," Bruce commanded, holding up one hand while the other pressed on the radio in his ear. His eyes narrowed, and he somehow got bigger.

"What's up?" Ethan asked, not liking the way his head of security was reacting to whatever news he was getting through his headset.

"Someone just tried to break into your house," Bruce stated.

Ethan felt his heart skip a beat. "What?"

"The alarm system was triggered when the fence was tampered with," Bruce explained. "The police are there. It looks like the perimeter alert was triggered and there's some minor damage to the fence, but nothing else."

"Cameras?" Ethan asked, not feeling particularly hopeful.

"Nothing," Bruce confirmed. "The intruder was wearing reflective material to blind the cameras. All we can see is a person, but no details. They knew what kind of cameras you have."

"And I'm guessing they are nowhere to be found?" Ethan asked, feeling annoyed that even with a million dollar security system this could still happen. What exactly was he paying all this money for?

Bruce shook his head. "He got away. But he left a picture of you with your eyes X-d out and your throat slit."

"Awesome. Just like the car." Ethan paced the hallway. This night had just gone from bad to worse.

"Can you think of anyone that would want to hurt you?" Bruce asked. "I'll go through the usual lists, but can you think of anyone recent?"

Ethan sighed and looked up at the ceiling, trying to think of someone who would hate him. "I don't know, Bruce. I piss off a lot of people."

"I don't mean to be indelicate, but how are things between you and Laura?" Bruce asked. "Could she have something to do with this?"

"Laura?" Ethan barked a laugh. "That's not who did this. She wouldn't know the first thing about the cameras. She doesn't even like getting her picture taken."

Something about that last sentence ticked Ethan's brain. Pictures. He sagged against the wall as he figured out someone who would hate him enough to destroy his car and want him dead.

"You think of someone?" Bruce asked, taking a step toward him.

Ethan nodded. "Janie. Janie must have seen the tabloid

picture in the newspaper of Laura and me. Janie'd be furious."

Bruce let out a long breath. "Jealous ex-secretary...." He shook his head, obviously remembering the trouble they'd had with her. There were restraining orders, police reports, and a slew of bad memories surrounding that woman and her insane idea that Ethan was supposed to love her.

"It has to be her," Ethan said. He felt like he might throw up. Janie had ruined his first chance with Laura, and now Janie was ruining his life yet again.

"Has anything else strange happened recently?" Bruce asked. "Things going missing? Gifts you weren't expecting? That kind of thing."

"Yeah. All of that," he said. His pens going missing. The tie in the mail. Ethan didn't think his heart could sink any lower in his chest, but those questions pushed it down another three inches.

"Shit." Bruce ran a hand over his bald head. "Janie would know our security protocols and where the cameras are."

"She helped with the house security once," Ethan remembered. "She came by and tripped one of the alarms. It was one of the perimeter ones along the fence."

Bruce looked at him. "I think you have a stalker, Ethan." The big man's face was grim. "I think Janie's pissed."

Ethan thought of Janie. She was tiny. He had thought her harmless. Annoying and disruptive, but he'd never thought she'd resort to something like this.

"Do you think she really means to hurt me?" Ethan asked.

"She's a woman scorned," Bruce replied. "She can do a lot of damage. Don't think of her size. Think of how angry she is. That's what we're up against."

Ethan shuddered. Janie had known everything about him as his secretary. He'd changed the locks and files since she'd left, but she still had knowledge of his habits that she could use.

"What do I do?" Ethan asked.

"Let me handle it," Bruce advised. "I'll get some guys to watch her. In the meantime, we're doubling your security detail, and you're changing your routines."

Ethan nodded. He had thought Janie was in the past. So much for that.

"We'll get to the bottom of this," Bruce assured him. "But until we do, you need to be cautious. You aren't safe. Has she tried to contact you?"

Ethan shook his head. "Not that I know of."

Bruce nodded. "Okay. You call me immediately if she does."

"What about Laura?" Ethan asked Bruce. "Do I need to be worried about her?"

Bruce paused and then nodded. "Yes. I'll tell the security team at the ranch to up their patrols and keep an eye on her."

Ethan hated the way his stomach twisted at the thought of her being harmed. He would do anything to keep her safe from this. She was innocent and didn't deserve Janie's wrath. She had too much on her plate with the kids to have to deal with this. It wasn't fair to put this on her too.

"Let's go back up to your office," Bruce said, putting a hand on Ethan's shoulder. "We need to come up with a plan."

Ethan nodded and turned down the hallway toward the elevator back upstairs. His thoughts flew through his mind like dark clouds blown on the wind.

This wasn't the same as what happened to Carter, but

the similarities were enough to make him nervous. He thought of Mia and how Carter's attacker had almost killed her and their unborn child. He couldn't let that happen to Laura. He couldn't let anything happen to Laura.

He sighed and ran a hand through his hair. How was he going to keep her safe from a secretary that knew his habits?

## Chapter 33

*L aura*

LAURA CLOSED her eyes and imagined herself at a mountain lake. There were horses, and the world smelled of pine and fresh rain. The lake sparkled in the sunlight and sunlight warmed her skin. It was peaceful and calm. Nothing could be wrong in this beautiful place.

And then a plane crashed into the lake, and everything was ruined.

Laura groaned and opened her eyes. Visualizing a calm space was not helping her anxiety. Ethan was getting on a plane again today, and all she could think about was his plane crashing and never seeing him again. It didn't matter that he'd survived the last flight just fine. It didn't matter than she knew it was irrational and stupid.

She was still anxious and upset about it.

She flopped onto the couch and checked her phone for

the millionth time. No messages. The kids would be home soon, and she welcomed the distraction. The kitchen was scrubbed to shining, the bathrooms sparkled, and the laundry was folded and put away. She was running out of household chores to keep her busy while she worried.

She was considering pulling out a cookbook and baking something when the door opened and Ivy and Dallas walked in. They were all smiles and energy, which was exactly what she needed.

"Hi, guys!" she greeted them, jumping up from the couch and rushing to the door.

"Hey, Laura," Dallas replied, dropping his backpack on the floor and kicking off his shoes. Ivy was slightly neater, placing her shoes by the door and hanging her backpack on the peg.

"How was school?" Laura asked, picking up Dallas' backpack and hanging it for him. She wasn't even going to bother him to pick it up she was so desperate to have something to do other than obsessively check her phone.

"It was field day today," Dallas told her. "We played zombie tag in the field."

"That sounds fun," Laura replied. "What about you, Ivy?"

"I won the Frisbee throwing competition," she said proudly. "We have a movie day tomorrow, and then Ms. Jackson says we will have a picnic for the last day of school."

"A picnic?" Laura asked.

"Uh huh. You're supposed to bring watermelon," Ivy informed her. She dug into her backpack and handed her a flier.

"Okay," Laura said, reading it over. She apparently signed up to bring watermelon. She would have to go to the store tomorrow. Dallas probably had something similar, so she opened his backpack and found that she was bringing popsicles for his class.

"I don't remember the last day having this much food," she said to no one in particular. She remembered field day and parties, but not like this. She also didn't remember school getting out so early in the year.

She wished she could ask her parents about it.

"Do you guys want to go to a park or something?" Laura asked the kids, pushing away the sad memories. She'd been thinking about her parents and their accident too much today as it was.

"It's too hot," Ivy complained. "Can we just watch a movie?"

Laura nearly said no, but both kids looked hot and tired. They had been outside all day for field day, she remembered. She smiled and nodded. Maybe a movie would help her take her mind off things. She could get lost in an animated world, and as long as the didn't want to watch the animated plane movie, she'd have a great distraction. "Sure."

The two kids hopped up on the couch as Laura searched for the remote.

"I wanna watch the ocean movie again," Ivy announced.

"I like that one," Dallas agreed. Laura nearly fell over in surprise. *They agreed on a movie? At the same time?* The two kids just smiled at her.

"I liked the beach Ethan made for us," Ivy said. "And he said it was like this movie. Can we go to a real beach sometime? I promise to try not to get scared."

Laura gave her a big hug, tears in her eyes. She was so proud of her little sister for wanting to try again with the planes. She knew exactly how much courage it took.

"You got it," Laura told her. She let go of her sister. "And you're sitting on the remote."

Ivy laughed and pulled out the TV remote. Laura turned and flipped on the TV. She set the remote on the arm of the couch and picked up the DVD case to take out the movie. The TV flickered to life and turned onto the last channel they had watched.

"... For those of you just tuning in, there is a luxury private jet that is missing over the skies of the western United States," the news anchor announced. Laura's head jerked up to see a reporter in a blue dress looking concerned at her through the screen. "We're keeping a live update going as we get more details."

"PRIVATE JET MISSING" read across the bottom of the screen in big bold letters that took Laura's breath away. The world dropped out from underneath her, and her heart forgot how to beat. Shivers of ghosts ran across her skin, and the roar of airplane engines filled her ears.

It was happening again.

She remembered seeing her parents' crash on the news. It had been the same reporter, but a different dress. The headline was different, but the feeling was the same. Images of the wrecked plane with smoke rising to the sky on the screen filled her mind.

"Laura?" Dallas called to her. She turned to see him staring at the TV in fear. Beside him, Ivy sat looking like she might throw up. They'd seen that news episode, too. They'd seen the fiery remains of what happened to their parents on the TV screen just like this.

She knew she needed to change the channel, but she couldn't move. She needed them to say whose plane was missing. She needed to find out more.

The reporter sounded like she was underwater to Laura's ears as she struggled to get past the sounds of the past in her head.

"A plane headed for Denver was rerouted through Las Vegas," the reporter announced. "It has failed to touch down and is no longer appearing on radar."

Laura's stomach heaved, and there was no stopping it. She ran to the bathroom and barely made it before her lunch came up. Breathing hard, she wiped her face and quickly washed her hands before coming back out.

Ivy was hugging Dallas as the two of them stared at the screen. Ivy was crying. Laura mentally berated herself for having left the TV on at all. The two kids had no idea that Ethan was on an airplane right now, but any news story about a plane was a bad idea for them to watch. The images of planes and the tone of the reporters brought back too many memories.

She quickly grabbed the remote and hit the auxiliary button. The blue DVD load screen took over the TV and Laura let out a small sigh of relief. She had forgotten to breathe while the reporter was on the screen. She put the DVD in the player.

"Laura, what happened to the plane? Why is there a plane missing?" Ivy asked, panic rising in her small voice. She held onto her brother like he might disappear at any moment. "Is it gonna crash?"

Laura quickly moved to the couch and took the two of them into her arms. "No, no, it's not going to crash," she promised. "I'm sure the plane is just fine. You know the news reporters always make it sound worse than it is."

Ivy sniffled but calmed down. She believed Laura's words. Laura just wished she could believe them herself. Ethan's plane was supposed to land in Denver. Just thinking about him on that plane made her want to throw up again. She wanted to scream, but she needed to stay calm for the kids.

"Don't worry, you guys," Laura said as the two kids snuggled into her. She clung to them as much as they did to her. "We don't leave each other. That's what we promised. We're okay."

"We don't leave each other," Ivy and Dallas both repeated solemnly. They nodded to each other, each affirming the promise.

"Okay, don't worry about it anymore. We're just going to watch our movie," Laura said, hitting the play button. The movie started with a flurry of color, and the two kids focused on the screen.

With them occupied, Laura pulled up her phone and quickly pulled up her news app. Her finger hovered over the icon. Did she really want to look this up? What if it was him? Did she really want to know? The idea that it was Ethan's jet missing terrified her. But, if she didn't look it up, she could pretend it wasn't him. It was someone else. He was safe until she knew for certain that he wasn't. It wasn't real until she read about it.

She pulled up her text messaging app instead.

*Please call me.*

SHE HIT send to Ethan and chewed on her bottom lip. She made it thirty seconds before opening up her news app and searching for the story on the missing plane.

The story was just coming out, so there weren't very many details yet. The owner of the plane and those on board hadn't been released yet. All that she could find out was that it was a private airplane leaving from Los Angeles to arrive in Denver. There was an engine issue, and the plane had rerouted through Las Vegas, but it hadn't shown up yet.

She peered at the picture, trying not to make it too obvious to Ivy and Dallas what she was looking at. The plane in the picture looked smaller than the one she'd seen Ethan get on. And Ethan wasn't technically flying into Denver, he was flying into the local Silver Springs Airport, but that wouldn't make as good a news story.

She sighed and put her phone away. She couldn't say that it was or wasn't his plane for sure. She wouldn't know until he texted her he was fine or the news announced the owner of the airplane. She was going to have just to wait.

She tried to focus on the movie, but she couldn't. All she could think about was how she was going to tell Ivy and Dallas that Ethan's plane was gone. That someone else they loved had gotten on an airplane and never come back. It didn't seem fair. She wasn't sure she was strong enough to go through it all again.

Her parents' death still made her wake up gasping in the night from nightmares of smoke-filled planes and looming mountain crashes. More than once, she'd dissolved into tears because someone would walk past her wearing her mother's favorite perfume. She couldn't drive past their old home without breaking her heart. How was she going to do this again?

She thought she felt the phone vibrate and quickly checked it, hoping for a message from Ethan. But it was just a notification that she had been invited to another game on Facebook. She nearly threw the phone across the room.

She needed to know if he was okay. She needed to know

he hadn't left her. Her heart struggled in her chest and her filled with tears. She needed him. She depended on him.

She loved him.

And he was going to leave her just like her parents did. He was going to disappear in a puff of smoke and leave her hurting and alone again. She wasn't going to have any say in her future yet again.

She should never have let herself get attached to him. She'd fallen in love, and he was gone. There was no happy ending for her because even if this wasn't his plane, even if he was fine, this was going to happen every time he flew

She would be a worried mess every time he left her to get on that stupid plane. She wasn't ready. Someday, she knew she would be able to handle it, but that wasn't today. Today, the wound her parents' death had left on her heart was still too fresh. She couldn't do this.

She needed to step away from him. She needed to put in some distance so that it wouldn't hurt so much if anything did happen to him. She wasn't ready to let someone into her life who could leave again.

She sniffled and wiped her cheek. She wasn't in a good place for a relationship. It wasn't fair to Ethan. He deserved someone who could love him without freaking out every time he got on an airplane. He deserved someone who didn't have abandonment issues.

She needed to end things, or it would only end up hurting them both. It was better if she just cut it off between them now while things were still forming. It would hurt less than if they waited.

She nodded to herself. It was the right decision. It was for the best.

The phone rang in her hand, startling her from her

thoughts. She quickly read the caller ID and let out the biggest sigh of relief. It was him.

"Hey," she said, answering the phone. She slid out from under the kids and went into her bedroom.

"Laura, you seriously don't need to message me fifty times during the flight," he told her, his voice frustrated. "My phone is off. I will call you when I get off the plane. My phone didn't stop chirping for thirty seconds the moment I turned it on. I was afraid something serious had happened to you."

His words only solidified that what she was going to do was the right thing. This wasn't a good match. She was too clingy right now. He didn't need her craziness.

"I know," she said softly.

"You know? Then why do you do it?"

She closed her eyes and took a deep breath. "There's a plane missing. It was supposed to land in Denver, and it didn't," she explained calmly. "It was on the news, and I freaked out. I thought it was your plane."

The silence on the other end was deafening.

"I'm sorry, Laura," he said after a moment. "I'm fine. My plane is fine. It wasn't me. Everything is fine."

"I know that now," she said. She paused. There was something in his tone that felt off. "Are you sure everything is fine? You sound... different."

He sighed. "Can we meet? I should talk to you about something."

His words made her heart sink. Those were never good words to hear from the person you were dating. They were actually the words she wanted to say to him.

"The kids are home," she said. "I can't go anywhere, but you're welcome to come here."

"I'll be there in fifteen minutes," he told her, and then he hung up.

Laura stared at her phone and felt the tears well up in her eyes. This felt like the beginning of the end. This wasn't going to end with rainbows and sunshine. No one was going to end up happy after they had the conversation that was coming. They would hurt, but hopefully, it would be a quick pain instead of an unsurvivable one.

Was she going to do the right thing? She wasn't sure. Then, she wiped her cheeks and thought of the fear that had just gripped her heart for the past twenty minutes. She thought of the terror she'd just experienced thinking he was gone. She couldn't do that anymore.

It was going to hurt. But, maybe it should hurt now so that there could be rainbows and sunshine later.

# Chapter 34

ETHAN LET out a long slow breath as the car pulled out onto the highway. He was doing his best not to be angry, but it was hard. It was hard not to be frustrated when she messaged him so constantly. Laura was so amazing in every other way, but her fear of him flying was the one thing that he did not enjoy about her.

He stared out the window, watching the mountains to the west rise and dip into the horizon. He knew that he would have texted her too if their positions had been reversed and he'd seen the news on the missing plane. It was just that there were so many messages. He had so many issues on his plate between the R&D department problems and now Janie stalking him and sending him death threats. Getting a million messages telling him to call her was not helpful.

He pulled up his phone and checked the news. The

other plane was a small personal aircraft, not nearly as nice as his was, but he could see how she would be worried. Luckily, the other plane had landed without injuries. It just had serious electrical issues and had shorted out several systems, making them late and difficult to communicate with.

He closed his phone and leaned back against the car seat. She was going to be upset and worked up because of this. He needed to tell her that it wasn't safe to be around him right now because of Janie. He didn't know what Janie would do if he saw the two of them together now. She could get seriously hurt because of him, and he would never forgive himself if she did.

The muscle in his jaw tightened. What about the kids? He could easily see Janie targeting Dallas and Ivy because they were Laura's. Janie wanted to hurt him, and right now, the easiest way to do that was through Laura. Janie had already disrupted his relationship with her once already. What would she do now that they really were together?

He didn't like thinking about it.

How was he going to keep Laura and the kids safe? What would he do if anything happened to them? He felt responsible now, and it was a lot of commitment. He needed to step back. He needed to slow down so they wouldn't get hurt.

"Take a right here," he said to one of his new security guards. Pete and Joe were a lot less chatty than Craig, but they seemed good at their jobs, so Ethan didn't mind. He hoped Craig was enjoying some time off while Pete and Joe drove him around. "It's the little townhouse on the left."

The car pulled to a stop on the street outside her home. He looked out at it. It was just a small townhouse squished between two others. There were two small aspen trees growing in the front yard, framing the view of the mountains. It was quiet and safe, but with Janie on the loose, he wasn't sure just how safe it was anymore. He didn't want to tell her this, but it had to be done.

"Wait here," he instructed the two guards as he opened the door and stepped out.

"Sir?" Pete asked, unbuckling his seat belt to follow.

"I'll be right at the door." Ethan motioned toward Laura's house. "If I go inside, you may come in. Until then, just wait in the car."

"Sir, I don't think that's the best idea," Pete replied.

Ethan rolled his eyes. "Are you really worried someone is going jump out from behind the tree and get me?" He motioned to the tree. A cat couldn't hide in the tree without being seen.

Pete sat back down. "We'll wait here for you, sir."

"Thank you," Ethan replied, turning away and walking up to her front door. Each step felt heavier than the last. He was freaking exhausted, and all he wanted to do was go to his hotel and sleep for a week, but he needed to talk to her. She didn't sound right on the phone. The closer he got to the door, the worse he felt about what was going to happen next.

He raised his hand to knock, but the door opened before he could make any noise. Laura held a finger up to her lips.

"I'll be right outside guys," she said. He could see Ivy and Dallas watching a movie. They were mesmerized and barely responded that they'd heard her. She stepped out onto the porch, closing the door behind her.

She wrapped her arms around herself and looked up at him. Her eyes were red and puffy like she'd been crying. Guilt pulled at him.

"You have bad news, don't you?" she asked, breaking the silence between them.

"How can you tell?"

"You get this line between your eyebrows and your shoulders tense up when you don't like something," she explained. She motioned to his body. "You're standing aggressively. If you were a horse, I'd be worried you were going to kick me. Or bite."

He consciously tried to relax his shoulders and found it harder than he expected. "I'm not going to bite," he assured her.

"So what's the matter?" she asked. Her voice was soft like she already expected the worst.

He sighed. He'd practiced in his head, but now he wasn't sure what to say. He started out with the easier intro to what was bothering him.

"Part of it is work," he replied. "Things are a lot more complicated. The California office needs me, and the R&D opening is having issues. Carter will be able to help, but…"

"But you need to be going back and forth," she finished. She lips thinned. "You have to fly more."

He nodded. She glanced around like she was looking for strength and her arms tightened around her.

"I can't handle that," she said softly. "I can't handle you flying all the time."

"Laura…"

"No, I know that it's stupid," she said, holding up a hand. "I know that it's irrational and that there are people with way riskier jobs. I know that. But I also know that when you get on that plane, the only thing I can think about is how I lost two people that cared about me most in this world."

"Flying is safe," he replied. He didn't know what else to say.

"I know. Believe me, I know," she said. "Did you know the odds of being killed on a flight are 1 in 29.4 million? The odds of being struck by lightning are 1 in 960,000. I was thirty times more likely to be hit by lightning than have just one of my parents die in a plane crash. I won the unlucky lottery not just once, but twice."

"I can't change that," he replied, feeling the need to defend himself. She was worked up and blaming him for something he couldn't do anything about. It wasn't fair.

"I know that," she snapped. "But it's still there."

"You know this isn't healthy, right?" He wanted to throw up his arms and yell at her to get over it. That she needed to move on with her life. She needed to confront her fear and live in the real world. This was irrational and insane. It wasn't good for her or the kids.

Her nostrils flared. She took a deep breath in and let it out slowly. "I can't lose any more people. And yes, I get that planes are safe, and almost no one dies in them. I get that. But it happened. And lightning usually strikes the same place every time. That's why lightning rods work. I am a lightning rod."

He rolled his eyes. He should have gone to the hotel and taken a nap before this. He wasn't in the right state of mind to be having this conversation, but it was too late now. He could feel his blood pressure rising.

"It sounds like you've made up your mind," he replied. He could tell what she was doing. She was going to end things. She couldn't handle his job, so she was going to push him away. He didn't know how to change her mind.

"I think we need to take a break," she said, carefully forming each word. "We need to slow things down."

He clenched his fists and then relaxed them. She wasn't in a rational place right now. She was still upset about the airplane going missing. He shouldn't have pushed it today. He should have just gone to the hotel.

"This isn't what I want, Laura," he said. "Can we talk about this later? When we're both calmer?"

"I am calm," she replied. "This is what I want. It's what's best for the kids. They saw that plane on the TV and freaked out. They didn't even know you were flying today. If they did, I don't know what they would have done."

"The plane crash was a freak accident," he told her. "It almost never happens."

"One in 29.4 million," she told him. She shook her head. "Once things are settled at your work, we can try again. Until then, I can't have you flying and scaring them and me. It's not going to work."

Panic at losing her clawed at his chest. "Laura, I care about you."

"I know. And I care about you," she whispered. "That's the problem."

He hated the way his throat was tightening. He had to do something.

He kissed her. He didn't think, he just pressed his lips against hers, hoping that he could convey the depth of his feelings through the motion. He didn't have the words to tell her how he felt, so he showed her.

She pushed him away and wiped at her mouth. "That's not what I want, Ethan," she told him. Her voice wasn't angry. If anything it was sad. "I want a break. I want to not worry about you, and I don't want to have to explain to Ivy and Dallas where you are. I don't want to lie and tell them that you're not on a plane."

His heart cracked. He didn't want to lose her. Not like this. He thought he was going to lose her because of Janie, but this?

Janie. The thought hit him hard. If Janie thought they were broken up, she would leave Laura alone. Perhaps this was a blessing in disguise. If Janie thought that Laura wasn't a threat, she would focus only on him. Laura would be safe.

He looked up into Laura's sad green eyes and knew what he had to do. He had to keep her safe. He had to push her away.

"Are you sure this is what you want?" he asked, his heart already breaking.

She swallowed hard but met his eyes. "Yes. I can't do this."

His heart shattered, but he knew it would keep her safer this way. At least until Janie was found and taken care of. He took a step away from her and lowered his eyes.

"I respect your decision," he said softly. "We'll take a break."

Her lower lip quivered, and he nearly lost his nerve.

"I'm sorry, Ethan." She swallowed hard.

"Me too," he replied. He took a deep breath and looked around. "Say goodbye to the kids for me."

And with that, he turned and walked away. He wasn't a safe person for her to be around. He needed to keep them safe, and this was the most efficient way. He'd make sure it leaked to the papers, and he'd have Pete and Joe tell Bruce to spread the word.

He felt like sobbing as he walked back to the car. He would fix everything as soon as he could, but for right now, he was protecting her. He walked away without looking back. There was no reason to be here now.

# Chapter 35

 *aura*

LAURA WALKED into Sandy's and was glad to see the place was mostly empty. It wasn't quite lunchtime yet, so the usual crowds weren't there. She'd dropped the kids off for their last day at school and headed over to the one place she knew would have comfort food and a friend.

"Hey you," Elena greeted her from the bar as she walked up. Elena's smile faded as she looked at Laura. "What's the matter?"

"I think I broke up with Ethan," Laura told her. The words felt like daggers driving into her heart.

"What?" Elena asked. She quickly walked around the bar and wrapped her friend up in a hug. "What happened?"

"I freaked out because he was on an airplane," Laura explained. "Like super freaked."

"Okay..." Elena let her go, motioning to two bar stools.

Together they sat down to talk. "How did that lead to you two breaking up?"

Laura shrugged. It sounded stupid now, but she still felt mad about the whole thing. "He's going to be traveling a lot," she explained. "He has to go back and forth between here and California. I can't handle it. I lose it just thinking about what could happen on the plane."

"You know planes are safe, right?" Elena asked. "He's fine."

"Oh, you're right," Laura replied, putting as much sarcasm into her voice as she could without snarling. "Soooo safe. By the way, how are *your* parents, Elena?"

"Whoa, Laura," Elena held up her hands defensively. "I'm not trying to attack you."

Laura sighed and ran her hands through her hair. "I know. Sorry."

"It's okay," Elena assured her. "So you told him this?"

Laura nodded. "Yeah. I told him we needed to take a break. That we were going too fast."

"Okay. How'd he respond?" Elena asked.

"He kissed me," Laura replied. "He said he didn't want to take a break. But, I made it clear that was what was happening."

"Then what?" Elena asked. Laura couldn't read her expression.

"He said okay and left. He just walked off. It was two days ago, and he hasn't called me or anything," Laura told her. Her throat tightened, and she played with a napkin left on the bar. "Did I do the right thing?"

"Did you do the right thing?" Elena snorted. "You pushed away a great guy you not only thinks you're the bee's knees, but he also doesn't care that you have kids. He actually likes your kids. Not to mention he's got a good job, to put it mildly."

Laura's mouth dropped open. This was not the reaction she was expecting from her friend.

"And you're telling me that you gave him up because he gets on a plane once in a while?" Elena continued. "There are way, way more dangerous jobs out there that deserve this reaction. The problem is all in your head, Laura."

Anger flared up in Laura's chest, hot and fierce. She crumpled the napkin and wished she had the power to light it on fire with her mind.

"You know I love you, Laura," Elena said shaking her head. "But I don't think this was the right move."

Laura got up, nearly knocking the bar stool over in her fury. She couldn't believe her friend was betraying her like this. She needed support, not criticism.

"Fine. You don't get it either," Laura spat, grabbing her purse and heading to the door. She threw open the door as hard as she could and stormed outside. She didn't need this. She already felt terrible. The last thing she needed was someone telling her she was wrong.

Tears stung at her eyes as she looked for her car. She couldn't remember where she parked.

"Laura! Laura, come back," Elena called, hurrying out of the restaurant after her. She stood in front of Laura with her hands open. "I'm trying to be a friend, but I'm coming across as a bitch, and I'm sorry. Honestly, I'm sorry, Laura."

Laura's lower lip shook, and a tear snuck down her face. "He hasn't called me."

Elena hugged her close. "Oh, honey. I'm so sorry."

"I think you're right, Elena," Laura whispered into her friend's shoulder. She was glad Elena hadn't released her from the hug yet. She needed to be held. "I think I screwed up."

Elena hugged her tighter. "It'll be okay. You'll see. I know he cares about you."

Laura sniffled. "I'm still terrified I'm going to lose him," she admitted. "I'm not ready for this, Elena. I don't want to feel all of this."

"Oh, Laura." Elena rubbed her back. "Come back inside. I'll buy you a drink."

"That would be good," Laura said, letting Elena go and wiping her face. She tried to smile, but it still came out as weepy.

"I'll buy you two drinks," Elena said, putting her hand on Laura's shoulder and guiding her back inside the empty restaurant. "Then you can tell me how horrible he is, and this time I promise to agree with you and tell you that all men are pigs."

Laura chuckled and wiped at her face again. "You got any ice cream?"

"I have a whole freezer full," Elena promised, holding open the door. "Come on."

Elena held the door for Laura and brought her back to the bar. She hurried around to the serving side and quickly started making up a drink.

"So, I bet he left the toilet seat up, didn't he?" Elena asked. "Men are terrible."

Laura chuckled and took the drink when Elena handed it to her. "The worst," she agreed. "The absolute worst."

**Chapter 36**

$\mathcal{L}$*aura*

"BYE, GUYS! HAVE FUN! LOVE YOU!" Laura waved to the kids as the car pulled away. She could see Ivy and Dallas waving back, as well as Grandma and Grandpa. The two kids were off to spend the weekend with their grandparents. Laura had forgotten about it completely until Grandma had called and asked what time to pick them up.

Laura had arranged for the weekend off of parent duty two weeks ago, back when she was still with *him*. She'd had this fantastic idea to steal him away for a sexy weekend adventure. Then they'd broken up.

That was a week ago.

She turned and went back into the empty house, and she immediately missed her siblings. She had no idea what in the world she was going to do by herself this weekend. If nothing else, the barn was going to get a good cleaning.

She sighed and glanced over at her phone. He hadn't called her. The only message she'd gotten from him since she told him she wanted a break was two days old.

> *I'm fine. Home in California safe. Don't worry about me.*

THAT WAS IT. It broke her heart that he knew she'd be worried. She'd tried to call him, but the first time it went straight to voicemail. She was too much of a chicken to try again.

Besides, she knew it was what needed to happen. They needed a clean break to keep from coming back together. They needed this. The kids needed this. It was the right thing to do.

But, oh, did it hurt.

It hurt so much more than she was expecting. The first few days had been rough, but it was the silence that was driving her mad. She kept thinking the pain would start to vanish, that she would want him less now that he was gone, but it was only getting worse.

She had thought that pushing him away would prevent the pain of losing him. Instead, it had made the pain of losing him real. She didn't hurt before, but she did now.

Laura was an idiot, and she knew it.

She sighed and looked around the house. It was so quiet and empty without the kids jumping up and down. She didn't know what to do with herself. Dinner was on her own tonight. She went to the fridge, and nothing looked appetizing. She looked over at the empty table and felt an immense loneliness crash down on her.

It was the last thing in the world that she wanted to feel. She didn't want to be by herself. If she were alone with her thoughts, she would end up changing her mind about what she'd done. She'd call him again. She'd have to deal with the pain.

She thought about going to the barn, but there wouldn't be any humans there. It was a Friday night, and all the ranch hands would be home. The camp kids weren't coming until next week, so she'd be just as alone there as she was here. Besides, she didn't want to have to shower again.

So, she decided to go to Sandy's. Elena was probably working since she always seemed to be working. It only took a couple of minutes to hop in the car and make the short drive to the restaurant.

The evening air was cooling quickly, and the sound of crickets filled the air. Everything smelled like pine needles as she walked across the full parking lot and into the restaurant. It was a busy night with plenty of locals and even more visitors enjoying the mountain evening.

Laura walked in and headed straight for the bar. She found an open seat and snagged it, checking around to see if she could find Elena.

"What can I get you?" the bartender asked. It wasn't Elena. It was a young guy with dark hair and matching dark eyes. She didn't recognize him, but he was probably just new for the summer.

"Is Elena here tonight?" Laura asked, trying not to sound too desperate.

"Sorry. She called in sick," the guy told her.

"Oh. Um, let me think about what to drink. Thanks."

Laura smiled at him, and he turned and went on to the next customer.

Laura chewed the inside of her cheek. She wasn't sure she wanted to stay in the crowded restaurant without Elena. Despite the room being crowded, she'd never felt more alone. But, if she went home, she knew she'd just spend the evening moping around and crying.

"Can I buy you a drink?" A man slid into the chair next to her. He was fairly good looking with shaggy blond hair and an easy smile. "It looks like you could use one."

"You really don't have to," she replied. The last thing she wanted was another guy who expected her to give something she wasn't ready to give.

The guy held up his hands. "No obligations," he promised. He leaned in. "I just don't want to drink by myself. Please?"

Laura hesitated. She was so lonely tonight that she was tempted. "I don't know."

"Look, I just broke up with my boyfriend," the guy admitted. "We were supposed to have this romantic cabin thing, so I drove all the way up here to meet him. And he broke up with me and is spending our time in that romantic cabin with another guy."

"Ouch." Laura winced. That sounded like a way worse breakup than hers.

The guy shrugged. "So, I need a drink. You look like you need one, too," he said. "And now you know you don't have to worry about me hitting on you."

She couldn't help but smile a little bit. The guy was charming. "Okay. One drink," she agreed.

"My name's Chad," the guy introduced himself, holding out his hand. She shook it and smiled.

"I'm Laura."

"Nice to meet you, Laura," Chad replied. "What do you like to drink?"

"Here? I like their Moscow mules," she told him. "Best in the state."

"Sounds good." He grinned and held up his hand to catch the bartender's attention. "Moscow mules for the two of us. Put it on my tab."

It only took a moment for the bartender to come back with two shiny copper mugs filled with delicious ginger beer and vodka.

"Well, your ex-boyfriend is an idiot," Laura announced holding up her cup. Chad clinked his against hers and smiled.

"Tell me about it," he agreed. "Cheers."

And they both drank. It tasted delicious. Laura wasn't sure what the secret ingredient was that Sandy's used to make theirs taste better than anyone else's, and Elena refused to tell her.

"So, why are you here drinking alone and looking like someone kicked your dog?" Chad asked.

Laura sighed. "I told my boyfriend we needed a break. He hasn't spoken to me since."

Chad winced. "That's rough."

"Yeah. In this case, I'm the idiot," she admitted, taking another sip of her drink.

"We're all idiots in love," Chad replied. He held up his glass, and she happily toasted again

"To idiots," she agreed, drinking deeply.

She went to set her cup on the counter and nearly missed, sloshing some of her drink onto her hand. She frowned at the cup, surprised at how strong the alcohol was. It certainly didn't taste that strong. Either that, or she was turning into a complete lightweight.

"So, do you think you'll ever find love again?" she asked. She made sure not to take another sip of her drink. When the bartender came back, she was going to order some food. It was probably hitting her harder than she thought because she had an empty stomach.

"I don't know," Chad said with a shrug. "I hate relationships at the moment. What about you?"

"I'm afraid I might have really screwed things up," she admitted. She turned the copper cup, so it caught the light. It was pretty. "This was our second chance. Do I really deserve a third?"

"We all deserve love," Chad told her. "I hope it works out for you."

"Thanks," she replied. "I hope so, too."

He took a deep sip of his drink and set the empty cup on the counter. "I need to use the restroom. You okay by yourself?"

"Of course," she told him. She frowned as she looked past him and saw a familiar face. Craig, Ethan's security guard, sitting in a booth by the end of the bar. What was he doing here? "Actually, I think I see a friend of mine."

She went to stand up from the bar stool, and the whole world spun. She couldn't seem to get her legs to respond to her commands. It was like she was swimming through jello.

"I think... I think..." she stuttered. She looked over at her drink sitting on the bar. She picked it up and nearly sloshed the remainder all over her front. "How strong were these?"

"Are you okay?" Chad asked, looking concerned as she nearly knocked her drink over.

"I think you need to go home now, Laura," Craig said, suddenly beside her. "I think you've had a little too much to drink."

"But I didn't," Laura protested, but no one heard her.

"Do you know this guy?" Chad asked her, motioning to Craig.

"Yeah," she said with a smile that felt way too big. She nodded, and her head felt like a bobble-head doll. "He's my boyfriend's bodyguard. He's good."

"Bodyguard, huh," Chad said, looking skeptical. He looked like he might have been sizing up Craig, like he might try to defend her honor in a moment. "You're sure?"

"She's sure," Craig assured her, putting her arm over his shoulder. "Thanks, buddy. I've got her."

"We're good," she told Chad. Her words slurred far more than she intended. "Thanks for the drink."

Chad shrugged. "Sure. Hope it works out for you."

Craig pulled her to a standing position, her arm over his shoulder and supporting most of her weight. She was fairly sure he was going to have to carry her out. It was a good thing he was strong.

"Thanks," she replied. "You too."

Craig nodded to Chad, and they started walking out of the restaurant. Laura's head spun, and the lights were too bright for her to look at. Luckily, Craig's car was parked right out front where it was easy to get into. He opened the door and got her in the passenger seat.

"Craig, I think that guy spiked my drink," she said. She couldn't believe it. He had seemed so nice. "It's a good thing you were here, Craig or I'd be in big trouble."

Craig reached over her and carefully buckled her in. She heard the seat belt click and her eyes started to close. She couldn't seem to stay awake. Craig smoothed the belt over her shoulder.

"He didn't spike your drink, Laura," Craig said. "I did."

And the world went black.

## Chapter 37

aura

LAURA'S HEAD THROBBED, and her mouth felt like she'd eaten fire. She shook her head, trying to clear out the ringing in her ears and figure out where she was. It took a moment for her eyes to adjust to the gray light and for the world to stop spinning long enough to get a clear image.

She was in some sort of empty warehouse. Pale gray light filtered in through windows on the second floor, but other than that she couldn't see much. Everything was dusty, so she assumed that where ever she was, it wasn't in active use.

She tried to rub her eyes to get the grit out of them but found them tied behind her. She was on a hard metal chair, the kind used for church get-togethers and elementary school concerts. It was not a comfortable thing to be tied to.

"Hello?" she called out. It hurt her voice to talk, but she

had to find out if she was alone. Her voice didn't seem to travel far.

She waited for a reply, but nothing came. She swallowed down her panic. She was alone and tied to a chair. The last thing she remembered was Craig's face telling her he had drugged her. He was the one who tied her up and left her here.

"Anybody?" she called out again. "Somebody, help me!"

Again, she was met with nothing but silence.

No one would even notice she was missing for at least two days. Dallas and Ivy were at their grandparents. Elena didn't know she wasn't home, and no one at work expected her to show up this weekend.

She struggled against the ties on her wrists, wrenching her shoulders and cursing as the ropes cut into her skin. She kicked against the zip ties on her ankles, but all it did was cause pain. She couldn't escape.

She was alone and tied to a chair by her ex-boyfriend's security.

She started to laugh. It was either that or cry, but she wasn't sure she had any tears left in her. Laughing worked just as well. After everything, she wasn't going to lose those she cared about. They were going to lose her, and airplanes had absolutely nothing to do with it.

Despite trying to keep everyone safe, she was the one in danger. There was no way she could have prevented this. She laughed as she realized there was one way she could have avoided being tied to a chair in the middle of an empty warehouse alone.

She should not have broken up with Ethan. If she hadn't pushed him away to keep herself safe, she'd be safe with him. They'd be at some romantic cabin somewhere with plenty of security and not a care in the world. By saving herself from the pain of losing him, she was going to get herself killed. That was certainly one way to prevent the pain, but not the one she had planned on.

Her laughter grew a little more maniacal. It was either that or burst into tears.

A door on the opposite end of the warehouse squeaked open, and Laura no longer felt like laughing. The sound died in her throat as she struggled to see who was coming to see her.

Craig stepped into the pale light from the window and smiled. He didn't look crazy. He looked just the same as he ever did. She had no idea what had made him do this.

"Good," he said coming closer. "You're awake. I brought you some water."

He came over and opened a water bottle. With gentle care, he brought it to her lips and tipped it up so she could drink. It was cold and quite possibly the most delicious thing Laura had ever tasted. She sucked on the bottle greedily.

"Whoa, whoa," he chastised, pulling it away. "Slow down. I don't want you to get sick."

Laura whimpered. She wanted that water. She would have done just about anything to get more.

"Please," she begged. "I'm just so thirsty."

"That's to be expected," Craig replied. "It'll pass. You can have more water as long as you promise to go slow."

She nodded, ignoring the pain that it caused to move her head. "I promise."

He put the water bottle back to her lips. She had to focus and use all her willpower not to chug the bottle. Instead, she took slow, careful sips.

"Good," Craig praised her when she had finished. "That's much better."

He put the lid back on the empty bottle and then frowned. He leaned over and carefully wiped a drop of water from her chin like she was a child.

"Thank you," she said, unsure of what else she could say to that. "Craig, what am I doing here?"

"You're here because Ethan needs to realize how much he needs me," Craig replied. He set the half-empty bottle down next to her chair and checked the ties on her ankles. He frowned at her. "You need to not hurt yourself."

"I'm sorry," she said quickly. He patted her leg as he stood back up. "But what do you mean, Ethan needs to know? I don't understand."

Craig sighed. "Did you know that he fired me?" he asked, hurt on his voice. "After everything I've done for him?"

"He fired you?" Laura could hardly believe. Up until a little while ago, she thought Craig was a model employee. "Why?"

"They said I had too much overtime," Craig replied. "He didn't even have the balls to do it himself. He had Bruce do it. He claimed I had too much overtime and needed to take some time off."

"Ethan told you to take some time off? Isn't that a good thing?" Laura asked, not quite understanding how that meant he was fired.

"No, it's not a good thing," Craig yelled at her. He took a breath and quieted himself. "He needs *me* to keep him safe."

"Oh." Laura nodded. "Even if you were working over-time, right?"

Craig smiled at her. "You get it," he said. "Do you know how many hours I didn't bill? I watched him sleep to make sure he was safe. I never billed for that."

"You watched him sleep?" Laura asked. She hoped he didn't notice the surprise in her voice.

"I'm his security," Craig explained. "I have to make sure he's safe. Even when he's sleeping."

"Well, that makes perfect sense," Laura replied, playing along. There was no way she was going to tell him anything otherwise. She needed him to want to help her, and the only way to do that was for him to like her. "But why did you kidnap me?"

"Because his current security team is a bunch of fucking idiots," Craig informed her. He knelt down so he could look her in the eye. He had beautiful eyes. "Do you know how easy it was for me to get you?"

She shook her head.

"I didn't even have to try," he told her. "I followed you for one night and was able to spike your drink and get you out here without a single one of Ethan's security team even noticing. It's like they weren't even paying attention. They're all too busy chasing stupid leads."

Laura bit down that they had broken up. If Craig hadn't brought it up, she wasn't about to. Her survival right now depended on Craig believing she was important to Ethan.

"I think you've made your point," Laura told him. "Can you let me go now?"

He smiled sadly and shook his head. "No, Laura, I can't. He has to see. He has to understand how much he needs me. I can't let you go."

It was a long shot anyway, she told herself. "What are you going to do with me?"

Craig rose back to standing and looked around the warehouse. "He's coming here so I can show him," he explained. "I told him to come alone. I'll know if he does."

"How?"

He held up his phone and tapped his earpiece. "I still

have all the security feeds. If he told his bumbling fuck-up of a security director, I'll know."

Laura swallowed hard. Despite the water, her mouth was dry again. "What if he doesn't come alone?"

Craig faced her. "I like you, Laura. You make him happy, and that's all I want. I want him happy," he told her. His face went dark. "But, if he doesn't listen to me, I have to prove my point."

Laura shrank a little in her chair.

"You understand, don't you?" Craig asked. "He needs to know that I keep him safe. That he needs me. I'm only looking out for his best interests."

"I'm sure he knows that," Laura whispered. She had to get out of here as soon as possible.

"I hope so," Craig agreed. "I don't want him to have to learn the hard way."

The way he looked at her made Laura's blood run cold. He looked at her the way a teacher looked at a difficult test. She hoped that Ethan was going to pass.

"When is he supposed to get here?" Laura asked. She had to figure out a way to escape before then.

"Soon." Craig pulled out a pocket knife and began to play with it. It made a metallic click every time he snapped it shut. She tried not to wince at the sound.

"Could you untie me until then? I promise not to run," she told him, already figuring which way to run to get away. "These ropes really hurt."

He shook his head and clicked the knife shut. "I'm sorry, Laura, but I don't trust you. No offense."

"None taken. I know you're just trying to do what's best for him," she told him. She had to keep him talking. The longer he talked, the better off she was. She got information and hopefully provided a distraction. "You mentioned the other team was following stupid leads? What lead?"

"They think his old secretary is the one they need to worry about," he said, flicking the knife open. She stared at the blade and tried not to shy away.

"The old secretary? You mean Janie? The crazy one?" She winced after the word "*crazy*" left her mouth. It probably wasn't the best word to use around him. "She broke into his house?"

He snapped the knife shut. She wasn't sure if it made her feel better or not.

"He just made me so mad," he told her. "After all, I've done, he just fired me."

Laura frowned. "I'm afraid I don't understand."

Craig sighed. "I keyed his car. I wasn't thinking. I was just mad." He shrugged like he was truly sorry for it. "I'll pay him back for the damage, I swear. I just lost it. It won't happen again."

She watched as he flicked the knife open again. She really hoped he didn't lose it.

"I get it," she told him, her eyes on the knife. "There are a ton of country songs about that very thing."

"There are, aren't there?" he agreed with a smile. "When his security team saw the car, they told him it was his crazy secretary."

"How very silly of them," Laura said, keeping her tone as neutral as possible.

"I know, right?" Craig closed the knife. "Like his secretary would know how to turn off the cameras? And then the whole house thing..."

"The house? What happened to his house?" She almost didn't want to know. Why hadn't Ethan told her any of this?

"I broke into his house," Craig admitted sheepishly. "I wanted to apologize for the car."

"So you broke into his house?"

"You say that like it's a bad thing." The knife flicked open.

"I'm sorry, Craig. I'm just trying to understand," she said quickly. "He didn't tell me any of this."

Craig fiddled with the knife for a moment before closing it.

"When did this happen?" Laura asked.

"About a week ago. We had just gotten back to California," Craig said, staring at his knife.

She nodded. That was probably part of why he was so upset when he got back. He wasn't just dealing with business while away. He was dealing with Craig breaking into his house.

"And Ethan thought it was Janie that was doing all this?" she asked. She had to keep him talking. If she'd learned anything from cop TV shows, it was important to keep the bad guy talking.

"That's what Bruce convinced him," Craig said the name like it was bitter in his mouth. "Stupid. She wouldn't know how to do any of it." He turned and looked at her again. "That's why Ethan needs me."

"I agree," she assured him. "He needs you to keep him safe."

"See? I knew you were good for him," Craig told her with a smile. "You should have some more water."

He picked up the water bottle and opened it again. He was so gentle and careful as he held it to her lips and let her drink that it was hard to believe he was the one who tied her up. She finished the last of the water.

"He should be here soon," he told her. "I'll get you something to eat when this is done. There's a decent hamburger place just around the corner."

"That sounds great," Laura replied. "Thank you."

He put his hand on her shoulder. "Don't worry, Laura. Once I show him how much he needs me, I'll keep you safe too."

She did her best to smile even though she was shaking on the inside. "Of course."

He patted her cheek and picked up the water bottle before walking off. The light was getting brighter, telling her it must be morning. She could now see the door that he was going out of. The door opened and closed and he was gone.

She stared after him, her entire body shaking.

"Please God," she whispered. "Please don't have Ethan bring anyone with him…"

## Chapter 38

$\mathcal{L}$*aura*

LAURA DOZED OFF. There was no way for her to keep time in the quiet of the empty warehouse. She watched as the sunlight shifted against the floor, but her eyes were still heavy from the drugs Craig had given her.

When she woke, the sun was at a different angle and more yellow than gray. She was thirsty again, and now she had to pee as well. She wondered what had woken her up when she heard the metallic thud of the warehouse door.

She prayed it wasn't Craig. She wasn't ready to pretend to be the compliant captive. She still hadn't found a way to get out of the ropes tying her to the chair. All she had to show for her struggles were bruises.

She watched with baited breath as a man came through the door. She wasn't sure if she could handle another conversation with Craig. She pressed her ankles and wrists against the ropes that held her to the chair, but the didn't budge. It felt like all she was doing was bruising herself.

The man stepped into the light and Laura gasped.

It wasn't Craig. It was Ethan. Her heart soared and stuttered at the same time. He was here to save her. She was being rescued. But, what if he had brought someone with him? What if he didn't do as Craig had asked?

Ethan glanced around the room before running across it to her chair.

"Are you okay?" he asked, checking the ropes. They didn't budge.

"I am now," she told him, her voice shaking with relief. She wished she could just collapse in Ethan's arms and have this whole nightmare be over.

"I'll get you out," Ethan promised, cupping her face in his hands. She looked into his green eyes, and she believed him. She nodded and did her best to smile.

*"I'm glad you made it, Ethan."*

Craig stepped out from the shadows. Laura didn't know how long he'd been there and it made her uncomfortable. She didn't like thinking of him watching her.

"Craig, come help me with these. She'll be back any minute," Ethan called to him, motioning to the ropes. He turned back to Laura, then did a double take on Craig. He frowned. "What are you doing here, Craig? Where's Janie?"

"He's the one who tied me up, Ethan," Laura whispered, her eyes on Craig. She could see the outline of the knife in his pocket.

Ethan's eyes went wide. "What?" He looked at Craig, then at Laura, then back to Craig in disbelief. "Why would you do that?"

"To show you how much you need me," Craig explained, taking a step toward him. "The rest of your 'security' team was so busy chasing after Janie that they failed to keep the woman you love safe."

"Janie didn't do this?" Ethan asked, shock filling his features.

"'*Janie didn't do this?*'" Craig mocked Ethan, using a high pitched voice. He spat onto the floor. "Of course she didn't. You're missing the point." Craig came closer. He pointed to Laura. "She's important to you, and they failed. Miserably. But I didn't fail. I keep you safe."

Ethan stood in complete shock. "It was you? The voice was disguised, but I would never have thought it was you." Ethan frowned, betrayal filling his eyes. "I trusted you."

"You should trust me, Ethan. You must trust me," Craig said. He smiled up at him as a dog would to his master. "I protect you. I keep you safe."

"Why are you doing this, Craig?" Ethan asked, hurt in his voice. "Why would you do this to Laura?"

"You fired me." Craig's voice was low and dangerous. Laura could hear the pain in it.

Ethan shook his head. "No, I didn't."

"Yes, you did!" Craig's voice echoed through the empty warehouse. He took a breath and visibly calmed himself. "Yes, you did. You had Bruce tell me you didn't need me."

Ethan frowned and shook his head. "Craig, I didn't fire you," he explained. "You had too much overtime. You couldn't work anymore this month."

"You left me behind," Craig shouted. "You left me!"

"He was worried about you, Craig," Laura cut in. Her heart pounded in her chest. If Craig got upset, he would lose control and hurt her. She softened her voice, trying to stay and sound calm. "He was worried you were working too hard."

Ethan's brows came together since that clearly wasn't the case but then raised as he figured it out. He nodded.

"She's right, Craig," he said, agreeing with Laura and going with what she said. "I don't want you to work too hard. That's what it was. I was looking out for you."

"Protecting you isn't work," Craig informed him. He took a step closer across the empty room. He was now close enough that if he brought out his knife, he could reach her. Laura's heart pounded in her chest.

If he decided to hurt her, there was nothing she could do. She pressed against the ropes, but all it did was hurt her bruises. Fear clutched at her throat. What would Dallas and Ivy do without her? Who would make sure that they got the right kind of ginger ale when they were sick? Who would tuck them in at night?

"I understand that now. I was wrong," Ethan replied. He motioned to Laura. "Will you untie her? You've made your point."

Craig shook his head. "Not yet. I need you to understand."

"Okay," Ethan said quickly. "I'm listening. You have my complete attention."

Craig swallowed, and his eyes went big. This was his moment. This was the moment that he'd been waiting for and needed.

"You need me, Ethan. I just want to keep you safe," he explained. "You're like a brother to me. I had to take her to show you that. I never meant to hurt her. I just need you to understand how much you need me."

Ethan nodded. "I see that now, Craig. I don't have an actual brother, but if I did, I would want him to be like you," Ethan said with a smile. He put his hand on Laura's shoulder. "Will you please untie her now? She doesn't need to be a part of this. I understand now."

"Will you hire me back on?" Craig asked in a small voice. He looked at Ethan with hopeful eyes.

"You will be my primary bodyguard," Ethan promised. "I need someone as dedicated as you. You've really shown me how much I can't trust anyone else. No one else can protect me. You've proven that."

Craig's eyes narrowed. "How do I know that you aren't just saying that?"

Ethan looked at Laura. "Do you know how it felt to hear she'd been taken?' He swallowed hard. "I love her, Craig. And I have spent the last twelve hours terrified that something had happened to her. I don't know what I would do if I lost her.

He met her eyes, and the weight of his words hit her. He loved her. She struggled down tears.

Ethan turned back to Craig. "You saw that. You were the only person on my security team to look out for all my interests," Ethan told him. "You're willing to go the distance. You saw what I needed, and you did it. I need you, Craig. You've proven yourself."

Craig considered Ethan's words. Laura's heart was an out of control freight train in her chest. This was the moment of truth. If Craig didn't believe Ethan, then she was dead. If he didn't believe that Ethan was going to hire him back on and that all was forgiven, she would never see Ivy and Dallas again.

Craig pulled the pocketknife from his pocket. Laura closed her eyes. If this was the end, she didn't want to see it coming. She was just glad she'd gotten to see Ethan again and know that he loved her.

"I"m glad you've seen reason," Craig announced. He

crossed the remainder of the room in six quick steps. Laura winced as the knife came close, but he only cut the ropes holding her to the chair. The ropes fell to the floor, and she opened her eyes. She was free.

"Go to the door, Laura," Ethan told her, helping her stand. Her legs wobbled, and she nearly fell. Her feet were both asleep from either the binding or sitting too long, or possibly both. She took a small, wobbly step of freedom.

The knife clicked shut as Craig put it back into his pocket. He grinned proudly at Ethan like he had done a good thing. Ethan held out his hand to him, and Craig happily took it.

"Thank you, Craig," Ethan said, pulling the man into a hug. Craig's face split into a broad smile, and he happily closed his eyes. It was then that Ethan plunged a needle into Craig's neck and pushed in the syringe.

Chapter 39

$\mathscr{L}$*aura*

SHE TRIED TO SCREAM, but nothing came out. Her lungs didn't seem to work. She couldn't believe what she was seeing. Craig looked up at Ethan with the biggest, saddest eyes. They were full of the ultimate betrayal as he collapsed to the floor. Laura even thought she heard a soft whimper come from the strong man.

Ethan caught him, guiding him down as gently as possible. Craig's eyelids fluttered as his knees buckled and the drugs took hold. Ethan lay Craig's head on the floor like he was tucking Craig into bed rather than knocking him out for the count.

"He's down," Ethan said to no one in particular. He sighed as he made sure Craig was safe on the floor.

Laura was such a mess of adrenaline and fatigue that she was having a hard time understanding what was going on. Things seemed to be going faster than she could track and her head still hurt from being roofied. She was afraid she might be hallucinating all of this and that she'd wake up still tied to the chair with Craig flicking his knife at her. This didn't feel real.

It didn't help when four doors all opened at the same time, and armed men ran inside. There were people in police uniforms, people in all black with SWAT stamped on the back, and unfamiliar faces of a security team. She stared at them as they ran past her, guns in hand to secure the room.

Two sets of EMT's came in through the door Ethan had entered once the police shouted an all clear. Each pair had a gurney and an oversized medical bag. One set went to Craig's fallen body and the other to her. She pushed them away and went to Ethan instead.

He hugged her to him, pressing his face into her shoulder. She, in turn, held onto him like she might float away at any moment. After the day's events, she felt like it was certainly possible. She closed her eyes and felt the tears of relief start to flow. He felt real.

Ethan held her tighter, his own breathing choppy. He was shaking in her arms, and she was holding him up as much as he was holding her. He repeated her name into her hair, keeping her safe in his arms. She felt safe for the first time since he'd left her house.

"Sir, we need to check her," one of the EMTs said gently, putting a hand on his shoulder.

Slowly, Ethan relaxed his grip on her. He wiped his cheeks with his shirtsleeve as they took her hand and had her sit down on the gurney. Her legs still didn't work right, but at least the pins and needles sensation was gone. Ethan hovered beside her, watching their every move to make sure she was being taken care of appropriately.

The EMTs did their best to work around him as they took her blood pressure and shined lights into her eyes.

"What just happened, Ethan?" she asked, blinking as the EMT removed the bright light. "You stabbed him."

"It was a sedative," Ethan told her. "He'll be fine. Well, he'll have a nasty headache, but it was better than the alternative."

Laura shivered. She didn't want to think about alternative ways this could have gone down.

"He said that he told you to come alone," she said. She looked around at the swarm of police, SWAT, security, and EMTs. "This isn't exactly alone."

"He did tell me to do that," Ethan replied. "I should begin at the beginning."

Laura nodded. "That would help."

Ethan took a big breath in before starting his story.

## Chapter 40

 *than*

*Eight hours earlier...*

"COME ALONE, or I'll kill her."

The electronic voice clicked off, and the line went dead.

A picture came through of Laura tied to a chair and address to meet.

Ethan stared at the phone in his hand. He was shaking. He never shook like this during business meetings or even when climbing over hundred foot drops. But this had him shaking like a leaf in a tornado.

Someone had Laura and was going to kill her.

He swallowed hard. It had to be Janie. The car, the break-in... and now she had Laura.

His knees buckled, and he sat down hard in his office

chair. The chair swiveled, nearly dumping him over and he cursed. He hated this Colorado temporary office.

"You need a plan," Ethan whispered to himself. He closed his eyes and started visualizing. It was what he did when he faced a difficult vertical mountain climb. He would visualize each spot his hands needed to go to and just how to grip the rock. He would plan the entire ascent up the rock face and anticipate any hidden obstacles. What if a rock breaks? What if his fingers slip? He visualized all of it, so there was always a backup plan.

He did this during business too. What if the acquisition goes south? What if the stock falls the day before a merger? Having a plan was critical. It was soothing in a way. He knew if he had a plan, he would know what needed to be done next. So, he looked at the problem and came up with solutions.

First, Laura was taken by an unknown entity. He assumed it was Janie, but just as a handhold could look secure and crumble as soon as he put weight on it, he knew better than to trust an assumption.

He was told to come alone to an address sent to his phone. There was no money ransom or business mention. This was about him and Laura. That told him this was personal, lending credence to the Janie theory.

He looked out the window at the darkening sky. The city lights started to flicker on as the sun turned the mountains orange. He wondered if Laura could see the sunset from where she was being held.

He picked up the phone to call Bruce and hesitated. He trusted Bruce, but something he had said bothered Ethan.

*"Someone knew the system. It has to be an inside job or someone who knows our systems."*

If he called Bruce, there was a very good chance that

Janie would find out. She either still had access to his security or had someone on the security team helping her. He couldn't call Bruce. Bruce and the rest of Ethan's team had to stay in the dark about this.

He thought about just going to the warehouse, but without knowing what was going on or having some basic plan, that was a terrible idea. Who knew what Janie wanted from him?

Ethan flipped his phone over in his hands, playing with the smooth features. He needed some sort of security. He needed help, but he couldn't use his own security team. He was afraid to use Carter's team as they often shared personnel.

He would have to use someone else's team. Someone who could contact the police without drawing attention and had experience with this kind of thing.

Luckily, he had just that kind of friend.

"Let's go over the plan one more time," Dean Sherman, head of billionaire Jack Saunders' security team said. He leaned forward over the small coffee table in Ethan's hotel room to listen to the response.

"I go to the warehouse alone," Ethan told Jack's head of security. "You and your team will be waiting in unmarked vans outside on the street."

Dean nodded. "The Denver police are already there making it look like electrical work is being done. It won't be strange to have several large vans in the area. The police are aware of the situation, but we're saying that it's Jack, not you on the radio. As far as everyone but you and I know, this is about him."

Ethan nodded. Jack was a good friend for letting him borrow his security team. Dean had flown out from New York immediately at Ethan's phone call to Jack. Ethan had met Dean at Mia's fundraiser and knew that the man was amazing at his job. He'd been part of the search for the missing boys.

"I'll have a syringe with a sedative up my jacket sleeve," Ethan continued with the plan. "If Janie searches me, it'll feel like part of the coat. I just have to make sure I don't stab myself with it."

"Yes, that would be bad," Dean replied dryly.

"I make sure Laura is safe. Then, as soon as I get the opportunity, I inject the sedative. The best is the neck, but the arm or glute will work if necessary," Ethan said. "Once I've done that, I say 'she's down' into the wire I'll be wearing."

"And what happens if you can't do that?" Dean asked, his bright blue eyes sharp as he waited for an answer.

Ethan didn't like thinking about this part of the plan. He wanted it to go easily and smoothly, but he knew that a plan for if things went to hell in a hand-basket was necessary and probably more important than the best case scenario.

"I say, 'boats and hoes.'" It was easy enough to remember, and a little bit funny, but it was a dark humor. Janie wouldn't know what it meant, but the team listening in on the wire would. A duress code. If he said that, then a full tactical team came in with guns blazing. If bullets started flying, they were just as likely to hit Laura as Janie. Boats and hoes full of holes. Ethan just hoped he could get Laura on the floor fast enough.

"It sounds like you've got it." Dean leaned back into the couch. "Try to stay calm. The calmer you stay, the calmer

Janie will stay. Play to her. Do what she asks. We're right outside if you need help."

Ethan nodded and sat back in his own chair. He needed something to drink. Or ten shots of whiskey. "I'm not ashamed to admit this to you, but I'm scared about this."

Dean smiled. "You should be. This isn't an easy thing. But, you'll do great. Just treat it like a hostile takeover, and you'll be fine."

Ethan chuckled. "Yeah, except I'm the one being taken over. I have to give the takers what they want in order to survive. That's not my usual meeting."

Dean checked his watch. "It's time. You ready?"

Ethan's stomach rolled with nerves, but his hands were steady. "As ready as I'm going to be," he replied. He stood up and put on his game face.

It was time to save Laura.

# Chapter 41

*L* aura

"LUCKILY IT WENT the way it was supposed to," Ethan told Laura.

She was still having a hard time believing this was all happening. She looked over in time to see the EMTs wheel Craig off strapped to a gurney. He was still out cold as they took him away with a police escort.

"What's going to happen to him?" Laura asked, following him with her eyes. She gripped Ethan's hand, drawing strength from him.

"He's going somewhere they can help him," Ethan answered, giving her hand a reassuring squeeze. "Don't worry about him."

Laura nodded and looked away. She understood that Craig didn't mean to hurt her, but she wasn't ready to forgive him for tying her up and threatening her life just yet.

The EMT checking Laura out cleared her throat. She smiled as the two of them looked over.

"You look okay," the EMT told Laura. "You're a little dehydrated, but your vitals are good, and you don't have any physical injuries."

"Can I take her home?" Ethan asked his hand on her shoulder.

"If you want to," the EMT replied. "She needs rest and fluids. If anything changes, you'll need to see a doctor."

"Thank you," Laura told the EMT and Ethan repeated the sentiment.

The EMT nodded. She quickly finished packing up her things, and she and her partner headed back to their ambulance. Laura stood from the chair. She didn't want to be on that thing anymore. Standing felt good.

A tall man with dark hair and piercing blue eyes headed their direction. He walked confidently and greeted them with a nod. Laura recognized him as Dean from Mia's fundraiser.

"How are you, Laura?" Dean asked. He didn't smile. She wasn't sure he knew how.

"Better now," Laura said with a smile. "Thank you."

"I'm just glad you're safe," Dean replied. He turned to Ethan. "It appears as though Craig was quite obsessed with you, Ethan. His car is outside, and it's full of items that belong you. Pens, neckties, napkins, t-shirts, and even a personalized phone charger."

Ethan's eyebrows went up. "So that's where that went," he said.

"We're just about finished here," Dean informed them. "You two are free to head home. I'll have one of my men drive you to the hotel."

"Thank you, Dean," Ethan replied. He reached into his

pocket and pulled out what Laura assumed with the microphone. "I can't thank you enough."

Dean took the microphone. "It's my job."

Laura hugged him. "Thank you, Dean."

A flicker of a smile crossed his face as he patted her back. "I'm just glad it all worked out. If you'll excuse me, I need to go check in with my team."

"I guess that's it," Laura said as the warehouse cleared of people. She turned to face Ethan. He stared at her like he was seeing her for the first time.

The controlled, assured mask of the billionaire cracked, and Laura could clearly see then man beneath the billionaire. Lines of worry stood out on his brow, and his eyes shone with tears.

"I was so worried," he whispered, pulling her into his arms. He held her close to him, his breathing rough with emotion.

"I'm okay." She raised her face to him and touched his cheek. "Will you take me home?"

He nodded. His green eyes were soft and only for her.

"Will you stay with me?" she asked.

He nodded again.

"Will you stay with me forever?" Her heart paused, waiting for his response.

"Forever," he promised. He smiled, and the worry vanished from his face. All that was left was love. Love for her. It made her warm with joy. It made her feel complete.

"Sounds good," she said, cupping her fingers under his chin and tugging gently. He leaned forward and kissed her, surrounding her in a wonderful kind of love.

**Chapter 42**

*Laura*

LAURA TRIED to keep the fear from bubbling up into a scream. She thought she was ready for this, but the closer she stepped, the more her body rebelled. If it weren't for the fact that Ivy and Dallas were holding both her hands, she would have turned and sprinted away.

Everything smelled of hot asphalt and jet fuel. It didn't help to settle her very nervous stomach.

"Is that the plane, Laura?" Ivy asked in a small voice as they stood on the tarmac. Both kids had a death grip on Laura's hands.

"Yes. It's very different than the one Mom and Dad was on," Laura said, doing her best to keep her voice steady. She felt like she pulled it off okay.

"I'm scared," Ivy admitted.

"Me too," Dallas agreed. "But, Ethan's on this plane, right?"

"Yes, Ethan's on this plane," Laura said. She gave their hands a squeeze. "I'm scared too, but this will be fun, okay?"

"Okay," both kids murmured, but neither one of them sounded convinced.

Ethan's head popped out of the plane door, and he waved to them.

Laura wouldn't have stepped toward the plane if Dallas hadn't pulled her. He wanted to see his friend. The small motion of his gentle tug on her hand was enough to get Laura's feet moving. It was slow at first.

Ethan took the stairs two at a time before jumping off the last one and jogging across the tarmac to meet them.

She remembered her parents walking along the tarmac. She remembered them smiling, just like this before they disappeared forever. Laura's courage failed, and she stumbled.

But Ethan was there. He smiled as she caught herself. Dallas and Ivy both let go of her hands to give him hugs. He happily pulled the two children to him.

That was when she realized that getting on this plane wasn't going to recreate the past. She wasn't her mother. Ethan wasn't her father. Getting on this plane was taking a step into the future, not reliving the past. They were moving forward with their lives, and it needed to happen. They needed to move on.

"You okay?" Ethan asked as she took her first confident step toward the plane.

"I am now," she said with a smile. He grinned at her and then raced the two kids up the stairs and into the private jet.

Laura took her time on the stairway up to the jet door. She was mostly prepared for this flight, but part of her was still afraid. This was how her parents died. It was only natural for her to be fearful, and she was doing her best. She took a deep breath before entering the plane.

The interior of the plane was not at all as she expected. She'd been expecting the tacky blue cloth chairs in rows with uncomfortable armrests and no room to move around. The jet was the exact opposite. It was open and spacious with a large couch and a big screen TV. There were comfortable chairs and space to move around. It looked more like a tiny living room than an aircraft.

"This doesn't look anything like the planes on TV," Dallas remarked. He ran to the back and immediately started exploring. "It even has a real potty!"

"Airplanes all have real toilets," Ivy told him, rolling her eyes. But, then she went to look at it too.

"This is your airplane?" Laura asked, looking around. It was certainly not what she thought of when he said she was flying.

"Yes. Well, sometimes," Ethan replied. He handed her a glass of champagne. "I have another one that's smaller, but it has a more comfortable desk."

Laura nodded. "Right. Because that's my usual criteria for judging an airplane."

Ethan chuckled and put his hand on the small of her back. "Let's get seated so we can take off."

Laura took a big sip of champagne. She could do this.

"Okay, guys," Ethan announced once Ivy and Dallas were on the couch. He stood in front of them. "I have a surprise for you. It'll make the trip more fun."

Dallas and Ivy's eyes lit up, and the bounced up and down. The fear of the plane was gone for them, replaced by excitement. Laura was trying. Another couple of glasses of champagne and she was pretty sure she'd be fine, too.

"Do you guys remember the preview we watched for the new Lego movie?" Ethan asked. He picked up the remote for the TV and spun it around in his hands. He pressed a button, and the Lego logo filled the TV screen. "We get to watch it."

The kids whooped and jumped up and down.

"But it's not even in theaters yet," Laura said. "It doesn't come out for another month."

Ethan shrugged. "I know a guy."

"You know a guy?" she repeated. She took another sip of champagne.

"Okay, sit back down so I can start it," Ethan told Ivy and Dallas. They both sat down, but excitement bounced in their little limbs as he hit the play button. He turned the volume up loud and sat next to Laura.

"I can't believe you got them this movie," she said, finishing her champagne.

"I thought it would be a good distraction," he told her. He motioned to the stewardess and almost instantly Laura had another glass of champagne in her hands.

"It's a good one," she admitted. The engines started up. Laura looked over to make sure the kids were okay, but they were so engrossed in the movie they hadn't even noticed. They were too excited about the movie to be afraid of the plane. Laura wished she could be that way too.

"You doing okay?" Ethan asked, taking her hand as the plane taxied out onto the runway. Her heart was pounding, and she was seriously considering just opening up the door and making a bolt for it before the plane got off the ground. She wasn't sure she could do this.

"I don't know," she whispered.

"Focus on me instead," he told her.

Ethan put her chin between his thumb and forefinger.

He looked deep into her eyes and then kissed her. She closed her eyes and focused on the kiss. She focused on the soft sweep of his tongue against her lips, the taste of the champagne and the warmth of his mouth. She focused on the feel of his skin against hers and the knowledge that he would always keep her safe.

That's when it hit her. She was safe with him. He had stabbed a man in the neck to keep her safe. He had come for her.

She set down her champagne and kissed him for real this time. The engines didn't matter. She wasn't sure if the feeling of flight was from the plane or from kissing him and knowing she was loved. She suspected it was the latter.

THE FLIGHT WAS FASTER than she expected. Maybe it was the two glasses of champagne, or maybe it was that the movie was really good, but the flight was quick and easy. She held her breath when they landed, but other than that, she barely had even noticed they were in the air.

The door opened, and Ethan took the three of them outside. The humidity and heat hit her first. Then the soft smell of flowers and clean ocean air. It was so different than the fishy smell of her first beach.

She stepped out onto a single runway and looked around. Cerulean skies and luscious palm trees filled her sight. She turned and gasped as she saw the ocean. Behind her, Ivy and Dallas stood in shock and awe.

A white sandy beach led to perfect turquoise waters that slowly darkened to deep blue. The water stretched out to the horizon, sparkling in the sun. Laura had never seen anything so beautiful. She realized now why Ethan wanted to show her this side of the ocean. This was nothing like what she'd seen in the city.

"Wow," Ivy whispered. "I want to be a mermaid."

"Me too," Laura agreed.

"Not me," Dallas said as they walked down the stairs. "I'm going to be Aquaman."

"Do you guys want to go swimming first?" Ethan asked. "Or have some food?"

"Swimming!" Laura, Ivy, and Dallas all exclaimed at the same time.

Ethan laughed. "Okay. Our bungalow is just over there. Our swimsuits should be all laid out in our rooms."

Together they walked off the private runway and down a sandy path to a little house sitting over the water. They walked along a bridge to the cutest little home Laura had ever seen. It was a three bedroom house sitting on top of the water with stunning ocean views from every window.

"Dallas, your room's over here, and Ivy's room is right next door," Ethan explained pointing to the first set of doors. "Laura, you and I are over here."

They crossed the kitchen and a beautiful living area to a big room with a huge king sized bed in the middle.

"I like that it's far enough away from the kids we can have some privacy," Laura said as they stepped inside.

"Yes," Ethan agreed. "I also rented the bungalow next door if we want more privacy. There's a private walk through that door."

Laura laughed, finally feeling relaxed. Ethan had thought of everything.

She hugged him. "Thank you for this. It's perfect."

He grinned. "Well, don't say that until you've gone swimming." He frowned and looked at the bed. Only his swim trunks were laid out. Laura's suit was nowhere to be seen.

"I guess I'm going skinny-dipping," she teased, looking around.

Ethan sighed. "It must be next door. I'll change and meet the kids. You take your time."

She kissed his cheek. "Okay. But if it isn't there, I am going skinny dipping."

His eyes dilated as he looked her over. "Don't tease me. I'd like you skinny dipping."

She grinned and hurried out the back door. The sun was warm on her face as she went to the next bungalow. It was much smaller than the first one with just one room with a large bed. Laying out was a brand new polka-dot bikini with a beautiful sundress to wear over it. She shook her head and smiled. Ethan really had thought of everything.

She quickly changed and freshened up in the bathroom before heading back along the path. Ethan was gone from the main bedroom, so she walked through the house and out to the beach. Everywhere she went she could hear the soft whoosh of the ocean. She loved it.

"Ethan?" she called as she walked through the house. "Dallas? Ivy?"

"Over here," Dallas called back. She exited the dining room and stepped out onto a porch suspended over the water and gasped.

It would have been a beautiful porch in normal circumstances. It was large and led straight out into crystal clear turquoise water, but today, it was covered in rose petals. Dallas and Ivy stood on either side of Ethan, each with a sign and big grins on their faces.

Dallas' sign read, "Will you" and Ivy's "marry me?"

Ethan grinned at her and dropped to one knee, holding out a black satin box. Laura wasn't sure how her feet moved, but somehow she was standing in front of him, looking down at the man she loved.

"Laura, I love you," Ethan said, looking up at her with those green eyes that made her melt. "I want to spend the rest of my life with you. It's tradition to ask the bride's father for approval, so I asked the two people that mean the most to you instead."

He nodded to Ivy and Dallas. "They said it was okay," Ethan told her.

Laura chuckled and smiled at her two siblings. They grinned and waved their signs at her.

"So, Laura Corbett, will you marry me and make me the happiest man in the world?

Laura couldn't breathe she was so happy. Her brain forgot how to use words.

There was a long silence, which Dallas broke. "You're 'posed to say yes," he whispered.

She laughed, feeling tears of joy trickle down her cheeks. She took Ethan's hands in hers.

"Yes, Ethan. Yes."

His face lit up like the Fourth of July as he stood up and kissed her. He spun her around in his joy, and her siblings shrieked with delight. Dallas threw his sign up in the air and Ivy clapped.

"Thank you," Ethan said, setting her down from their spin. He kept his face close to hers. "I can't believe I found this kind of love."

She grinned and kissed him, her heart full. "We have a wonderful kind of love. We have the best kind of love."

Escape With Me: A Midlife Love Story

"I gave it all up to be happy. I'd give it all up again for you."

They say life begins after 40, but Cassie ain't feelin' it. Divorced and feeling trapped by her job, she wants to let loose for her friend's tropical beach wedding. She decides to let her hair down and get a little unpredictable. That's when she meets a handsome bartender, Wyatt.

Despite a few grey hairs, Wyatt's the liveliest man that Cassie has ever met. She knows that there's got to be more to his life story than just being a bartender, but this is just supposed to be a vacation fling. And after sunny days spent breaking all the rules on the beach together, Cassie realizes that nobody has ever listened to her the way that Wyatt does.

His carefree life is enviable, his kisses are intoxicating, and she can almost imagine a life with him. But all vacations come to an end. And when Cassie invites him to visit her hometown, Wyatt reveals that he can never go back. Not to her town. Not to America. Not to civilization.

Cassie leaves, confused and heartbroken, wondering just who she got herself involved with. Suddenly, her predictable life gets turned upside down when she sees her picture splashed across the Internet. And when the tabloids come looking for the mature woman who found the lost billionaire, she has no idea what to do...

...until he comes back.

Escape With Me: A Midlife Love Story

# ABOUT THE AUTHOR

New York Times and USA Today Bestseller Krista Lakes is a thirtysomething who recently rediscovered her passion for writing. She is living happily ever after with her Prince Charming. Her first kid just started preschool and she is happy to welcome her second child into her life, continuing her "Happily Ever After"!

Thank you for supporting an indie author. Anything you can do, whether it be writing a review, or even simply telling a fellow reader that you enjoyed this, helps me out immensely. Thanks!

Krista would love to hear from you! Please contact her at Krista.Lakes@gmail.com or friend her on Facebook!

Further reading:

*Bad Boys and Babies*
    Family Doctor's Baby
    The Billionaire's Baby Arrangement
    Crime Boss Baby

*Kinds of Love*
    A Forever Kind of Love
    A Wonderful Kind of Love
    An Endless Kind of Love

*Billionaires and Brides*

Yours Completely: A Cinderella Love Story

Yours Truly: A Cinderella Love Story

Yours Royally: A Cinderella Love Story

*The "Kisses" series*

Saltwater Kisses: A Billionaire Love Story

Kisses From Jack: The Other Side of Saltwater Kisses

Rainwater Kisses: A Billionaire Love Story

Champagne Kisses: A Timeless Love Story

Freshwater Kisses: A Billionaire Love Story

Sandcastle Kisses: A Billionaire Love Story

Hurricane Kisses: A Billionaire Love Story

Barefoot Kisses: A Billionaire Love Story

Sunrise Kisses: A Billionaire Love Story

Waterfall Kisses: A Billionaire Love Story

Island Kisses: A Billionaire Love Story

*Other Novels*

I Choose You: A Secret Billionaire Romance

His Every Desire: A Billionaire Seduction

Wolf Six's Salvation: A Shifter Love Story

Burned: A New Adult Love Story

Walking on Sunshine: A Sweet Summer Romance

An American Cinderella: A Royal Love Story

Mr. Darcy's Kiss: A Contemporary Pride and Prejudice

www.ingramcontent.com/pod-product-compliance
Lightning Source LLC
Chambersburg PA
CBHW051638180726
48284CB00006B/1784